MOONLIGHT DUET

By

J.E. Taylor

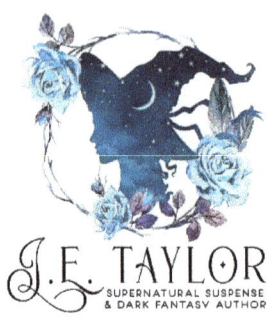

Moonlight Duet © 2024 by J.E. Taylor

All rights reserved under the International and Pan-American Copyright Conventions. No part of this book may be reproduced or transmitted in any form or by any means, electronic or mechanical, including photocopying, recording, or by any information storage and retrieval system, without permission in writing from the publisher.
This is a work of fiction. Names, places, characters and incidents are either the product of the author's imagination or are used fictitiously, and any resemblance to any actual persons, living or dead, organizations, events or locales is entirely coincidental.

Warning: the unauthorized reproduction or distribution of this copyrighted work is illegal. Criminal copyright infringement, including infringement without monetary gain, is investigated by the FBI and is punishable by up to 5 years in prison and a fine of $250,000.

MOONLIGHT DUET
Book 1
WOLF MOON

Alessandra and Hunter have a price on their heads. Can they escape their fate, or will the sins of the past lead them to their death?

In the eyes of the werewolf council, Alessandra Tate and Hunter Blaez committed the ultimate sin. Humans were killed at the hands of a werewolf, and the price for taking a human life is death.

After being on the run for three months, Alessandra's nightmares are still plagued with the acts of that evening. Never again will she trust a man to get close enough to betray her, even Hunter Blaez, her beta wolf and protector.

Hunter has other ideas. He has been in love with Alessandra for years, but all she ever saw was her second in command. Even rescuing her from certain death and following her into damnation wasn't enough for her to see him as a man.

When the council catches Hunter, Alessandra must choose between surviving without him, or risking her life to save the only man she truly loves.

WOLF MOON
Preface

"HEY ALLY, WANT TO come up and party?"

His casual invitation interrupted her stride. Alessandra looked up from the sidewalk, hugging her books. Frat house boys ogled her from the balcony. At least twice a day since the semester started, she heard the catcall, but so had every other sorority girl on the block who walked by the Alpha Beta Pi house.

Jeremy leaned against the railing with a beer in his hand, smiling down at her, his bright green eyes reminding her of a wild mountain lion, and she suppressed a shiver. He raised his beer and, with a slight tilt of his head, said, "Come on, Ally. We won't bite. His smooth voice caressed her ears, and she paused, inhaling deeply and memorizing his musky scent.

Yeah, but I might.

"Why should I?" Alessandra turned fully toward the house, flipping her long black hair over her shoulder and placing her hand on her hip, waiting for an answer.

He drained his beer and put his index finger up before he disappeared. Stepping out the front door moments later, he trotted down the sidewalk, stopping a few feet in front of her. "Come party with me." His gaze drifted over her in that hungry come-hither expression, matching the seductive tone in his voice.

She batted her eyelashes and tilted her head to the right, studying his cocky sureness. His reputation of slam, bam, thank you ma'am, the equivalent of a male whore ran through her head, and now his sights were set on her. "Again, why should I?" Alessandra asked, toying with him.

"Because I've wanted you since I first set eyes on you." Jeremy leaned in as he spoke, his breath reeking of Corona. "And I can tell you feel the same." A knowing smirk spread over his lips.

Alessandra took a deep breath and let out a husky laugh. "Yeah, right." Even though Jeremy was one of the better-looking men on campus, arrogant and sexy as hell, she would not let him take advantage of her. Not with the risks. Not even if her dreams *were* filled with visions of lapping every inch of his six-foot sculpted frame.

"I have class," she answered and took a step toward campus.

His hand clamped down on her arm, stopping her. "At least come to the party tonight. It's homecoming."

Alessandra sighed and chewed on her lip, considering his invitation. All her sorority sisters were going, along with everyone who was anyone on campus. She didn't think the grin on his face could get any bigger, but when she agreed, it widened. She looked at the hand clasped around her upper arm and he let go, taking a quick step back as she raised her gaze to his.

"It starts at eight." The wind kicked up, wrapping a cool breeze that promised a bitter winter, and he dug his hands into his pockets. "See you then." He turned and disappeared into the frat house.

ALESSANDRA FIDGETED IN HER seat through the entire class. Hunter texted at least a dozen times about a camping trip tonight, and she ignored each silent buzz of her phone.

Why did he always show up at the wrong time with the rest of his ragged pack? Her sweet sixteen, her first date, her prom—all screwed up for the sake of a "family" trip. Family? Ha! Not so much. More like unwanted chaperones. God, couldn't they let her have a normal life?

Her phone buzzed again, and she tore her gaze from the professor to the demanding words blinking on her phone. With a couple of quick keystrokes, she sent her defiant answer. She wasn't going this time. She'd meet up with them tomorrow. They could go one night without her leading the party.

She turned the phone off and focused back on the front of the classroom.

EVEN THE SIDEWALK VIBRATED from the hip-hop beat as she approached the front door of Alpha Beta Pi. She traded a glance with her sorority sisters, and they squeezed through the crowded house into the rear courtyard. Bodies crammed into the open space, moving like a sea of Mexican jumping beans.

She scanned the crowd and couldn't see Jeremy. A quick sniff brought several mingled scents, mostly booze and sweat, but another sweet scent laced the air: an undercurrent of marijuana—all the normal byproducts of a college frat party. Moments later, that musky aroma reached her, and she turned to see Jeremy approaching.

"Hey, Ally, want a beer?" He offered her one of the two opened Coronas in his hands.

"No thanks. I really shouldn't drink."

His eyebrows creased, and he bit his lip. "Why not? Are you an alcoholic or something?"

"Something like that."

The crease smoothed out, replaced by arches that rivaled McDonald's, and she chuckled at the incredulous look gracing his handsome, chiseled face.

"I'm actually allergic to alcohol."

The arches remained. "Really?" he grunted and handed the bottle to a wayward fraternity brother. "What, do you swell up like a balloon?"

This time, she laughed. "No, no spontaneous swelling." She didn't care to elaborate further.

"Want some punch instead?"

"Sure," she answered, licking her lips.

His gaze traveled between her mouth and her eyes, and he nodded, disappearing into the crowd. A few minutes later, he slipped next to her, handing her the plastic cup full of red fruit punch. A lovely orange ring decorated the edge, along with a glistening cherry.

She slid the cherry between her lips, severing it from the vine in such a way that he sucked in his breath, his chest rising and falling with the desire pumping through his blood, emitting a scent she adored, the tang of feral wanting.

Lifting the glass to her lips, she sipped the drink. Her thirst flared, and she downed the delectable liquid. "This is fantastic. What's in it?"

"Fruit punch, pineapple juice, Sprite, along with the fruit, of course," he answered. "Do you want me to get you some more?"

"Sure."

Before she knew it, he was back with a drink in each fist, both for her.

"This way, I don't have to run off again for at least another five minutes." He flashed his dazzling white teeth in her direction.

Halfway through the third glass, the room tilted, and she blinked, staring at the wavering liquid in her glass before bringing her gaze back to Jeremy's expectant grin.

"Why don't you finish that, and I'll take you outside? It's getting warm in here," he said, pointing to the glass, and she downed the rest and setting the glass on the nearest table.

Instead of heading out front as she expected, he pulled her up the stairs, corralling her out onto the balcony, and cornered her against the siding, pressing his body to hers, his lips finding the curve of her neck and his hands wandering over her silky shirt.

"Jeremy," she whispered, blinking away the slow spin that gripped her.

"What?" He brought his mouth away from her skin and raised a questioning eyebrow. His green eyes shimmered in the moonlight.

"What was in that drink?" Her tongue felt fuzzy in her mouth and she swallowed, scraping it along the dry roof of her mouth. She squelched the craving for another drink, especially considering her dulled senses. She struggled to perceive his musky scent or his beer-laced breath, even though he was inches away, and a constant buzz filled her ears, distorting all sound.

His grin widened, and his eyes twinkled. "It's a grain punch."

A measure of fear spun up her spine, chilling her warm skin. Her father's words echoed in her ear.

"Drinking will eliminate your ability to recognize trouble and stunt any opportunity you might have of escaping danger." His staunch parental glare punctuated the statement, and she never once questioned the hereditary reaction to alcohol.

After all, he had been right about everything else.

"Don't look so upset, angel. Enjoy the buzz." His lips found hers, drowning all her protests, drowning all logic, drowning all thoughts of her father's warning.

His kisses, along with the stroke of his hands and his whispered promises of forever, were as intoxicating as the drink, and she allowed him to lead her into his bedroom. The door latched behind them and he navigated her toward the bed. Helping her undress, his hands never stopped their exploration, fanning the flames in the pit of her stomach, and she matched his fervor, nipping at his neck and chest and stomach. He stopped her when she reached for his belt.

"I understand what you truly are." His sinuous tone filled her ear just before his tongue swiped it, sending chills through her lithe form. Before she could blink, he had her wrists bound behind her back and a blindfold covering her eyes.

"I know what you are." This time his voice held contempt and the back of his hand slammed into her cheekbone, sending her to the floor with flares of pain resonating through her jaw.

With her senses dulled with shock and alcohol, he yanked her to her feet and covered her with a rough blanket that reminded her of the old potato sacks they used to use for the sack races at camp rough and scratchy, to the point it itched. She struggled in the bonds.

She found her voice as the noise dissipated and she stumbled on the curb. "Jeremy, what the hell are you doing?"

The slide of a door dispelled her question, and he threw her into a cramped space. The clang of the door closing behind her confirmed her suspicions. She was inside the infamous Alpha Beta Pi van.

According to campus rumor, the fraternity brothers took turns filming their sexual encounters in this van. But she didn't think that's what he had in mind. No, she thought his motivations were a little darker than a sexual romp.

The van lurched forward, and hands tore the rough blanket from over her head. Lights bled from under the blindfold. "Jeremy?" She hated the twinge of fear in her voice.

The blindfold ripped from her face and she squinted under the intense lights. Blinking until her eyes adjusted, she made out his form just out of camera shot and he wasn't the one driving the van.

"What do we do with her?" someone behind Jeremy asked. She thought she recognized the voice, but before her brain could form a coherent thought, a needle jabbed into her leg.

Jeremy came out of the shadows and depressed the plunger, sending burning liquid up her thigh. Pain spread from the injection site, traveling through her system at mach speed. Her heart, already taxed by fear, pumped the poison through her bloodstream, creating a blazing agony in every cell of her being, and she screamed. The wail echoed through the small metal chamber and her muscles clenched into tight balls of anguish.

"Belladonna," he said, holding up the empty syringe. "That ought to keep her under control until the cougars find her," he said to the shadows over his shoulder.

Belladonna? Did he say Belladonna? Terror washed through her faster than the pain and her chest hitched breath after painful breath.

Belladonna was one of the deadliest substances to her kind. This agony crippling her would only increase and if he spared her a fatal dose, at the very least, she wouldn't be able to function for the next few hours, never mind defend herself against this maniac.

"Why?" she hissed, straightening into a sitting position.

Sliding into the light, he crawled toward her like a predator. "Because I can't stand freaks of nature like you," he said, punctuating his statement with another backhand that sent her sprawling onto her side.

"Bastard."

His laugh filled the van, and he straddled her, the sound of multiple zippers barely audible above her ragged breath.

CLOSE TO TWO HOURS of rough sexual contact passed before the van pulled to a stop, gravel crunching under the wheels. Covered with their sweat, saliva, and semen, she nearly collapsed when they hauled her out of the van. Before she had a chance to recover and study her surroundings, the blindfold covered her eyes.

The late October wind lifted strands of her long black hair, whipping it around and smacking her face with each gust. Her once creamy skin turned into a relief map of gooseflesh among the bruises. Her feet protested with every sharp stone that pierced her sole. Each scratch of a branch tore at her skin, milking the pain and snapping her into instant sobriety.

Jeremy had a grip as strong as a vise on her upper arm, his fingers digging cruelly into her flesh. He dragged her along, impatiently correcting each of her stumbles with a yank.

Hot tears stung her eyes and coated the back of her throat; she stifled the sob, locking it in her chest. Her muscles still hadn't recovered from the Belladonna or the brutal rape she endured, but she refused to collapse. Not here, not in the mountains. Not with the wild cats roaming these woods, just looking for the chance to rip someone like her to pieces.

The sudden lack of sticks digging against her along with the soft moss-like grass underfoot signaled a break in the forest. Dull light bled under her blindfold, the full harvest moon illuminating the clearing. They walked another hundred paces from the wood line before they stopped.

Her bound wrists yanked toward the ground, almost knocking her to her knees, and then the slack returned and her hands again rested at the small of her back.

Shivering in the night wind, she stuttered, "W-w-what are y-you d-d-oing?" Her teeth chattered through every word.

"Setting the bait," Jeremy whispered close to her ear. His breath caressed her cheek and then a cool substance spread from the crown of her head, dripping through her hair, covering her bare skin, tickling as it traced paths down her legs. The air filled with a sweet tang, reminding her of a fine cut of venison cooking on the grill and she licked her lips despite the bone chilling cold settling into her already exhausted limbs.

It took a second to recognize the substance, and between the flavor on her lips and the overwhelming scents accosting her, primal fear jump-started her adrenaline. "What are you doing?" The shiver was less pronounced as panic overtook her senses.

Another prick pierced her shoulder, and the pain flared again. "If the mountain lions don't kill you first, the wolves will. They always attack my poisoned offerings and when they do, the Belladonna in your system will kill them just as surely as it'll kill you."

The shuffle of feet followed his harsh statement, their pattern speeding up and drawing farther away.

"You son of a bitch!" she called after them, taking a step toward the diminishing noise. Her bound arms stopped her, anchored to something in the clearing. She struggled to break the binds. She battled against the burning poison traveling through her bloodstream and she struggled against the need to curl up into a tight ball of agony.

Barely able to remain standing, she dropped to her knees. "I will kill you!" Alessandra cried once more and then listened until the distinct footfalls on the forest floor vanished, along with their laughter. A car ignition sparked, followed by the fading sound of the engine. A sob welled up from her bowels, the long forlorn moan echoing in the small clearing, cascading over the trees into the heart of the forest, a calling to the carnivores searching for sustenance.

Adrenaline faded, and her teeth chattered, the cold soaking through her skin again and leaving her numb. Rolling her shoulder, she attempted to dislodge the blindfold, failing. After a few tries, an exasperated growl escaped between the constant click of her teeth.

An owl let out a screeching hoot and her heart lurched in her chest, her whole body following suit. The cry of a wildcat in the distance set her heart into a frantic beat, one that left her dizzy and warm despite the cold.

Fear-laced rage wound around her, and she forced herself to her feet. She didn't want to die out here in the woods. Not at the claws of a wild beast, not on the eve of the harvest moon. A guttural roar of frustration leaped from her lips and she struggled to break the binds holding her in place, but the rope wouldn't budge. "Son of a bitch!" she repeated over and over and over at the top of her lungs until she had no voice left.

That's when the leaves shuffled under padded feet.

Alessandra crouched low to the ground, bringing her face to her knees, praying and shimmying the blindfold far enough to uncover her eyes. Gleaming bones, whole rib cages and skulls, along with disembodied arms and legs, littered the ground around her and her breath hitched in her chest.

Anchored to a metal bar planted in concrete in the center of the perfectly round clearing, she studied the discolored rope binding her in place. Glimmering black liquid dripped from the twine.

The shakes that gripped her this time around were not from the cold.

The ground surrounding her feet was soaked with blood. It pooled in small divots, shimmering black in the moonlight. It dripped from her torso down her legs, and it filled the night with a succulent scent of fallen prey. Marked with deer blood, she was fair game to the scavengers in the woods.

Thoughts of bears and any manner of wild cats, especially cougars, made her skin break out with droplets of perspiration, announcing her fear to any beast surrounding the clearing.

She raised her eyes to the wood line. Golden eyes peered out from the dark, dozens of them, and a low grumble surfaced in unison. Her eyes darted to the bones on the ground and back to the eyes.

The first wolf stepped into the clearing, baring his teeth and keeping his dark hungry eyes locked with Alessandra's. The mammoth wolf stood close to six feet, his fur a mass of gray, black, and white markings swirled together to form a pelt worthy of a hunter's gun.

Alessandra stopped shaking and struggling with the binds around her wrist. "Come on." The words came out in a low rumble from her chest and the wolf paused, its slow stalk forward, halting, his teeth no longer bared.

The pack stepped into the circle, lining the woods.

Alessandra broke the stare with the alpha wolf, glancing around the clearing and counting. She brought her focus back to the first animal, tilting her head slightly. There were fifteen wolves, including the magnificent gray wolf in front of her. They sniffed the air, bringing their tails between their legs, and lowered their heads in unison. A low growl broke the silence.

The mighty beast resumed his approach, slowly crossing the distance alone. The rest of the pack hung back, watching their leader.

He sniffed the blood surrounding her feet and lapped at it without breaking eye contact, the rumble still building in his throat.

Alessandra dropped to her knees in front of the wolf. "Hunter, get me the hell out of these binds," she whispered.

The harvest moon reflected red in the wolf's eyes as they moved from her face to the soft tissue of her neck.

"Belladonna," Alessandra warned, causing the wolf to return his gaze to hers.

His eyes widened in understanding and sadness filled the deep blue eyes.

"You can't bite me. None of you can. If you do, you'll die, too."

Teeth grazed her wrists, and she cut her gaze back at the pristine white pelt of another wolf. Its powerful jaws clamped on the rope, and she offered a half-baked tilt of her lips to the silver eyes before she focused back on Hunter.

The pack closed the distance but was too skittish to partake in the spilled blood surrounding Alessandra, the blood the gray wolf lapped, his tongue soaking up the thick substance with each stroke before it disappeared between his giant teeth.

"It's okay," she whispered, glancing at the circle.

Tentatively, they lowered their snouts to the blood and began to drink.

The ties holding her wrists loosened, and she shifted so the white wolf could break the binding the rest of the way. A few minutes later, she rubbed her wrists, scanning the surrounding pack.

"There is a way." She stood. She traded a glance with Hunter, and his eyes narrowed in dissent. Even so, when she stood, they parted, letting her through.

Wolf Moon

Without looking back, she walked into the thick woods, her head tilted low, her teeth grinding together and her eyes glimmering with the red moon.

She had a score to settle and before she stepped out of the woods onto the edge of the road, she tilted her head back, letting out a haunting howl. The pack followed suit.

She lifted her nose to the air and caught the scent, heading in the same direction they had a few hours earlier after leaving her in the clearing. Jeremy mentioned a camping trip tonight. That was before he drugged her, before he bound her and left her for dead.

She walked, ignoring the burning ache in her muscles and the sharp pain in her feet, heading downwind and reaching their campsite at almost four in the morning. She didn't have much more time before the Belladonna seized her heart, leaving her in a death spasm. His musky scent mingled with the smoke of burning pine and hickory was a welcomed relief.

They were still up, laughing and toasting their success at bringing another shape-shifter into the woods, wondering how long she lasted before the animals attacked and if anyone heard her dying screams.

She stopped, still hidden by the thickets, her anger coiling inside, warming her near frozen skin. Reaching her hand out, she found Hunter's soft fur at her fingertips. Stroking his massive head, his tongue flicked her calf, cleaning a small patch of dried blood from her silky skin.

"I am aware we made a promise, but it's the one and only method that will counter Belladonna," she whispered under the crackling of the fire. She slashed her gaze to his deep blue eyes. "It's the only thing that'll save me, and that bastard deserves it."

She whistled at a frequency too low for the human ear, sending out her command. The pack silently padded through the woods surrounding the clearing.

She stepped into the opening, accompanied by the mammoth gray wolf.

The laughter died as three pairs of wide eyes stared in her direction.

Jeremy shot to his feet, eyes darting between a blood-soaked Alessandra and her companion. He put his hands out in front of him. "You, you, you should be dead," he said, taking a step back. A wet spot spread across the front of his jeans, filling the air with an acrid stench mingled with fear.

The full moon hung low in the sky as the collective growl of the pack filled the clearing and they stepped into view, blocking any chance of escape.

The alcohol that prohibited her from transforming had finally worked its way through her system, and Alessandra broke out in a feral grin. Cocking her head, her teeth transitioned from blunt incisors to razor-sharp fangs.

"You *do* know human blood counteracts Belladonna, right?" Her teeth gleamed in the moonlight; the long canines glistened, saliva dripping at the prospect of her next meal.

WOLF MOON
Chapter 1

ALESSANDRA TATE STOOD ON the balcony of the old cabin, staring out into the woods with a cup of hot chocolate in her hands. Her thoughts kept drifting to the night she was attacked. As much as she wished she could shut the memories down, they kept crawling to the surface. She shivered. Hands came to rest on her shoulders, and she jumped, nearly spilling the scalding liquid down the front of her.

"How are you doing?" Hunter's deep baritone whispered.

His concern grated on her nerves. "Fine," she said, even though she was anything but. She had crossed the line and was now a fugitive. Killing a human for any reason was taboo.

The tribal community didn't care that Jeremy and his fraternity brothers had beaten and raped her. They didn't care. The bastard had injected her with belladonna and left her for dead.

All they cared about was that she had spilled human blood.

"Bull," he said.

She turned. Hunter's sharp blue eyes held her gaze. He was as handsome a man as he was a wolf, but she had always seen him as her right hand, her beta in charge of the pack when she wasn't around. She had alpha blood running through her veins. Hunter Blaez didn't.

Besides, he was six years older, and had always viewed her like a little sister who needed to be protected. The night they attacked her, he crossed the line with her, tearing into those frat boys with as much feral fury as she had, while the rest of the pack looked on in horror.

The only reason she was alive today was because of the human hearts she'd ingested. That was the only thing that reversed the deadly effects of the belladonna.

"Why did you do it?" she asked, searching his eyes.

His lips twitched, and his eyes honed to the woods, scanning the trees as if the answers she was looking for were carved into the bark. When his gaze returned, he sighed and gave her a single shoulder shrug.

Hunter wasn't much for small talk, and Alessandra had been thankful for that during the days following the massacre, but that was three months ago. Now, his quiet demeanor just made her want to scream and shake him. She needed more than silence and sullen glances.

It was one reason she had fled her home to go to college.

She needed active participation in conversations, not blind followers.

She needed someone who would debate issues with her.

She needed someone who challenged her.

"Hunter, talk to me," she said, using the alpha tone he had to obey.

He snarled and turned away. "I hate it when you do that."

"Why did you spill their blood when you didn't have to?"

"Because what they did to you pissed me off." He glanced over his shoulder at her, with eyes full of hellfire. "Shits like that don't deserve to live." He ran his hand through his dark hair. Hunter's mouth opened as if he wanted to say more, but then his lips clamped together.

Alessandra set the hot chocolate on the table and crossed her arms. "And?"

He stalked to where she stood, towering over her. "If you haven't figured it out by now, you're as blind as you are naïve." He spun and disappeared into the house, leaving her staring after him.

She charged in after him. "What the hell does that mean?"

He stopped halfway up the stairwell. "Ally..."

"No, Hunter. I need to know. I need to understand why the hell you would damn yourself to a life on the run?"

"I didn't want you going through this alone. Besides, your innocence wasn't theirs to take."

She didn't disagree, but there was something deeper in his gaze, more personal. He trudged up the stairs without saying more.

"Hunter?"

He stopped but didn't turn.

Alessandra wanted to push him for more, but the tight set of his shoulders kept her quiet. "I don't think I've ever said thank you," she finally said.

His slow up and down tilt of his chin warmed the chill between them, and then he disappeared into his room.

She blinked as the conversation settled into her and his words finally sank in. She crossed to his door on the far side of the house. Hunter had his back to her and was in the middle of peeling his sweater off. His muscles rippled as he tossed the garment into his hamper.

"What do you mean by 'if I haven't figured out by now'?"

He spun in her direction, and she stared at his bare chest and carved six-pack. Alessandra tried to recall the last time she'd seen him bare-chested. She thought it might have been when she was in middle school and he was a senior in high school. His physique distracted her, and she completely forgot the question she just asked.

"You really don't understand, do you?"

Her gaze snapped from his chest to his eyes. "Huh?"

He raised an eyebrow.

Alessandra shook her head to clear her mind. "I don't understand what?"

Hunter crossed to the door and grabbed the doorframe with his hands, blocking her from entering farther. "You don't want to get into this with me right now."

His tone ruffled the alpha in her, and she straightened with a glare. "Yes. I do."

"Alessandra," he said, his tone held a warning as clear as the use of her full name. He dropped his arms and stepped back, putting distance between them.

She encroached on his space. "Hunter, what is with you?"

His jaw clicked closed and the blaze in his eyes turned feral. "You can't be this close to me right now."

"Why not?"

"Because," he growled, and his hands curled into fists.

Alessandra looked up into his electric blue eyes and something inside her fluttered. His musky scent mixed with the aggravation radiating from him. "Because why?" Her question came out in a soft whisper.

"Because I can't get that shit out of my head. I wasn't there to stop them, and it burns more than you can fathom. Every night I hear you screaming in your sleep and that just magnifies my failure." He turned away from her and his hands slowly uncurled.

The tension in his back remained, and she reached out, placing her palm on his shoulder.

"I was the one who blew you off that night. It's not your fault."

Hunter sighed. "I should have been close enough to do something," he whispered. "I should have known."

Alessandra stepped to his side, taking in his profile. He side-eyed her, but he didn't turn to meet her gaze. "Hunter, there was no way you could have known. I didn't even sense it until it was too late."

His lashes brushed his cheeks. "You were too absorbed in trying to be normal to sense the danger."

His tone was harsh enough to draw her hand away from his skin. Hunter glared sideways. "You are always too caught up in Alessandra to see anything beyond your narrow view."

"What the hell…"

He turned, grabbed her by the arms, and slammed her against the wall, pressing his form to her with a low growl. "I've always been your equal in speed and strength out there." He jutted his chin towards the window. "And I did a damned good job leading the pack while you were away, but you never even acknowledged it. Just like you've never acknowledged this."

Alessandra stared wide-eyed into his angry features, but that wasn't what clouded her mind. It was his hard body pressed against hers, all of it, including parts she had never associated with her beta. She gasped as his hips pressed into her, making his point clear.

"That is what you do to me. Now, do you understand why I damned myself alongside you?"

Alessandra couldn't speak, she just searched his eyes. Flashes of pain and want echoed in his irises like a warning signal, and her breath hitched.

"They took what I have wanted for years. They hurt you in ways I don't have a clue how to heal. They made it so that when I brush against you, you flinch. That is harder than your naïve ignorance ever was."

"I just never…" Alessandra started.

Hunter lowered her and stepped away. "You never saw me. I get it." He put his hands up, increasing his distance.

She blinked and took him in as if staring at a stranger. "That's not it. I guess I always assumed your interest lay elsewhere, so the thought of you and me being more than just an alpha and her second in command never entered my mind."

His eyes narrowed. "But you see me now, right?" He held his arms wide.

Heat filled Alessandra's cheeks. "It's kind of hard not to."

His lips thinned as he pressed them together like he was trying to keep a comment to himself. He rolled his eyes and reached for the t-shirt on the edge of the bed.

When he covered his chiseled chest, a measure of disappointment filled her. That reaction sent a jolt of electricity from her fingertips right into the center of her soul. She had never viewed him as mate material before, and now that he had finally laid his true intentions out before her, it sparked a fiery current. One that she was deathly afraid of.

Alessandra took a step backwards, putting a buffer of space between them, and Hunter sighed.

"Really?"

Her eyes darted around the room as the discomfort built inside her like a wildfire, turning her confidence into fear. The panic attack squeezed her lungs and all her mind focused on was the abuse she'd endured in the van. The thought of another man touching her made her stomach roll, and she bolted into the hallway and nearly dove at the toilet in her bathroom, reaching it just in time for the contents of her stomach to paint the bowl.

"This is why I shredded their throats," Hunter said from behind her.

His hands gently pulled her hair away from her face and he kneeled beside her, rubbing her back as the memories overwhelmed her once more.

WOLF MOON
Chapter 2

Hunter sat in the dark, staring out into the deep woods. He had cleaned Alessandra up and tucked her into bed before retiring to the living room and the fifth of vodka he had stashed away. Alcohol wasn't a werewolf's friend, as Alessandra had found out. It shut down their senses and made it impossible to shift.

But it was also something that numbed the pain.

Alessandra's reaction tonight was not what he thought it would be. He thought by now she would have warmed up to him, or at least have seen the possibilities, especially with the spark that had filled her eyes at the sight of him shirtless.

Instead, the thought of being with him made her vomit.

He scoffed, and drained the glass, letting the bite of the vodka settle his nerves.

"What the hell did you expect?" he asked his reflection. No answer came, so he filled the glass and repeated, grimacing at the slow burn sliding down his esophagus.

He downed another drink and picked up the bottle, pouring the last few drops into his glass. His hands tingled, as did his cheeks, and he let out an enormous sigh.

"Hunter?"

He stiffened on the couch but didn't turn. The fact he hadn't heard her pad down the stairs or caught her scent in the air gave testament to the risks of alcohol for their kind.

She stepped into view, her gaze glued to the now empty bottle. Instead of drowning in the last half glass himself, he offered it to her.

She stared at it before shaking her head.

"Suit yourself." He hammered the last of the vodka back and slammed the glass on the table.

"What are you doing?"

"Getting shitfaced." He licked his numb lips. "Duh." Her incredulous look crawled under his inebriated skin. "Don't look so disappointed."

"I just..." She waved at him.

"You just what? You just thought I'd stick my tail between my legs and follow you around like I have for the last ten years?" Sarcasm rang in his voice.

"Just be a good boy and not make any waves?" Anger flared at the rise in her eyebrows. "Fuck you."

She huffed, and instead of glaring at her, he returned his gaze to the world outside.

"I've wasted ten years, hoping you'd come around, and when I finally tell you what's in my head, the thought of being with me makes you throw up," he growled and stood. The ground seemed to shift, and he reached for the couch to steady himself. "I damned myself for you. What a fucking idiot."

He stumbled to the sliders and opened the door to an arctic blast of air. He shivered and turned in her direction.

"So, just keep your opinion to yourself right now, because I don't need a lecture or some bullshit excuse. I needed a drink, so I had one."

"Do you get what they did to me?" she asked, her voice holding controlled anger.

"I don't care." Hunter went to step outside.

"You understand what a gang bang is, right?"

He paused, fighting his own memories of their stench saturating every cell, making her reek. The demons were back, and his stomach lurched. He reached the railing and leaned over, using the cold wood to catch his breath and calm the violent spasm in his belly.

"They made me swallow their dicks until I choked. They fucked me until I bled from both my vagina and my ass, but that didn't stop them. They continued to rotate until they were too tired to get it up anymore."

Hunter spun towards her. "I know," he bellowed, as his fists clenched.

"Then how the hell can you possibly think I would willingly let another man touch me ever again?" she yelled back, her voice echoing off the thick pines.

Hunter blinked, and his hands uncurled as the depths of her pain squeezed his heart to the breaking point. He didn't know how to answer her, or how to erase the horrors. But he had to try.

With a speed that belied his drunkenness, he closed the distance and pulled her into his arms, crushing her lips under his. She gasped and went rigid in his arms. He took advantage of the situation, dipping his tongue into her open mouth, tasting a hint of the mint toothpaste she had used.

The snarl that came from her, along with a shove that sent him across the porch, stopped his heart cold. She shifted in a blink and darted towards him with her teeth bared. Instead of cowering like he should have, he jumped to his feet and charged at her, still in human form.

Anger pulsed in his temples and he ducked under her snap and turned, throwing himself on her back, wrapping his arm around her neck in the process and dragged her to the ground with him. He held her spine to his chest and clamped his hand around her snout.

"Don't you dare bite me," he growled in her ear. "You may have been the alpha queen of the pack, but you aren't running a pack anymore."

She tried to dislodge her snout by shaking her head.

"It's just you and me, but I'll gladly leave you the hell alone if you keep this shit up."

She stopped moving, even relaxed against him. He loosened his grip. She twisted and stood over him with her teeth bared, the feral growl shocking him as much as her limberness had.

Hunter stared into her fiery eyes. "Go ahead." He leaned his head back, exposing his throat.

Her growl subsided, and she licked her chops before letting out a huff. She settled on top of him, nuzzling her nose under his chin. He took a deep breath and sighed, wrapping his arms around her.

He stroked her silky fur while staring at the stars above them. After a few minutes, he lifted her muzzle, making her meet his gaze. "I'm not subservient to you. If you want me to stay, we are equals," he said. "If you don't want me, then you have to cut me loose."

Her soft whine shot his nerves, leaving them raw and exposed.

"I can't stay if there is no future here." He rolled her off and headed inside. The alcohol hadn't numbed the pain piercing his heart.

"Hunter?"

He turned, taking in her tear-stained face.

She stumbled, and then the sound of the gunshot echoed. Red spread across her shoulder and his breath locked in his throat. He moved, tackling her before a second shot shattered the glass door.

She panted in his ear as he rolled her out of the sightline of the woods. His chest constricted and he could hardly pull air into his lungs. His gaze shot to the opposite side of the cottage where the car keys sat on the counter, and the door to the garage where their jeep had sat for the last couple of months. He had no idea if it would even start, but if they didn't hightail it out of here, they would be dead.

"Looks like our brief reprieve is up," he said, and met her gaze. "Time to run." He pulled her to her feet, and she winced. With her hand clasped in his, he darted across the opening, using the furniture as a barrier. He didn't slow down as he passed the counter, swiping the keys and catapulting both of them through the garage door.

Darkness flooded his vision, and he cursed the alcohol he'd just drunk. Without it, he was truly human, truly without the extra wolf's senses that kept him alive and out of danger. The buzz evaporated the moment Alessandra had launched at him, and now his heart pumped with a frantic need to purge the drug from his system, but he ignored the burn of it and swung the door open.

Alessandra climbed in and he bolted to the driver's side, fumbling with the keys. He slid them in the ignition and closed his eyes, saying a little prayer before he turned the key. The jeep jumped to life and Hunter didn't wait for the garage doors to open. Instead, he pressed down hard on the accelerator, hitting the center of the barn-style doors, knocking them wide and scraping the sides of the jeep.

He flipped on his bright lights, hoping to blind anyone wearing night vision goggles. He tore down the road, almost standing on the gas pedal. His knowledge of the roads and all the possible escape routes proved essential, and they didn't encounter anyone, which meant they had attacked from the woods, not the road.

"You okay?" he asked when they were a fair distance away and his heart rate had finally come back to normal.

Her wheezing pulled his attention from the road. He nearly ran off the blacktop at the sight of her struggling to breathe. Hunter pulled off at the next turnaround and slammed the brakes, shifting the vehicle into park before he gave her his full attention.

"Silver." Alessandra barely whispered, and Hunter reached into the back seat, pulling out the first aid kit he had stowed away.

His hands shook as he ripped through the package, looking for the scalpel. That bullet would kill her as surely as the belladonna would have if he didn't get it the hell out of her. Metal glinted, and he grabbed the scalpel, his heart slamming back home now that he had a means to dig it out.

The dread in her eyes revealed that she was already aware this was going to be painful, so instead of wasting words, he tore her shirt off and examined the wound. The blood on the front of her shirt was not an exit wound. It was from splintered fragments of her shoulder and collarbone.

"Shit," he muttered and met her gaze. "Stay in this form, no matter how much this hurts. Okay?" He waited for her nod and then went to work. She cried out, but to her credit, she did not squirm under the pressure.

Sweat speckled her forehead and the tightness of her jaw was enough to rip another patch of his heart, but he finally pulled the silver out with his fingers, ignoring the fiery burn against his skin. He looked at the cause of her agony and let out a snarl as he pitched it out the window.

"Drive," she whispered.

"I need to patch you up first."

"No. Drive. Trust me; they are close enough for me to catch a scent on the wind." Her weak voice tore his resolve, and he slid back into the seat, doing exactly as she asked until they were another fifteen minutes down the road. He turned off on a barely visible side road, parking under an overgrown pine thicket. The dull green of the jeep blended in, and he prayed they were hidden enough for him to stitch her up.

He turned on the overhead light, hating the fact he needed it. Alessandra's face was bathed in sweat and her eyes had that dull quality of shock.

"I have nothing to give you," he said, and pulled a needle and thread from the medical kit. With a deep breath, he leaned in and began the painstaking work of closing her wounds.

"I'm glad you're a doctor," she whispered as he pulled the last stitch.

He delivered her a small chuckle and met her gaze. "I never actually finished my residency."

Her eyebrows arched and he offered her a shrug.

"I only had a couple of weeks left and my final medical exam had already been scheduled..." He placed a bandage over the stitches before packing up the medical kit and stowing it away in the back seat. "But then everything went to hell... And here we are."

Hunter flipped the overhead light off and slid back into the driver's seat.

"I'm sorry. I didn't know," Alessandra whispered.

He huffed and put the car in drive. He had no idea where to go next. This was the only safe house he had bought after his father went missing, and while he had an exit strategy in place, he had hoped they wouldn't need it, because he was all out of ideas.

"Just get some rest," he said, trying to keep the annoyance churning in his stomach alongside the vodka from creeping into his voice, but he failed.

"What is your issue?" she asked.

"I can't fucking see. I can't catch a scent, either. Not with the damned alcohol in my system, and I have no idea where the hell to go."

"What about—"

"—There's nowhere left for us to go." He sent her a glare that matched his tone. With the edge of the vodka fading, anger replaced it with a relentless burn.

"No need to get bitchy. After all, I was the one who got shot," she snapped.

He swerved off the main road, barely staying on the blacktop of a nearly hidden road. The jeep jumped with every pothole and frost heave, jostling them both in the seats. The hiss from between her teeth pulled his glance her way, and he eased up on the gas pedal.

"Sorry," he muttered.

"It's okay," she said, her voice soft and full of the pain he was sure was pummeling her shoulder.

"Motel or side of the road?" he asked.

She remained silent for longer than he expected. When he looked her way, she sighed.

She sucked her lower lip between her teeth and met his gaze. "What is safer?"

"Damned if I know."

Alessandra scanned the wooded landscape. "Think we could break into one of these cabins?"

"I don't want to leave fresh tracks in the snow." He focused on the road. "But if I come across something that already has tracks, maybe that's an option."

"Is that really wise?"

He huffed a laugh. "None of the options are wise, but we might be able to get away with holding up in a cabin with people. It could mask our scents and it's something they wouldn't look for. Besides, we can say we are almost out of gas and saw the tracks. Instead of freezing out in the car..."

She kept chewing on her lip. "How do you explain this?" Ally nodded at her shoulder.

"You need to change and we need to bury the clothes in the snow."

"You've got blood on you, too."

"Then we both change." He pulled the jeep to the side and got out, making his way to the back where the emergency bag sat. It held clothes for at least a couple of days. He shuffled through the clothing, pulling out jeans and a sweater for Alessandra and a clean sweater for himself. He stripped his blood-splattered shirt and tossed it on the ground behind the jeep before going to the passenger door. "Do you need some help?" he asked, as he handed her the spare clothes.

Alessandra shook her head and shimmied on her pants under the nightshirt she wore. Hunter turned away, but her sharp intake of breath pulled him back around. She had the shirt partially off and was struggling to get her injured arm and head out of the cloth. He reached in and gently pulled it over her head, exposing her bare chest.

Hunter focused on getting the fabric off her shoulder, but the awareness that her perky breasts were inches away from his hands sent a tremor of heat through him. He dropped the bloody shirt on the ground outside and picked up the sweater from her lap, helping her to thread her injured arm into the sleeve before slipping the shirt over her head.

At that moment, he stole a glance at her sweet chest. Desire boiled in his blood and he forced himself to step back. If he stayed that close, he would do something he would regret. Instead, he picked up her nightshirt and closed the passenger door.

With every step away from the door, the burn inside him cooled. Hunter collected his shirt and jogged the way they'd come until he found what he was looking for. A snow bank big enough to hide their scent.

He squatted and started digging at the frozen snow until he had a sufficient tunnel for the two shirts. With numb fingers, he shoved the clothing as deep as it would go before filling in the hole. By the time he got back to the jeep, his hands were numb enough to sting from the warm air of the car.

Squeezing and opening his fists, he got the blood pumping until his hands tingled. Finally, he glanced at Alessandra. "Feeling better?"

She shook her head. "That really hurt."

"Just hang in there. I'll find us a safe place to get some rest. Okay?" Alessandra needed sleep to heal and being in this car would not give her the opportunity to rest. All she needed was eight hours of deep sleep and that gunshot wound would be gone. By that time, he would be back to himself as well, and no longer vulnerable like he was without his wolf's senses.

WOLF MOON
Chapter 3

IT TOOK HUNTER ANOTHER hour and a half to find a place that was occupied and had a driveway only big enough for one set of tire tracks. He carefully traced over the same tracks until he got to the garage, and instead of pulling up behind the garage, he pulled into a space next to it that would keep their vehicle hidden from the road.

"How many?"

Alessandra sniffed the air. "Four. One adult and three kids."

"Damn. A family is less likely to help."

She closed her eyes and concentrated, focusing on her good hand. Feeling the transformation start, she swung, catching his forearm, leaving four deep slices.

"Jesus," he gasped and grabbed his bleeding limb as she reined the beast back, pushing it down inside her. "What the hell did you do that for?"

"Take your shoes off," she demanded, and he did as she asked. "Now they'll help." She climbed out of the car before he could comment and waited for him to step by her side. He stared at her, holding onto his bleeding arm, and they continued to the front door. With a deep breath and a quick glance at Hunter, she knocked and waited.

She knocked again, this time getting herself set to pour out a fictional story about camping and a run in with a bear. It would also give her an excuse for why she was barefoot in the snow. A hasty retreat from a tent... and voilà.

Lights came on and she braced herself. "Just follow my lead," she said to Hunter before the door opened.

A man with a shotgun and sleep-tousled hair stood on the other side of the door.

"Oh, thank god!" Alessandra said, her voice full of panic along with a hint of relief. "My boyfriend got attacked by a bear while we were camping and I've been driving forever looking for someone to be home. I prayed that the tracks to this cottage were people coming in and not going out. Can you help us?" She kept shifting her feet, and he finally looked down.

His eyebrows rose and his gaze jumped to Hunter.

Hunter held his arm close to his chest and shrugged. "We kind of left everything in the tent, and then she proceeded to get very lost."

He lowered the shotgun a fraction, and the man glanced over his shoulder before looking back at the two of them.

"Maybe we should keep on trying to find a gas station?" Hunter said, looking at her and shifting his feet.

Alessandra looked from Hunter to the man inside. "Can you point us in the right direction?" she asked, knowing that the closest one had to be a fair distance away. Far enough for her not to pick up any gasoline scent on the light wind shuffling their clothing.

He lowered the gun a little more. "The nearest one is about thirty miles to the north. You just take a right out of the driveway and keep going."

Alessandra turned to Hunter. "I think we have enough gas to get there," she said. "Thank you," she said to the man, sending her warmest disarming smile in his direction before she turned to head back to the car.

"Wait a second," the man said, lowering the gun all the way. "What's your gas gauge on?"

Alessandra chewed her bottom lip and her gaze bounced between Hunter and the man in the doorway. "It's on E, but the light hasn't gone on yet."

The man ran his hand down his face and then sighed. "Look, I'm not comfortable with strangers in my house, but I can't, in good conscience, send you off when an empty gas tank in anything worth a damn on these roads won't make it thirty miles on empty." He stepped aside and waved for us to come in. "Why don't you come in and we can look at your friend's arm, and then we can figure out what to do about your car situation."

Alessandra gave him a grateful smile and entered the house, glad to be out of the cold. She turned when the door closed. Hunter stood on the entry tile, giving her a raised eyebrow. Her gaze dropped to her wet bare feet, leaving an imprint in the plush fibers, and she nearly jumped back onto the tile.

"Do you happen to have a towel and a first aid kit?" Hunter asked.

"You don't need to stand by the door, son. Why don't you come in and take a seat," the man said.

"I don't want to ruin your carpet," Hunter replied.

The homeowner gave him a once over. "Well, then, I best get to it." He stepped into the far hallway.

Alessandra looked at Hunter. His face had lost most of the bright color it had when he got back in the jeep after making them change. He leaned against the door, meeting her gaze with a trace of a smile.

She stepped towards him. "Are you okay?"

"I'll be fine," he said, but he certainly didn't look fine.

"Maybe you should sit."

"That's not a bad idea. The adrenaline is definitely fading." He slowly slid down to the floor and crossed his legs. "Way too much excitement for one night," he mumbled.

Alessandra let out a soft chuckle. He wasn't kidding. She was just as exhausted as he looked, and her shoulder pounded. Sleep was beginning to be a necessity, not just something nice, and she yawned.

"I'm tired, too," Hunter said, just as the man came out with a couple of towels and a first aid kit.

Wolf Moon

"The name's Stan," he said, handing a towel to Alessandra and then to Hunter.

"I'm Hunter, and my girlfriend's name is Ally," Hunter said, pointing in her direction.

The way he said girlfriend sent a warm flush through Alessandra and she tilted the edges of her lips ingo a semblance of a smile to mask the chill Hunter had created in her. It was almost as shocking a reaction as the way his lips had felt earlier.

"Let's look at that arm." Stan crouched down next to Hunter, inspecting the tears in his shirt. "You might need to take that off in order for us to get an idea of the severity of the wounds."

He attempted to shed the sweater and got his arm stuck in the fabric. Alessandra moved closer to help like he had done for her. Her hand grazed his skin as she peeled the sweater over his head and the connection lit a fire inside her. One that scared the shit out of her. His words from earlier echoed in her ears and she moved back so Stan could take a look at the damage she'd done to Hunter.

"I'm not sure I have what you need in this box," Stan said.

Alessandra eyed the cuts. She had gone deeper than she meant to.

"At least it wasn't my throat," Hunter said, trying to lighten the mood as he inspected the wounds. "I'll just need to clean the wounds and use some butterfly Band-Aids." He sucked on his lower lip and turned his eyes upwards, meeting Alessandra's gaze. "If you have a small tube of liquid band-aid, that would help as well."

"All I have is what's in this kit," Stan said, and flipped open the case.

Hunter took a deep breath and laid the towel across his lap. "Do you have hydrogen peroxide?"

Stan shook his head.

"Whiskey?" Hunter asked.

Stan nodded and disappeared into the kitchen.

"You're not drinking that, are you?" Alessandra asked.

Hunter' shoulders jerked in a sloppy shrug. "That might dull the pain when I flush the wounds with it."

The sting of irritation raked through her, but the flash in his eyes daring her to say more kept her silent. She had caused his pain. All of it, and nothing she could say would stop him from his current self-destructive path. At least nothing she was willing to admit to.

Stan came back with the bottle and handed it to Hunter. Alessandra pressed her lips together as he unscrewed the bottle. The man actually hesitated and closed his eyes for a second. When he opened his eyes, his blue irises shone, and he clenched his jaw, pouring the scotch across his arm. Air hissed between his teeth. Then he brought the bottle to his lips and took a hefty sip before handing it back.

"Thanks," he said, and then patted the broken skin with the towel, blotting both blood and alcohol from the wounds. Hunter looked at Alessandra. "I need you to put the butterfly band-aids across the cuts where I tell you."

Alessandra stepped closer, putting his shirt next to him on the floor. Both she and Stan fished through the kit, pulling out a dozen of the small elastic sutures. They carefully patched Hunter's arm at his direction, and when the worst of the wounds were closed, they wrapped his arm in gauze from his wrist to his elbow.

"That should do it," he said as Alessandra taped the end of the gauze with a small band-aid. "Thanks," he added.

Stan stood, gathered the remnants of their triage session. "I have a guest room downstairs, if you two want to catch some sleep. We can figure out what to do about gas in the morning."

Her gaze linked with Hunter's and she gave Stan a nod. If he had meant them harm, he probably would have done something by now. "That would be nice. I think, now that the adrenaline has faded, we both could use a little rest before we deal with anything else."

"Much appreciated." Hunter climbed to his feet.

Stan brought them into a partially finished basement that held a double bed. He waved towards the opposite corner. "There's a powder room over there where you can clean up. There're a couple of hand towels for you. The bed's already made. My son's friends are supposed to be swinging in tomorrow, so…"

"We hope to be out of your hair before your guests arrive," Hunter said. "Thank you for your hospitality. It is a rare quality these days."

Stan's cheeks bloomed at the compliment. He left them to their own devices, closing the door at the top of the stairs. The click of the lock caught her attention.

"He doesn't trust us," she said.

Hunter lay on his back on the bed. "He's just being cautious." He waved toward the bulkhead doors to their right. "We can still get out, but with the door upstairs locked, we can't get to his family. He's compassionate, but not blind to what could happen."

Alessandra stood staring at the small bed, and Hunter sprawled out on the mattress. Finally, he lifted his head and met her gaze.

"I'm not sleeping on the bare floor," he said, and she cocked an eyebrow at him. "We both need sleep to heal. I'm not tossing and turning on the floor, so you choose. You can share the bed with me, or you can have the floor."

"What if I order you?"

He slowly sat up. "If you order me? What the fuck? I saved your ass tonight. I deserve a soft mattress. Don't worry, princess, I'm not in the mood for anything other than sleep tonight."

"Hunter," she started.

"Once I get you somewhere safe, I'm not sticking around," he said, and rolled to his side, giving her a view of his back.

Alessandra stared at the remaining space on the bed and then the hard industrial carpet on the floor. Instead of immediately dealing with the situation, she stepped into the bathroom to relieve herself and wash up as best she could.

When she returned, his soft snore filled the room, and the tension in his back had relaxed. His injured arm hung over the edge of the bed and the small red stains in the bandage tugged at her. With no more arguments, she climbed under the covers, facing away from Hunter.

Heat from his close proximity bathed her with a strange comfort. Alessandra sighed, letting the exhaustion finally drag her under.

WOLF MOON
Chapter 4

H**UNTER WOKE AND BLINKED** at his surroundings. His shirt was balled up on the floor and his senses were back to their heightened wolf level. Alessandra's arm draped around his waist and he stared at it for a moment before turning his head.

The movement made her stir, and she pulled her arm with her as she rolled onto her back. The absence of her skin against his almost pulled a groan from his throat. If she didn't address this attraction, he had to cut her loose for sanity's sake.

She made the sweetest noise and stretched. It took everything he had not to pounce, and he took a deep soothing breath to staunch the fire burning in his soul.

Alessandra's eyes popped open, and her head snapped in his direction. She nearly jumped from the bed, her gaze jumping from him to their surroundings. He could almost see the click in her mind as the memory of where they were, and why, flooded her brain. Red bloomed in her cheeks, and she rolled her shoulder.

It was amazing what solid rest did for a werewolf. His arm had the faint itch of healing. If he peeled back the gauze, there would be nothing but light scratches, and he ventured to guess Alessandra's shoulder was healed. He'd have to remove the stitches after they got out of here.

"You didn't yield," she said, and her hands found her waist.

Just like that, the serene morning turned to shit, and aggravation braised every inch of him. He climbed out of bed and swiped the shirt off the floor, passing by her without a word. When he finished his business and rinsed the sleep from his mouth, he opened the bathroom door.

Alessandra stood, shifting from foot to foot, and almost ran him down in her bid to get inside the washroom. Hunter straightened out the bed and cocked his head, listening for signs of life upstairs. Nothing stirred.

He rested his gaze on Alessandra when she stepped out of the bathroom and then headed up the stairs. He tried the doorknob and let out a small sigh of relief when it turned easily. The morning sun spilled into the living room and the note sitting on the nearest table caught his attention.

"They unlocked the door?" Alessandra said from behind him.

"Yes. And left a note. They went to get us some gas. They said to help ourselves in the kitchen." He held the note so she could see. "I guess he didn't want us alone with the kids," he added with a shrug.

"You didn't answer me downstairs," she said, returning to her scolding.

"I'm not yours to command, Ally. We had this discussion yesterday before the shooting started."

"Bullshit. I'm the alpha here."

Her domineering tone set him off, and he spun on his heel. "You really want to challenge me right now?" he barked.

"I want you to snap out of this shit. Now," she said.

"In all the years we've known each other, have you ever seen me just bow down to you because you told me to?" he asked.

"You always did what I asked."

He laughed. Miss high and mighty needed to be set in her place. "I did what was right for the pack, and most times that coincided with your requests. Jesus, do you really think I'd blindly follow anyone? Are you that fucking naïve?"

She glared at him.

"You don't know a goddamned thing about me, do you?" he snarled. "I bet you don't even know my real name?"

She blinked at him. "Hunter Blaez," she said meekly, and it burned right in the center of his core.

"No. It's actually Jacob. Jacob Randall Blaez. Hunter is a fucking nickname my dad gave me when I was younger, and it stuck." He towered over her, glaring down into her upturned face, torn between walking away and taking her in his arms.

"Well, I bet you don't know anything about me." She crossed her arms. Her lips pressed together in that smug way that sent him over the edge.

"Your name is Alessandra Elizabeth Tate," he said, with no hesitation and her eyes widened. "Your favorite color is blue, and your favorite food isn't steak, like it is for most wolves. It's actually spicy chicken. You talk to your dead mother every night before you go to sleep, asking her to guide you, and you curse your father for leaving you behind and taking the council's side. You pretend to hate chick flicks, but you secretly love them as much as you do action films. And while you flinch at the thought of a man touching you, deep down, you want someone to make that pain disappear. Do you need me to continue?"

Her eyes narrowed, and her jaw tightened. He stepped closer, and she backed into the wall. Hunter planted his hands on either side of her head and leaned forward so his eyes were level with hers.

"I'm also aware that you sense whatever the hell this is between us."

The sound of the garage door pulled him away, and he stepped into the kitchen, finding two coffee cups along with sugar and creamer waiting next to the pot. He poured both cups and fixed Alessandra's the way she liked it and left his black, hoping it was strong enough to fuel him for the day.

He turned and handed the cup to her, and she raised an eyebrow.

Wolf Moon

"I'm mad, not a dick," he mumbled as the door to the house opened.

"I see you found the coffee," Stan said as three teenagers bounded into the house. Two girls and a boy came in and the girls stopped short at the sight of him.

"We hear you got attacked by a bear," the boy said from behind the two stunned girls.

Hunter pulled his shirtsleeve up to show the bandage. "Yeah and I lived. Can you believe it?" He sent a grin their way and sent a side-eye at Alessandra. "Your dad was kind enough to help us out." He reached into his back pocket and pulled out his wallet. "How much do I owe you for the gas?"

Stan waved his hand. "Don't worry about it."

Hunter's senses prickled. Alessandra was too busy sipping her coffee to catch the nuance of fear from Stan. The kids headed down the hall and Stan watched them go before he turned back to Hunter.

"So..." Stan's eyes darted between Hunter and Alessandra.

Hunter put down his cup. "We should be going. We've taken up too much of your time and kindness already," he said. "Come on, honey," he said to Alessandra, and held his hand out.

Alessandra still clutched her coffee, and she stared at his offered hand for a second before she slid into character. She set the cup on the counter and slipped her hand in his. Hunter's chest loosened as she smiled at Stan.

"Thank you so much for your hospitality," she said.

"Why are your boots in the jeep?" Stan asked before they passed, and Hunter stopped.

He bit his lip and sighed. "Would you really have permitted us to come in if I had my boots on?" He waited, meeting Stan's gaze.

"It was my idea," Alessandra added. "We needed help, and Mr. Skeptical here said no one in their right mind would let us in their house that late at night."

Hunter raised an eyebrow at her, impressed at her improv skills.

Stan huffed. "So, why did you have shoes and she didn't?"

Hunter shifted and looked down at the ground. "I was getting a little too close to nature," he said, and smirked. "And she struck back."

Stan pressed his lips together. "Really?" Sarcasm laced the question.

"I didn't realize a mamma bear was hibernating in the brush I relieved myself in." He shifted, wondering if they should have chosen some other animal. It was rare for bears to be out and about at this time of year, and if he had been thinking straight, he might have chosen something else, instead of a bear attack.

Stan reached out and grabbed the rifle leaning on the wall. "You sure it has nothing to do with that home invasion a couple of towns over?" He turned his phone towards them, and their pictures graced the screen with a wanted sign underneath.

Shit. "Yes." Hunter said as he moved his gaze from his picture to Stan. "My arm wasn't torn to shreds by a person."

Alessandra squeezed his hand. "That was our house," she said, drawing Stan's attention. "Someone attacked us."

"This says there's an outstanding warrant for your arrest." He waved his phone at them.

Wolf Moon

Hunter pulled the side of his lip between his teeth. The gun wasn't quite level, but Stan had his fingers near enough to the trigger to keep Hunter from trying to rip the weapon from him.

Noises behind them caused Alessandra's hand to clamp down on his.

"We didn't come here for trouble," Hunter said softly. "We needed some rest, and now we'll get out of your hair."

The cock of a gun behind them made him close his eyes.

"You really don't want to do this." Hunter met Stan's gaze.

"Why not?"

Hunter took a gamble. "If someone you loved was raped and beaten and left for dead, what would you do?"

The gun lowered, and Stan's jaw tightened.

"I took justice into my own hands. That's why I have an outstanding warrant."

Alessandra's head lowered and her shame and horror swept over him. He gave her hand a squeeze, glad she still held tight.

"And some son of a bitch bounty hunter shot us out of our home last night."

"Your arm?" he asked, pointing the barrel of the gun.

"To be honest, I'm clueless about what happened," he confessed because he had run out of lies. "I didn't even know I was bleeding until we pulled into your driveway." He sighed.

"Please, just let us go," Alessandra said. "We really don't want any trouble."

"What about the reward, Pa?" the boy behind them said.

Her hand tightened around Hunter's, as if she had an inkling of the question that would be asked next.

"Is he telling the truth about what happened to you?"

Hunter glanced at her, and the shame was visible in the heightened color of her cheeks, but the single tear that escaped her right eye said more than her slight nod. It broke his heart, and he took a deep breath, blinking back the wetness in his own eyes.

Stan seemed to be affected in the same manner. The barrel of the shotgun dropped to the floor. He looked beyond them to the boy. "I understand you wanted that reward, son, but I can't, in good conscience, hold these two."

"They could be lying," he said, and both Alessandra and Hunter turned to look at him.

The boy's gaze moved from Hunter to Alessandra. The gun slowly lowered. Somehow, he could see the damage reflected in her eyes, and relief washed over Hunter. He let out the breath he wasn't aware he had been holding.

With no more words, he led Alessandra out the front door.

Alessandra took the driver's seat, moving his boots to the back seat. "I'm driving," she said. "Want to put the gas they got into the tank?"

Hunter peered at the gas can on the ground near the entrance. His feet were already cold, but he could deal with the snow biting his flesh for a few more minutes. He grabbed the container and emptied the contents into the Jeep's gas tank. Before jumping into the car, he put the empty container back where he'd found it and then slid into the passenger seat.

Alessandra had the heater going, and the flow of warm air on his cold feet felt good.

"Where to?" she asked.

Hunter digested the question as she pulled to the end of the driveway. Heading back in the direction they came would most likely be a death sentence.

"North and West is really where I want to go, but there is no way we can cross the border with our faces plastered all over the news." The Canadian border was less than a two-hour drive from their current hiding place in central Maine. "It's also the direction they will assume we've gone since they tracked us here."

"Then we go the opposite direction."

"We can't go much farther East, honey," he said, glancing at her.

Her lips pressed together, and she shot him a glare.

He couldn't suppress his grin fast enough, and looked out the window instead. "Where do you think the last place they'd look for us would be?"

"The Florida Keys," she said.

He laughed. Werewolves were not known for their fondness of heat, and the Keys were the last place he wanted to go. Just the thought brought sweat to the surface, and he wiped his neck, shuddering at the thought. It also meant no hunting grounds. They'd have to actually work to buy food in order to survive.

"The only other place hotter is probably Arizona," he said. At least the desert would give them a chance to hunt.

"Yeah, but they'll look there. They won't look at the islands, where we can't hunt."

Hunter sighed and gave a nod. "The Florida Keys it is."

WOLF MOON
Chapter 5

ALESSANDRA'S EYELIDS DROOPED AND her right leg ached. She had been driving a little over twelve hours, and the Washington, DC traffic had nearly done her in. Hunter slumped in the passenger seat. He had slept most of the drive. The lack of conversation between them wasn't exactly ideal, but at least he hadn't brought up the argument from this morning.

She had only stopped for gas, paying cash from Hunter's stash. And at each stop, he woke and asked if she'd like him to drive. She had needed to concentrate on the road, otherwise all the thoughts and feelings bottled inside her would overflow, and she had no idea what that would bring.

"You need to let me drive."

She startled when she heard his voice and the car swerved, narrowly missing the truck in the next lane.

"Jesus!" she snapped, as her heart pounded in her throat. That pleasant lull of hypnotic driving had disappeared at the sound of his voice.

"Why don't we get off at the next exit, grab some food, and then I can drive for the next stretch," he said, in that perfectly reasonable tone that made her want to growl at him, despite her stomach being in full agreement.

"Fine," she said.

He raised his eyebrow at her. "You're the one who insisted on driving," he said, picking up on her irritation.

Alessandra took a deep breath. He was right. Her foul mood really had more to do with her internal reflection over the last twelve hours.

"Maybe we should find a place to sleep for the night." She didn't want to sleep in the passenger seat. While Hunter could drop to sleep almost anywhere, she could never sleep soundly in a car.

"I'll be good to drive for a while."

"I need a bed, not an uncomfortable bucket seat."

He raised an eyebrow. "I slept just fine."

"You could sleep anywhere. I can't."

"Fine," he said, and shifted in the seat. "We can find somewhere off the next exit. If we're going to just hang out for the night, I may go out for a bit."

"Why?" she asked, giving him a sideways glance.

Wolf Moon

"Once I fully wake up and eat, I'm not going to be able to fall asleep right away. Not after sleeping for this long. I'll have too much energy and I'll need to burn some of it off."

"How?" she asked, keeping her eyes peeled for an exit sign.

"I don't know. Maybe I'll go for a run. Or maybe I'll find a bar and get drunk."

She snapped her head in his direction and the grin that he tried to hide surfaced. He was needling her on purpose.

"Fuck you," she muttered.

"That's another way I can release some energy," he said.

"Stop it." This obviously was the end of her peaceful drive.

"We need to finish our conversation from this morning," he said, and stretched in the passenger seat.

All things considered, Alessandra had ended up with a protector who was very easy on the eyes. She shook her head, trying to clear that thought from her mind.

"Was that a no?"

His voice carried a challenge she wasn't prepared to face. She also wasn't ready to deal with the truth of his words this morning. She'd had a long drive with him sleeping. A long time to think about the chemistry that had always seemed to exist. She just mistook it as some strange brotherly-type overprotectiveness.

Hell, he had dated, even flaunted his girls to the pack. She had always been highly skeptical of the women he brought to meet them. None of them were ever good enough for him. Not in her mind, and now that she looked back, it seemed to stem more from jealousy than her alpha scrutiny.

She had dated as well, and he had been just as critical of the guys she'd introduced to the pack. Jeremy was a gross misjudgment, and Alessandra was sure if she had introduced him to her pack, they would have picked up on his dark intentions. Jeremy had stripped her of any trust of the male population, including Hunter.

She wasn't sure she'd ever find that trust again, despite any attraction that might be there under the surface.

Instead of answering his question, she took the next exit and followed the lodging signs. She pulled into a seedy-looking motel on the main strip, and grinned at the sign.

The Hunter Motel in Newington, Virginia, certainly wasn't the type of hotel she would normally stay at, but it had a little restaurant attached, and it was the only place visible on the strip.

Hunter's dimples appeared when she pulled up next to the office. He went to step out of the jeep.

"Maybe I should go in," she said. "You look the same as your wanted poster."

"And you don't?"

"No. Not like you do." Alessandra took her long hair and rolled it into a bun. Hunter raised an eyebrow at her when her lips curved up at the corners in a sly smirk. She scanned her reflection in the mirror and secured the tight bun. With her hair pulled away from her face, she looked less like the girl in the poster.

"I'll be right back." She grabbed a handful of bills from the box hidden in the console.

She strode into the office and stifled a yawn with her hand. A pimply guy sat at the desk, gaping at something she couldn't see. She cleared her throat, and he jumped.

"I need a room for the night. Preferably ground floor near the restaurant, if possible," she asked.

"The only one I have on the first floor near the restaurant has a single king. Is that okay?" he asked, as he pushed aside whatever had captivated him.

As much as she would prefer separate beds, the location of the room was more important. "That's fine."

With the key in hand, she slid back into the jeep. She studied Hunter's beard and shoulder-length hair. He looked exactly like the wanted poster, and she had never seen him without scruff on his face or a short haircut.

"You need to change your look." She speared a look in his direction as she pulled into the parking space in front of their room.

"What's wrong with my look?" He sent her a sideways glance before he slipped out and opened the back.

She waited at the door while Hunter grabbed the oversized suitcase. He followed her inside, and she closed the door before he could comment on the accommodations.

He set the suitcase down on the dresser and flipped it open. "I need a shower before we eat." He didn't even peek in her direction; instead, he grabbed clothes out of the suitcase and disappeared into the bathroom.

She needed to clean up as well and stepped to the bag to see what he'd packed in their emergency exit kit. She retrieved a sundress and spaghetti strap sandals, smiling. It wasn't quite warm enough in Virginia, but Florida would be perfect for this. Jeans, shorts and t-shirts were the only other things left in the suitcase, along with nightclothes. She pulled out a second pair of jeans and a plain blue t-shirt that matched Hunter's eyes. He had packed underwear and a couple of bras for her as well. His stash was mostly the same. Jeans and t-shirts, but under it all, he'd also packed a suit and dress shoes. The dichotomy of the different clothing tickled her.

She climbed on the bed and switched the television on while she waited. Another yawn caught her off guard, especially with the accompanying stomach rumble. The shower had gone off a while ago and Alessandra wondered what the hell he was doing in there. She needed food and sleep, and if he didn't come out soon, she was going to march in there and take over the bathroom.

She stood up to do just that when the door opened. The man standing there didn't look at all familiar. His short, dark locks were slicked back, and his clean-shaven cheeks glowed in the dim light. His bright blue eyes sparkled under the frame of deep black lashes. He was stunningly handsome.

"Hunter?" she couldn't help but ask.

His teeth shone pearly through his grin. "Better?" He waved at his face.

"Holy shit," she said, and before she could stop herself, she crossed and ran her hand down his cheek. It was as smooth as she imagined it would be.

He captured her hand, holding it in place as he stared down at her. "I gather you like the new look?"

The heat from his breath tickled her wrist, and she pulled it from his grip.

"I may have ruined your razor, though," he said as she slipped past him.

She closed the bathroom door and leaned on it, trying to catch her breath. She had never seen him clean shaven. Nor had she ever seen him with short hair. With long hair and a beard, he looked more like a free-spirited hippie, but with what he looked like now, he could easily walk into a modeling agency in New York and be given a contract on the spot.

Her gaze landed on the sink and the stray hairs he had missed in his attempt to clean up. The scissors from the first aid kit sat on the edge of the sink, along with her razor. She huffed a laugh, hoping the razor had a little sharpness left, but she doubted it.

She undressed and peeled off the bandages on her shoulder. The bullet hole was gone, but the stitches were still there. Alessandra wrapped a towel around herself and opened the door.

"Did you want to take these out before I jump in the shower?"

Hunter's gaze jumped from the stitches to the towel wrapped around her before he gave a nod and climbed off the bed. He took a seat on the closed toilet and grabbed the scissors from the sink before pulling her close.

"And you couldn't do this because?" he asked as he snipped each stitch.

"Because it freaks me out a little." She met his gaze and then looked at the ceiling. The pull on her skin sent a chill through her and she shivered.

He shifted her closer and continued to remove each thread. When he finished, his hands landed on her waist, pulling her gaze from the ceiling to his. Warmth radiated through her.

"All done," he said, but he stayed put and she didn't move from between his knees.

The moment stretched as she searched his eyes. There was no denying the attraction that lived between them, but it terrified her. His hand cupped her cheek and the fondness that filled his eyes brought a lump to her throat.

"Do you feel it?" he whispered with such desperation that her heart ached.

She leaned into his hand, unable to say yes, and unable to deny the electricity flowing through her entire form. He slid forward and pressed his lips to hers. The soft contact set her heart on overdrive and broke through her paralysis.

She stepped away, grasping at the towel to keep it in place. Hunter leaned back and took a deep breath before the hardness returned to his features.

"Clean up. I need food just as much as you do," he said, and left the bathroom, slamming the door behind him.

Alessandra stepped into the shower and dialed it to the coldest setting her skin would allow, staunching the heat that had encompassed her the moment Hunter's lips found hers.

WOLF MOON
Chapter 6

Hunter sat on the edge of the bed listening to the water run. His heart still hammered in his chest. Alessandra hadn't flinched. She had actually kissed back for a moment before she stepped away. The woman hadn't refused to acknowledge the presence of something, so all his posturing at Stan's house must have sunk in.

He glanced at the door and sighed, running his hand through his short hair. The whole situation left his nerves raw and his libido chomping at the bit. The beast in him wanted to storm in and take her to heights she'd never experienced, but the man kept him in check. If he gave in to his animal instincts, that would ruin everything.

As much as she infuriated him, he longed to break through her barriers. He yearned to be the one who fixed her. He wished to be the one to erase the nightmares. The truth of being in love with Alessandra had always been rough, but now that she was aware, she was seeing him as a man and not her backup wolf.

The door finally opened, and she stepped out. Her wet hair hung loosely around her face, and she avoided his gaze.

"We need to figure out what to call each other."

Her gaze snapped to his. "What do you mean?"

"Well, with the outstanding warrants looking for Hunter Blaez and Alessandra Tate, we should probably start calling each other something different in public."

Her arms crossed. "Why didn't they use your real name?"

"Because the dipshits don't know it. I've got my original birth certificate and my social security number with me. My driver's license was mistakenly made using my nickname, and I never corrected it. Because of that, all my credit cards and loans and shit were made out to Hunter Blaez."

Her eyebrows went up.

"Yeah. My father decided I should leave it alone, and he made sure I had my documents before he died. He said to keep them close in case I needed to make a run for it. I guess he was aware that I'd get myself in trouble someday."

"But how did you figure out to take them with you?"

Hunter chuckled. "My dad never trusted the council, and he taught me to be prepared for anything. Why do you think I have a hidden compartment in my car?"

Alessandra studied him. "It's like you're a complete stranger to me."

"I'm a survivalist, Ally. And I had the forethought to grab my personal shit before I left my house that night." He laughed. "I remember second guessing myself, trying to laugh away the urgency in the pit of my stomach. But I still listened. I still packed up my father's fortune and anything that would do me any good on the road. When I left the house that night, I knew I was never going back home." He paused and closed his eyes. "I'm not sure if it was the wolf thing between us, or if it was some kind of warning from my father, but my heart was in my throat that entire night. The pack wasn't all that cooperative, either. They just wanted to go hunting and have some fun, but I couldn't. I said we needed to track you down, especially when I couldn't get hold of you on your cell. They thought I was fucking nuts until we caught your scent in those woods."

"I didn't know," she whispered, and crossed to the suitcase, depositing her dirty clothing on the side.

He stood and stepped behind her, looking at her reflection. "At least you have something to call me." Her lips twitched into a smirk, and she met his gaze in the mirror. "And it's not asshole."

"Aww. I kind of like that," she whined, pulling a grin to his face.

"Seriously. What do you want me to call you? Sandra?"

She wrinkled her nose in response and then chewed her bottom lip. Just the motion of her lip sliding into her mouth distracted him. "How about Leigh?" she asked.

His eyebrows went up as he considered it. Instead of reacting to the visceral need to kiss her, he concentrated on the name, framing it in his mind and silently saying it in his head.

"I actually like that," he said, and she turned towards him, looking up into his eyes.

"I'm glad," she said, and licked her lips. "Jake."

"Jacob," he said, correcting her. He wanted her to call him by his rightful name, not another nickname.

"Jake," she repeated, challenging him.

He rolled his eyes. "Fine. You ready to go grab some food, Leigh?" He had mixed feelings about her new nickname for him, but he certainly liked the way Leigh rolled off his tongue. From the pink hue in her cheeks, she seemed to like it as well.

They were seated at the little diner, and he looked over the menu. The bacon cheeseburger looked like it would hit the spot, and he closed his menu. Alessandra had her hands folded neatly over the menu and she was fixated on the moving traffic out the window.

"Leigh, we need to talk about earlier," he said, figuring the restaurant was a safe space, one that neither of them would make a scene in.

She blinked at him, pointing her finger at her chest in such a way that Hunter wanted to drag her from the restaurant and put her over his knee. He clenched his teeth.

"This is not the place," she said, eyeing the approaching hostess.

Hunter turned his attention to the perky waitress, leveling the sizzling smile he had been told would make Mother Teresa take him to bed. The waitress reacted, smiling back and nearly ignoring Alessandra. Out of the corner of his eye, he saw her bristle. If she had been in wolf form, all her hair would be standing on end and her teeth would be bared. Hunter couldn't help it. The jealousy radiating from her stroked his ego in a way it hadn't been stroked in years.

"What can I getcha?" the waitress asked, her sole focus on Hunter.

"My girlfriend will have a spicy chicken sandwich with fries and a vanilla milkshake."

At the mention of girlfriend, the waitress' leer faltered.

"And I'll have three bacon cheeseburgers, along with a vanilla milkshake."

The waitress wandered away with their order, and he focused back on Alessandra.

"Girlfriend?"

"It's better than alpha bitch."

Her eyes narrowed.

"I have half a mind to kick your ass," she muttered under her breath. It wasn't quite low enough for him not to pick it up.

"Maybe we can do that when we get back to the room," he teased, in the same low tone.

Her lips twitched up at the edges, and for the first time in a very long time, her eyes sparkled with mirth.

The waitress came with their vanilla milkshakes, and she gave a tight facsimile of a smile to the two of them and dropped the straws in the middle of the table. Hunter waited until she was out of hearing range before picking up the straws and offering one to Alessandra.

"Aren't you tired of pretending?" he asked, after he took a sip.

The shine in her eyes dulled. He silently kicked himself.

"I haven't been."

All his good humor disappeared. "What do you want to do when we get to Key West?" he asked, changing the subject because her denial was just as infuriating as her cluelessness had been. There was no use in arguing in the restaurant.

"Swim in the ocean," she said.

"I was thinking about getting a boat. Maybe a cabin cruiser." He sent her a sideways glance.

"Don't you need a boating license?"

He leaned closer. "Jacob has one in his name." He met her gaze and leaned back, relishing her open-mouthed stare. He had played shadow, and then nursemaid, for way too long. It was time to peel back the layers of who he really was. It might be a risk, but everything they did now was a risk.

"As I said before, I don't know a thing about you."

He grinned and took a sip of his milkshake. "The key question here is, do you, or do you not, want to find out what truly makes me tick?" He challenged her with a raise of his eyebrow.

Blush crawled through her cheeks, and she couldn't meet his gaze. The waitress came with their food, and he swore she exhaled with relief. Instead of focusing on her, his mind, as well as his stomach, pulled to the plate in front of him. A small voice in the back of his head reminded him to mind his manners. He was in a public venue, not in the middle of the woods devouring a fresh kill.

Alessandra must have been thinking the same, because they ate like civilized adults. When the plates were cleared, and the meal done, he wiped his mouth with a napkin and met her gaze.

"I'm going to have to go on a run after this," he said.

"I need sleep." She covered the yawn that followed.

"You don't want to go for a short run?"

She shook her head.

After peeling off enough cash to cover the bill and a decent tip, they left the restaurant and headed back to the room. Stepping inside, he closed the shades and locked the door, before sitting in the chair near the table, while she changed in the bathroom. His light mood at the restaurant had darkened. He didn't want to leave her alone in the hotel room, but he needed to get rid of this pent-up energy inside him. His fingers drummed on the table while his knee bounced.

Alessandra stepped out of the bathroom and his entire form went still. She wore a spaghetti strapped nightshirt that came down to her mid-thigh. The sweetheart neckline showed some of her cleavage. He'd completely forgotten he had thrown that in the suitcase and seeing it on her turned the fire inside him into an inferno.

He stood to leave.

"Please don't go."

He stopped with his hand on the chain, fully aware that his body had reacted to the sexiness of the outfit along with the plea in her voice.

"Ally, you really don't want me to stay."

Silence filled the space long enough for him to look over his shoulder. The way she hugged herself and stared at the ground clawed at him and he sighed.

"You really think I'm a bitch?" Her gaze lifted, but this time, there was a feral challenge in her eyes.

He turned to face her. "So, you really want to kick my ass?" He crossed the distance and stared down at her. "Go for it," he whispered, sensing the beast bristling within him.

Without any warning, he was suddenly on his back on the ground with Alessandra straddling him. She also had his wrists pinned to the ground on either side of his head. The growl in the back of her throat was the sexiest thing he had ever heard, and his body responded. He ambushed her with a smile.

She blinked down at him. "You're not supposed to be enjoying this," she snapped.

"I disagree." He rolled, pinning her underneath him, using her grip against her. He stared down at her. His smirk faded at the fear now present in her eyes. "I'm not going to do anything," he breathed, and rose to his knees, letting her scuttle out from underneath him.

Her breath remained ragged as she sat on the corner of the bed. He climbed to his feet and took the space next to her. The mattress vibrated. Alessandra's entire body trembled, and her hair blocked her face.

Hunter reached out and tucked the strands behind her ear. This time, she flinched away from him.

"Fuck," he growled, and sprung to his feet. A silver knife slicing through his abdomen would have been a lot less painful. He headed straight towards the door.

"Jacob," her shaking voice stopped him, along with the use of his real name.

Wolf Moon

"What?" His heart squeezed with disappointment and a level of fury he could hardly contain. If he could turn the clock back, he would relish every scream and dying gurgle that came out of those bastards.

"I'm afraid," she whispered.

"Of what?"

"Of everything."

He leaned his head against the door and asked the only question that really mattered. "Do you ever think you could love me?"

"Yes," the softest whisper reached his ears, and he turned, meeting her tear-stained eyes. "But I'm not sure I will ever trust anyone again."

A part of him growled inside. He was uncertain about what else he could do to earn her trust. Instead of heading out for a much-needed run, he collapsed in the chair next to the door. He would not get any relief from the pent-up emotions locked inside him. What he really wanted to do was rip that negligee off her and lick every inch of her skin.

Alessandra just stared at him. "What's going through your mind?"

He huffed a laugh. "You really want to know?" he asked.

She slid under the covers, pulling the sheet up to her chin. She looked like a terrified child, and he cursed the want pulsing in his blood.

"Honestly?"

She gave a single nod.

"I was just thinking about licking every inch of your skin."

Her eyes widened and her cheeks turned bright pink.

"You asked."

She let out a nervous laugh and her gaze found the ceiling.

"But I'll stay right here for the night because the thought freaks you out."

The red in her cheeks blotched and tears slipped from the corner of her eyes.

He leaned his head back and stared at the ceiling. His hands gripped the arms of the chairs so hard the metal under the fabric groaned. "Someday, I'd like to be the one to replace those nightmares with something tender and loving."

"I have nightmares it's you hurting me," she said, through a hitched breath. "Those are the ones that undo me every time."

His gaze found hers and it took every ounce of willpower not to cross the room and take her in his arms. Every detail of her pain scraped at him and he pressed his lips together, blinking away the mist that covered his eyes.

"No one is going to hurt you like that ever again," he said. "Not while I'm breathing."

When she held her arms out for him, he scrambled across the distance and pulled her into his chest. Her sobs shook her form, and he stroked her silky hair, softly cooing in her ears until her last hitching breaths wound down.

"On a lighter note, at least you didn't vomit when I kissed you earlier."

Her halfhearted laugh brought a spark of hope to his heart. She pulled away, and he met her gaze, wiping the tears from her cheeks with his thumbs. A tear came to rest at the corner of her mouth and before she could catch it with her tongue, Hunter leaned in and delivered a kiss that caught the tear.

She gasped, and the opportunity presented itself. He slid his tongue into her mouth, exploring. Alessandra stiffened under his lips, but her tongue tentatively swiped his, slowly rolling in a sensual circle. He groaned with the sweetness of it.

She planted her hand on his chest and the kiss deepened right before she pushed him away. He met her gaze, and they stared at each other for what seemed an eternity. For the first time, he saw the spark of want in her eyes, but alongside it was her fear.

He planted a kiss on her forehead and headed into the bathroom, locking the door behind him. As he stripped his clothes, he debated between a cold shower or satisfying his need for release. He didn't think a cold shower would do anything to quell the pent-up energy in the center of his being. So, he dialed the water to hot and stepped under the spray. With his hand soaped up, he closed his eyes and imagined all the decadent things he wanted to do to Alessandra.

He sped his stroke as the energy pooled in his belly. In his mind's eye, Alessandra moved under him with the same fervor, her hips rising to meet his. He clenched his mouth closed and squeezed his eyes tight as his body responded. He kept stroking, his body jerking with the force of each spurt. He slowed his stroke and opened his eyes. His jizz dripped from the wall and he let out a light chuckle at how much had come out. It had been way too long since he'd had any form of release. Hunter cleaned both himself and the shower walls and then dialed the water into the frigid zone to cool the heat still burning inside.

By the time he stepped into the bedroom, he had his libido in check. Alessandra's soft breathing told him she was sound asleep, and he sighed and changed into a pair of running shorts. Halfway to the door, her soft groan stopped him. The acrid stench of fear spread through the room.

Her moan became a muffled scream, and he closed his eyes, turning around and stepping close to the bed. Gently, he ran his fingers through her hair, starting at her temple.

"It's okay, baby," he whispered. "It's okay."

"No!"

Her scream shot to the depths of his soul, and she shot up to a sitting position, panting. Her eyes darted around frantically, finally landing on him kneeling by the side of the bed.

"You died." Her voice shook. "They found us and I watched you die."

Hunter sat on the edge of the bed facing her. "It was just a dream," he said, trying to keep his voice soft and calm, like he always did when she had nightmares. Although the subject of this one differed from the others. Usually, her nightmares revolved around the horrors that happened to her in the fraternity van.

Her arms encircled his neck, shocking him into momentary inaction. When his brain caught up, his arms wrapped around her as tightly as hers were around his neck. Her trembling turned his nerves into raw receptors, and he pressed his lips to the edge of her throat, nuzzling her neck. His fingers grazed the sides of her breasts. "It was just a dream," he whispered in her ear, but held fast, not wanting this intimate moment to end.

Her trembling subsided, but her grip on him didn't loosen. Instead, her lips found the side of his neck. Her butterfly kisses nearly made him lose all the control the cold shower had given him.

"Don't start something you have no intent on finishing," he warned, and her teeth clamped down on his earlobe. Chills rippled through him and his grip tightened. "Ally, please," he whispered. He wasn't sure if he was asking her to stop or asking for permission to ravage her.

"I need you."

Her whisper tickled his ear. He pulled her away, making her meet his gaze. "This isn't what you want," he said. Her fear still radiated like a poison in the air.

"I need this," she said, and her eyes filled with tears.

"What do you need?" he asked, making sure he understood her clearly. An assumption right now would kill their entire future.

"You. I need you to make the nightmares go away." She wrapped her hand around to the back of his head and pulled him to her lips.

The urgency in her kiss erased any logic from his mind and before he had any awareness, he had laid her back on the bed and his hand had already traveled under the hem of her nightshirt. His lips moved from hers to the v between her breasts. She arched into it, letting out a purr that shot his heart into his stomach. He peeled her shoulder straps down her arms and pushed the fabric of the night shirt below her breasts, taking a moment to caress each one before he lowered his mouth to her nipples.

Her fear remained, but mingled with the scent was yearning, and he continued caressing and kissing her skin. When he sat up to pull her shirt the rest of the way off, her entire body went rigid. He stared at her, at her clamped eyes. He thought twice about removing her underwear. Instead, he lowered his mouth to her stomach, licking a path from one side to the other.

Gooseflesh rolled across the path he'd just kissed. The closer he got to her underwear, the tenser she became. While he just wanted to bury his face between her legs, he avoided that for now. Instead, he kissed his way down each of her thighs.

When he reached the top of her feet, she had relaxed enough to seem to enjoy his pampering. He met her gaze. "Roll onto your stomach," he said, and alarm flashed in her eyes. "Trust me," he whispered, and took her toe in his mouth, sucking it gently before relinquishing it. He knew how hard those two words were for her and he remained in place, massaging her foot while he waited for her to comply. If she didn't, the exploration would be over for tonight, and every cell in his body did not want this to end.

He kept eye contact and when she rolled onto her stomach and looked over her shoulder, he just sent a ghost of a smile her way. The mistrust in her eyes, along with the mix of emotions in her scent, held him in place for a moment.

ALESSANDRA STARED INTO HIS sparkling blue eyes, wondering if trusting him would be a mistake. But the sincerity in his gaze told her otherwise. Her entire body throbbed with adrenaline and desire, but

Wolf Moon

the thin veil of fear covering her held her back from truly enjoying Hunter's touch.

He closed his eyes and brought the foot he had been massaging to his lips, running his tongue down her arch. Her foot tingled from the contact, spiraling up her leg right to her core. She bit her lip against the moan and curled her arms around the pillow, resting her cheek on the soft fabric.

When he moved to her ankle, she moaned at the sensations his mouth and tongue created. His hands were gentle as they kneaded her calves, melting away the tension. As his hands and mouth drew close to her ass, the tension returned, but this time, it was in anticipation of his touch, not dread.

Her breath hitched when his tongue followed the line of her panties. His hands continued to massage the back of her thighs and all she wanted was for him to slide them between her legs and massage her clit. Hunter's touch was intoxicating, and his avoidance of the only area clad in fabric was driving her mad.

By the time he got to her neck, she was genuinely panting with need and shuddering with every swipe of his tongue.

"Roll onto your back," he whispered.

This time there was no hesitation, and when his mouth traveled from her shoulder to her hand, she closed her eyes, silently willing him to travel lower again. When he sucked her index finger into his mouth, she opened her eyes. Every muscle trembled when he straddled her and a measure of disappointment laced her stomach when he took her other hand, exploring her with his mouth.

He followed the line of her arm to her neck before planting a kiss on her lips. Hunter pulled away and stared down at her. "I think that's enough for one night," he said. His voice was huskier than she'd ever heard it.

Alessandra whined. She couldn't voice what she wanted, but she pleaded with her eyes, praying he could read her as deeply as he professed.

His slow smile sent a shiver up her spine. "You have to say the words, Leigh," he said, and the use of the new name they'd agreed on did something to her insides she didn't understand. Warmth flowed through her.

Alessandra licked her lips. "Please, don't stop," she said. Her voice trembled.

He lowered his mouth to her breasts, sucking the hard nubs until she moaned. He moved lower in as slow a progression as before. His tongue traced her stomach along the edge of her underwear. His legs still straddled her, although he had moved down over her knees.

Hunter slowly looked up, meeting her gaze as his hand slid between her thighs. His thumb slowly circled over her clit, creating an inferno inside her. Alessandra pulled her legs out from between his and spread them wide, almost ensnaring him with her limbs. Her intent was as clear as she could make it without words.

Hunter's breath caught in his chest. The want in his eyes was as all-consuming as his touch.

"Are you sure?" he asked, even while his thumb kept circling.

"You wanted to lick every inch of me," she said, empowered by the heat consuming her.

Hunter groaned in response and the ripping of fabric followed. He dropped between her legs, even as his thumb kept that insane circling. He licked the inside of her thigh, and then the other, teasing, circling everywhere but where she wanted him.

When his mouth replaced his thumb, Alessandra sighed. "Jacob," she whispered, because somehow that was more fitting of the moment. The sensation of his name rolling off her tongue nearly matched the pleasure of his mouth playing with her clit.

Every motion of his mouth, every swipe of his tongue, brought her closer to letting go. Her heart slammed against the wall of her chest, her toes curled as the heat built inside her core. She grasped at the sheets, balling them up in her hands. When the wave crashed, she screamed with it, cum shooting out of her like a geyser.

Hunter's fingers slid inside her as he leaned back on his heels. His free hand disappeared inside his shorts, stroking with the same urgency as his fingers plunging inside her.

"Jesus fucking Christ," he groaned, squeezing his eyes shut and shuddering.

His hand slowed and then stilled inside her and he opened his eyes, meeting her gaze. Both of their breaths huffed, and she marveled at the magic he had just created. Alessandra had never had a true orgasm before and the old adages of it being an earth moving experience weren't exaggerated.

"I'm sorry. I got a little carried away," he said, removing his hand from between her legs. He grabbed his discarded shirt and wiped the hand that had been down his shorts before stretching out next to her.

She just stared at the ceiling, still too stunned at what had transpired to speak.

He rolled onto his side and propped his head up on his hand. "Are you mad?"

His question pulled her gaze to his. She shook her head and his lips curved into that devilish grin that sent a shiver down her spine.

"Just speechless?" he asked.

"Yeah." She kept his gaze. Her muscles were the consistency of an overcooked noodle, and she forced herself to raise her hand, cupping his cheek. She ran her thumb along the smooth cheekbone before she traced his lips with it.

Hunter sucked the tip between his teeth before just kissing the pad.

"Jacob," she whispered.

"Leigh," he replied, and rolled his eyes. "It really is weird calling you something other than Ally."

"I like it better than my real name. Either that, or it's just the way you say it that I like better."

"I gotta admit. Hearing my given name from your lips turns me on something fierce." His cheeks turned red.

As the limpness faded from her muscles, they ached with exhaustion. She reached down, grabbed her discarded nightgown, and slipped it on before curling into a ball on her side. Hunter's hand idly traced her back, and her eyes refused to remain open.

WOLF MOON
Chapter 7

HUNTER SLOWLY TRACED HER back for a long time, long after she fell asleep. Guilt bit at him yet again, and he wondered if everything that had happened to them was his fault. The slow cadence of his fingers across her skin did nothing to soothe his unease, and when he was certain she wouldn't wake, he climbed out of bed and straightened the covers before heading into the bathroom.

He splashed cold water on his face and brushed his teeth before staring at his reflection. "What were you thinking?"

Of course, his brain had not been the one in control, so thinking had nothing to do with any of it. Although he had to give himself a little credit. He'd refrained from making love to her like he wanted to. Instead, he purged that need with his hand. Again.

"I just hope she doesn't have any regrets in the morning," he mumbled, and headed back to the bed.

He crawled on top of the blankets and stretched on his back, tucking his hands behind his head. Hunter contemplated turning on the television until Alessandra rolled into the crook of his arm. He stared down at her. The peace in her features drew a smile to his lips, and he wrapped his arm around her, nuzzling into her hair.

Hunter thought back to the day he met Alessandra. He was thirteen and had gone hunting with his father. They were stalking a deer and before he had a chance to take off after his prey, an arrow pierced the ground in front of him, stopping him in his tracks. The shock shifted him back to human form, and he looked up into the tree behind him. Lying on the branch was a cute girl who was probably half his age.

"Mine," she hissed, and refocused on the deer. A second arrow flew true, and the deer dropped.

"That was our meal," Hunter said as she climbed down.

She gave him a cockeyed tilt of her mouth. "Go ahead. I'm sure my parents have something for me at home."

Even back then, the alpha in her was as apparent as her dark hair. He could also sense that she didn't seem to want the role. At least, not the way the other alphas projected it. He had seen his fair share of alphas, and none of them had ever given up a kill, not without a fight. She was different, and he knew at that moment he would gladly stand beside her and protect her from the bad in the world.

He was also aware she would likely be the death of him.

He closed his eyes, kissed the back of her head, and took a deep inhale, reveling in her sweet scent, drifting off into a satiated sleep.

SUNSHINE BROKE THROUGH THE crack in the curtain, shining right in her eye. She blinked and then lowered her gaze to the arms wrapped around her. Hunter's soft snore tickled her neck. She couldn't budge. He had her pinned by the blankets. Every muscle in her body tightened, and the air refused to fill her lungs.

The flood of memories of what his mouth and hands were capable of sent a shiver through her. In the light of day, the decisions she'd made last night didn't seem real.

"Hunter," she whispered, and the man shot up to a sitting position like someone had zapped him.

His gaze bounced around the room while his brain caught up to where he was. When his gaze dropped to hers, his mouth formed a crooked smile.

"Good morning," he said.

"Leave after breakfast?" she asked, rolling onto her back.

"Sounds good," he said, and slipped out of bed. He made a beeline right for the bathroom and Alessandra sighed, sitting up. Her gaze fell on her torn underwear lying in the middle of the carpet and heat filled her cheeks.

She crossed to the suitcase and filtered through the pile. If they traveled the same distance today, they'd be in Florida before the night was over, so she grabbed the sundress instead of jeans or shorts.

Hunter came out a few minutes later with a towel around his waist, smelling like fresh soap. Her gaze lingered for a moment before she stepped inside for a quick shower.

By the time she finished, Hunter had the suitcase closed and was ready to go. His eyes sparkled as they scanned her from head to toe.

"What am I supposed to do with this?" she held out her nightshirt and the small toiletry bag that held her razor and brushes. He stuffed the night shirt and bag into a side pocket before zipping it up.

"We have everything?" he asked, glancing around the room.

Both their gazes fell on the discarded underwear and then snapped to each other. His lips pressed together, trying to hide a grin, and her cheeks heated.

"Should we just leave it there?" Alessandra said, and Hunter's eyebrows arched. He opened his mouth to answer and then grinned.

"You are naughtier than I expected," he finally said.

"Perhaps you've awakened a beast," she said, and crossed to the door, swinging it open. A bolt of electricity hit the center of her chest and she froze in the doorway. She licked her lips and refused to look away from the dozen guns aimed at their hotel room door.

"Jake?"

He stood less than an inch behind her in the same state of shock she was in. His scent didn't alter as he scanned the Virginia State Police surrounding them.

"Put your hands up slowly, Leigh," he said from behind her, his voice steady.

"Keep your hands where we can see them and step out of the hotel room," the nearest officer demanded.

They complied.

"Hands on the wall," the order came from deeper in the group.

Hunter stepped beside her and placed his palms against the wall. She followed his lead, but her heart thundered in her chest. His gaze met hers, but he didn't make any promises or excuses.

When the police approached and started patting them down, Hunter asked, "What's this about, officer?"

No one said a word. When the officer grabbed her wrist and slapped a cuff on it, she winced at the burn of the metal. The cuffs weren't iron. They were silver. Before she could struggle out of the cop's grip, they secured her other wrist behind her back.

Hunter's gaze met hers as they turned him around and slammed him against the wall.

Her breath locked in her chest at the pain radiating from her wrists. The crowd parted, and a visceral need to run gripped every muscle. The head of the national council, Ken Winters, stepped forward, but that's not what made her blood freeze in her veins. It was the look in his eyes as he stared at her, like he had horrifyingly painful plans for her.

His gaze landed on Hunter and a satisfied smirk surfaced. "I warned you." He pointed at Hunter.

"Fuck you," Hunter growled.

The exchange between the two men sparked a curiosity in Alessandra, but before she could ask questions, Winters gave the cops a nod and the closest officer hauled them into the back of a cruiser.

The officer who took the driver's seat in their cruiser wasn't human. He was a hybrid, and he glared in the rearview window.

"You have dodged us for the last time," he said with a drawl, his gaze locked on Hunter.

"Who do you think we are?" Hunter asked, his voice reasonable enough for the man to glance back.

"Fugitives."

Hunter laughed. "My father's a lawyer and he's going to have a field day with you." The deadpan glare he leveled made the driver shift. "Unlawful arrest. No one read us our rights, you just hauled us away with no explanation. Your men have the cuffs on so tightly the metal is cutting into my skin. I'm sure that could constitute police brutality."

"Shut your mouth. I can detect your scent."

"I took a shower, dipshit," he said.

The fact the cop wasn't human didn't help her unease. Hunter's little play acting, along with his strange interaction with Winters, made this much harder for her to deal with. All she could think about was the nightmare that had led to their night of passion. The certainty that he was being led to his death ate at her insides as much as the silver was burning through her wrists.

"I smell damned good," Hunter added, like he didn't understand what the driver was getting at.

"He didn't do anything," Alessandra said.

The cop glared back.

"He killed humans," he said.

"Stop talking, Leigh," Hunter said.

"They arrested us, Jake." Her voice rose. "They think we're someone else," she added, playing along with whatever game he was trying to play.

The cop's brow creased, and he reached for the radio. "Boss, are you sure these are the ones you're looking for?" he asked real softly.

"That's the killer we've been tracking. Bring them in and we will take care of them once and for all."

Hunter's eyes conveyed the same dread pummeling her muscles.

"Do you know why I'm wanted?" she asked, after he had put the radio back in place.

"You harbored a fugitive. A fugitive who killed for sport."

Now she was thoroughly confused, but she pressed on. "I did not kill for sport. I killed to survive."

"It doesn't matter."

"So, I just should have just let the belladonna they injected in me run its course? Kill me like they intended?" She didn't want to go down without a fight, and if her dream was any indication of reality, Hunter was going to be ripped to shreds by the council pack before they turned on her.

He glared in the mirror. "Yes. Killing humans is not tolerated for any reason."

"Even if the filthy pigs deserved it?" Alessandra said.

"Stop talking, Leigh." The anger flared in Hunter's voice, turning it into a feral growl. "It won't change a thing. This fucker's been paid off."

The cop's glare moved to the mirror and then back to the road. "You understand the price for taking a human life."

Alessandra's fear morphed, sending a dose of adrenaline through her entire form. If she didn't do something, they both would die. She hauled her knees to her chest, catapulting her feet into the back of the driver's seat with all the strength her alpha blood allowed. The impact threw the driver forward onto the steering wheel. A loud crack filled the car, and the driver remained slumped over the wheel.

The car sped up, and Hunter tackled her on the seat, driving her down with his shoulder. Screaming metal filled the small space, and the cruiser flipped. She had no idea how many times they hit the cage or the ceiling, but when the car finally came to rest, not one window remained.

"Hunter?" she whispered, her head still spinning enough that she wasn't sure if they were upright or not.

"Fuck," he whispered from under her.

Alessandra rolled off him, landing on the hard metal roof next to him.

"We need to get out of here," she said.

"No shit." His voice strained with pain.

"Are you okay?"

"No, but we need these cuffs off before I can tell just how fucked up I am."

Alessandra rolled towards the open window. Once she was on the ground, she curled into a ball and forced her hands under her butt. She managed to get her arms in front of her before she crawled to the front driver's side window.

Hot liquid dripped into her eye, stinging. The keys hung from the ignition and the cop's dead stare looked off towards the passenger side. His nose looked as if someone had pressed it inside his face. The impact with the steering wheel had killed him instantly.

She reached for the keys, pulling them out. It took her a minute to find the right one and once she did, her cuffs were easily unlocked. She crawled back to Hunter. He lay face down on the roof, his hands still locked behind his back. She unlocked his cuffs, but he didn't move.

"Hunter?" She rolled him over and gasped. The side of his face was covered in blood. She reached under his arms and hauled him out the window, falling back with his head in her lap. "Please wake up," she whispered. The panic created a flush through her, fueled by adrenaline. Even though she sensed life still present, she leaned over and put her ear to his chest. His heart pumped, but it wasn't strong like the beat that had filled her dreams last night.

Their only hope of escape was to shift and make a run for the woods, but she wasn't leaving without him. She scanned the ravine they'd ended up in and up the hill towards the road. No one peered over the edge. At least, not yet.

"Hunter, wake your ass up!" she growled low. She was aware of the dangers of shifting to the human body if it was broken, but in wolf form, they would heal faster. She covered his lips with hers, planting a kiss. "Wake up," she commanded.

He groaned under her, and his eyes flittered open. "You need to run," he said. "Keys are in my pocket. Go."

She laughed.

"I can't feel my legs," he said, meeting her gaze.

"Shift and run with me." Her heart squeezed in agony.

"I'm already dead, Leigh. You aren't. Please," he pleaded.

Tears blurred her vision as he fumbled in his pocket. He slid the keys into her hand. "Go."

"Jacob Blaez, shift your ass and run with me!" Her breath hitched in her chest.

"Run, before they get here. If I can smell them, so can you. Now go." His voice held the power of an alpha command and she backed away.

"Damn it, Jacob, I love you."

He stared into her eyes. "I love you, too, and if I'm not as bad off as I think I am—I'll find you. I promise."

She blinked the tears away and pressed her lips together to keep her chin from trembling.

"Go," he commanded.

Alessandra turned and placed the key ring between her teeth. In two strides, her large paws came into view, and she was flying down the ravine as fast as her wolf's legs would take her.

The freedom of the run usually gave her a rush, but this time, each bound away from Hunter squeezed her midsection tighter. She skidded to a halt at his scream of pain, but his command to go still rang in her ears.

By the time she slinked behind the row of hotel rooms, she was unsure what would greet her in the parking lot. Lifting her nose in the air, the lingering odor of humans remained. She needed the Jeep, and that clinched her decision. She shifted back to her human form and took the keys from her mouth. Barefoot and windblown, she stepped around the corner of the hotel into the nearly empty parking lot.

Hunter's Jeep still sat locked where they had left it. Beyond it sat a couple of empty sedans. Guessing she had a small window of opportunity, she trotted to the car, unlocked the door, and slid into the driver's seat. She checked the console and sighed in relief that the box of cash still remained.

Alessandra pulled out of the parking lot, turning south, just like Hunter had wanted, but she didn't get far. The pains in her stomach nearly doubled her over and her breath started catching in her throat. Sobs spilled, and she had to pull over to the side of the road.

She couldn't leave him to the council's mercy. She couldn't let him pay for her sins.

Alessandra turned the car around and headed towards the accident site.

WOLF MOON
Chapter 8

Hunter stared after the stunning gray wolf as she galloped away at a pace even a car wouldn't be able to keep up with. He wanted to be running alongside her, but with how broken his body was at the moment, he wasn't sure he'd ever walk again, never mind run.

A car skidded to a stop at the top of the ravine and the first of several faces peered over the side. When the head of the council joined the row of police, Hunter let out a low warning growl. He couldn't help the reaction. This man was the one his father had evidence against. This was the fucker who had killed his dad.

The old man hopped over the bent guardrail and slid down the ravine wall, coming to a stop inches from Hunter.

"Where is it?" he growled, as he hunched over to look in the car.

"Damned if I know," Hunter whispered. He meant for it to come out with some strength, but his was slowly seeping away. "Why don't you go crawl back into your hole?" he asked.

Ken Winters, the grand chairman of the werewolf council, sneered at him. He pointed his finger at Hunter and a sharp nail grew from the blunt tip. In a motion that belied his age, he jammed his fingernail into Hunter's shoulder.

The brittle pain caught him off guard, and he clamped his mouth as quickly as he could, but it wasn't fast enough to catch his initial cry of pain. He wouldn't let that happen again, especially with the master's sadistic smile beaming above him.

"I will find what your father gave you."

"Fuck you," Hunter said from between clenched teeth. He wasn't in any condition to fight back and he knew this line of questioning was going to get worse before he finally accepted death. The wolf in him bristled at the thought, unwilling to just lie down and die.

Winters crouched down next to him, twisting his finger, digging the dagger deeper into Hunter.

Hot agony gripped his shoulder, and he concentrated on drawing a breath through his nose instead of his tightly clamped lips.

"You seem fond of the girl. I'm sure once I have her, you'll sing a different tune," he said, after studying Hunter.

The dagger embedded in his shoulder retracted, providing temporary relief. He closed his eyes, ignoring the orders Winters barked at the men surrounding them. This was a walk in the park compared to what would come next. The council didn't care about their wolves. All they gave a damn about was power and wealth. And anyone who got in their way was trampled.

Alessandra did not get just how corrupt Winters was. But he knew only too well. His father paid the price when he attempted to expose the bastards for killing at will. Humans and werewolves alike. Sometimes the council wiped out entire communities just because they wouldn't conform to their rules.

Now, it looked like he would follow in his father's footsteps.

He closed his eyes. The proof that he had to bring these assholes down was buried under the moncy box right alongside his birth certificate. He wished he had shared it with Alessandra before the shit hit the fan, but he hadn't figured out who to send it to. There wasn't anyone who could challenge the council and win.

He finally opened his eyes to two of Winters' lackeys arguing over how to get him out of the ravine.

"I want him alive!" Winters yelled from the road.

Of course, the bastard wanted him alive. He wanted a spectacle, one that was sure to draw Alessandra from hiding. Hunter just hoped that she would heed his orders. The need to call her back had almost overwhelmed him, but if she had stayed, Winters would have everything he wanted.

The two men hauled him up the ravine and threw him into a truck bed. The impact drew a grunt from him. They splayed him out using silver shackles and left him staring at the bright sky. He didn't ask where they were taking him. He didn't care.

Each bump created a host of agonies through his body. He closed his eyes, willing either sleep or unconsciousness to come so he could attempt to heal. The silver ensnaring his wrists and ankles made either choice nearly impossible. Every now and then, Alessandra's scent drifted into his nostrils, like a promise of a dream, pulling him back into consciousness.

By the time the truck turned off the interstate, the sun had moved across the heavens and the deep blue sky of late afternoon greeted his exhausted gaze. Hours of torture seemed like child's play compared to the jolting bumps the side roads contained. Crunching sounds of gravel along with a thick canopy of trees made his heart race. Just by the heavy pine scent, he placed them in the mountains.

This was where the council carried out sentencing. He had heard rumors, and despite his injuries, the thought of being drowned in silver sent an involuntary shiver through him. His father had once told him that Winters had a trophy room for all those he'd sentenced to death. Screaming faces cast in silver lined the walls.

Hunter's throat closed, and he forced a breath into the tight space. If he panicked now, he might unwillingly give up Alessandra just to avoid that kind of death. The trees thinned until all he saw was the open sky and a variety of cranes. The truck came to a stop under one of the crane hooks.

Wolf Moon

Without a word, the driver got out, hooked the crane to something over Hunter's head, and gave a twirl of his index finger. An engine roared to life and chains rose, pulling a bar that they clasped Hunter to up into the air. Hunter glanced down to see his legs had a similar bar, and that one was attached to the truck. The crane didn't stop when he was fully extended and the pull in his abdomen yanked a cry of pain.

The driver made a cutting motion with his hand and the pressure abated, but didn't stop. Pain filled every inch of his abdomen. His arms ached, and he was glad he couldn't feel anything from his waist down. His brain hadn't had time to register his surroundings before the driver hopped up on the back of the truck and pulled out a hunting knife.

"Why are you doing this?" Hunter asked, and the man leveled a glare.

"Because beasts like you need to be put down," he said, and pulled Hunter's t-shirt away from his body before cutting the fabric off, leaving his chest and back exposed. He slid an ear-bud into Hunter's ear and stepped behind him.

A large clearing stretched before him. In the center of the clearing sat the werewolf council, lined up in a horseshoe around the focal point of the clearing—a giant vat filled with boiling silver. The metallic stench burned his nostrils, and he closed his eyes. An array of covered cages lined the outer edges of the woods, and Hunter wondered who else was being executed today.

"Ladies and gentlemen, we are gathered here to confirm sentencing, and carry out executions for the most heinous offenders of our species." Ken Winter's voice rose over the gathering crowd.

With a wave of his hand, the covers on the cages were pulled away.

The earpiece buzzed. "Look closely, Mr. Blaez. They are paying for your sins," Winters' voice whispered in his ears. "Tell me where the girl is and I will set them free."

Hunter's chest squeezed. Every member of their pack was behind bars, along with a few others he didn't recognize.

The loudspeaker crackled. "This pack, led by that man on the back of the truck, attacked a group of human campers without provocation, killing them just for the bloodlust thrill of it!"

"Bullshit," Hunter said, loud enough for the crowd to hear him.

Pain seared Hunter's back, followed by the crack of a whip. Heat traveled down his spine into the numb zone.

The man behind him chuckled. "You just keep your mouth shut or I'll put a gag on you."

Winters turned to the council. "Have you reviewed the cases put before you today?"

"Yes, sir," they said in unison.

"What say you?" he asked.

"Execution!"

There was no hesitation in any of the council members. Winters glanced at Hunter and an evil grin found the corners of his lips before he turned back to the crowd.

"They did nothing to deserve this fate!" Hunter cried, and received another lashing.

Winters gave a crisp nod to the executioner on the platform. The first criminal, thankfully not one of Hunter's pack, was dragged from the cages to the platform behind the vat. He struggled in the chains,

Wolf Moon

but there was no use against the silver holding his arms behind him or his shackled feet. The crane hook lowered until the hooded executioner could drag it to the chains holding the poor bastard's feet.

"I promise; your pack will have just as slow a death as this man's." Winters' voice whispered in his earpiece.

A burning anger rippled through his muscles, and just because both Winters and the man behind him was a sadistic bastard, the shards of the whip ripped through his skin.

"I'm sure the stench of your blood will bring your little whore running. And just for the record, I will not kill her like the rest of these misfits. I'm going to chain her in a room with your silver coated remains, just so she remembers her place in the pack."

Hunter growled, and the chain above him pulled, yanking the air from his lungs. The struggling criminal rose into the air at the same time. Hunter watched in horror as the man was dunked headfirst into the boiling vat, his scream cut off almost as soon as it started. The crane stopped when the man's shoulders hit the surface, but his death throes continued.

Hunter could almost hear the screams below the surface as silver invaded all the orifices, burning as much as sulfuric acid. He shuddered. At least this death was quicker than lowering someone in feet first. That would be a slower death, one that would be wrapped in agony. Headfirst, there was perhaps two to three minutes of agony before that first inhalation of silver.

They splayed the next criminal out in the same form as Hunter. The bar attached to his hands hit the silver first and the moment the poor bastard's hands dipped below the surface, the choking screams began, along with sobbing pleas. Hunter swore to himself that he would not so much as whimper. He would not give the council the satisfaction of his screams.

WOLF MOON
Chapter 9

ALESSANDRA NEARLY RAN THE jeep into the opening behind the crowd watching the council. Instead, she shot down a smaller side path to the right that seemed to dwindle to nothing but brush. She parked next to a fallen tree and closed her eyes. The ride had taken forever, and her body ached from sitting in the same position for so long. Her bladder was near exploding and she jumped out of the car and squatted behind it, relieving herself.

Hunter had to have weapons she could use in the jeep and now that she was parked, she opened the back and searched through the trunk. Nothing beyond a crowbar was visible. She took a chance, lifting the carpet liner to the wheel well below.

Warmth flushed her skin at the crossbow lying in the well instead of a spare tire. She reached down and touched the arrow tips, yanking her hand away at the burn of silver. Jesus, she expected a hunting rifle or something. Not silver-tipped arrows. Where the hell had he gotten these?

Never mind where, when had he gotten them?

She pulled the quiver from under the crossbow and jammed the dozen arrows in before hauling it over her shoulder. The only other weapon she was aware of was the scalpel in the medical kit.

As she opened the door, the first scream caught her attention. She lifted her nose, catching scents in the light wind. She couldn't tell how many werewolves were in the clearing, but the scents on the wind made little sense. Her heart clanged into overdrive, creating the tingling sensation of urgency through her. The overwhelming need to get to that clearing gripped her. She made sure the quiver was secure and slung it over her head. The handle of the crossbow barely fit in her human mouth, but within a blink, her canine jaws had no issue carrying the bow.

With the wind in her favor, she opted for speed instead of stealth. She stopped just short of the woods line, horrified by the scene in the clearing. She transitioned back into human form and readied the crossbow with shaking hands.

They had stretched Hunter between two bars on the back of a truck. A man with a psychotic leer held a bloodied whip in his hand. But that wasn't what had her throat locked closed. It wasn't even the screaming man being slowly immersed in what had the aroma of boiling silver that had her heart racing.

It was the sight of her pack in the execution line that burned away any hint of fear, replacing it with an all-consuming anger. How could the council hold them responsible for what she did? What. The. Hell?

She moved toward the clearing, and Hunter's head turned in her direction. She swore he could see her, but he closed his eyes and tucked his chin in, like he was hiding from the horror in front of him. The whip cracked.

Alessandra had an arrow fitted to the crossbow before she finished her next breath. She drew it back, wondering if anyone would notice if she took that fucker out. She had close to fifty yards from where she squatted to where Hunter was chained.

The man on the execution track was still screaming, and all eyes were on that spectacle. If she miscalculated, the arrow could kill Hunter. It had been years since she shot a bow, but she didn't think she had lost her touch. She aimed, exhaled and depressed the trigger.

The whistle on the wind pulled Hunter's gaze back in her direction, but the screaming of the criminal had reached an earsplitting note that completely masked the clunk of the jerk in the back of the truck.

"Place is rigged."

Hunter's voice traveled to her ears and his tone carried both agony and anger. He glanced sideways toward the woods before refocusing on the gruesome death in front of him.

The screams stopped abruptly, but the body continued to struggle. Alessandra refused to think about what that meant. Soon, it was clear, as the youngest member of her pack was led to the executioner circle. Charity had been the one who had freed her from the rope tying her in the clearing.

"Winters, I swear if you do this, I'll see you dead before the moon rises tonight," Hunter growled from his perch. His voice sounded strong, but she had a deeper insight. He smelled like death, and her heart squeezed at the thought.

The head of the council laughed at him. "That will be a very neat trick, Mr. Blaez. You seem to have the same dementia that your father had just before we executed him."

Alessandra gasped. She thought his father had died in a hunting accident.

"They didn't do anything. I was the one who killed those kids," he said, and Alessandra almost stepped out of the woods.

She had already fitted another arrow into the bow, but she was unsure of where to aim this one.

"That is precisely why they are here. They did nothing to stop you and your mate."

"She was my alpha, not my mate," Hunter said, and then cried out.

The screech of metal grabbed her attention. The chain above Hunter creaked as it tried to pull tighter. His skin on his abdomen stretched thin, and she knew damned well where she had to aim. It would give away her position, but if she didn't, her nightmare of him being torn in half would come true.

She repositioned herself closer to the crowd where she could get a view of what held him to the truck bed. She climbed a tree to get a better vantage point, ignoring Charity's panicked pleas. With the ankle braces in view, she held her breath. When the girl's first scream shattered the afternoon, Alessandra let the arrow fly. Silver slammed against silver, and Hunter looked down. One ankle hung untethered.

The second arrow unclasped the other ankle bond, freeing both his feet. Yet they still dangled in place. Relief flooded his features, and he closed his eyes, hanging his head.

Her gaze jumped to the dying girl. They dipped her arms into the silver up to her elbows. The skin above the silver blackened at the burn. Her long hair touched the liquid and sparked an inferno that engulfed her head. Her screams pressed on her chest like a giant crushing her.

She strung the next arrow and let it fly. The silver tip pierced right through Charity's heart, ending her suffering in one motion. Chaos erupted. The crowd behind the council dispersed as if being near the council was dancing with death.

Winters pushed a button on the box he was holding. Hunter was yanked high into the air.

All the strength in her limbs gave out.

The crane turned until Hunter hung right over the center of the boiling pot of silver.

Her heart squeezed. She couldn't lose Hunter. Not now. Not after letting him in. She needed him by her side. She stared at the only man on this earth she was willing to die for and made a vow to herself. From this moment forward, they would be together, whether it was in life or in death. Alessandra reached for another arrow and strung it in the crossbow.

Winters barked orders.

Alessandra jumped to the next tree and climbed to a larger limb, one that gave her a greater view of the landscape. Guards, both in human and wolf form, ran towards where she stood. She had the advantage of being upwind and detected the scent of fear even from this distance.

Her muscles clenched with terror as one of the human guards raised a rifle. She aimed the arrow and pressed the trigger. He went down before he could find her in the scope.

She reached into the quiver behind her and her heart lurched. She only had one arrow left. With a trembling hand, she pulled it out and loaded it into the crossbow. Three concurrent snaps made her jump and nearly lose her balance. The empty quiver slid down her arm and fell before she could catch it. When it hit the ground, another metal snap sounded.

Howls of pain filled the meadow, and she scanned the landscape. Three wolves were trying to pull free from sharp teeth spring traps. Alessandra detected the scent of the blood flowing from each trapped leg. Those traps had been meant for her. A chill ran down her spine.

Hunter's lips formed the word run, but she couldn't leave him and her pack to die. Not for her sins.

The loudspeaker crackled, and Alessandra's gaze jumped towards Winters, the head of the werewolf council. He held a box with a red button over his head, his thumb inches from Hunter's demise. "Alessandra Tate, you are surrounded. Surrender or I will personally press the release button holding Hunter Blaez. I will give you ten seconds to comply."

Her heart pounded in her ears and she judged the distance between where she perched on the branch and where he hung over the vat. It was a distance she could cover in mere seconds if one of those traps didn't get her, but she wasn't sure she could get there in time to save him. Not with gravity pulling at him.

Between each number, Winters' lips moved, but the speaker didn't pick up his words. Winters announced the number five in the microphone, still looking up at Hunter with a sadistic smile.

Hunter bellowed an angry growl, and he glared at Winters with such violent intensity that Alessandra reacted.

She hopped to her feet and bolted down the length of the thick branch, using the bounce at the end like a diving board. Throwing herself in the air, she twisted enough to aim and pull the trigger of the crossbow before she released it from her grip. She didn't wait to see if she hit her target. Instead, she shifted, stretching out her front paws and aiming for one of the poor bastards in the traps.

She landed on the wolf closest to the clearing, using him as a springboard, landing a few paccs shy of the pot. The chain holding Hunter to the crane released and her chest constricted, pushing the burn of adrenaline through her. He fell straight towards the vat, and she launched herself in the air.

The heat from the boiling silver singed the fur on her stomach, but it paled compared to the rush of terror racing through her bloodstream. She had one chance and when her mouth clamped down on the metal pole he was tied to, another burst of energy flowed through her, and she flung him towards the executioner's platform. He slid to a stop and her front paws hit the wood, but her back paws missed.

She let out a bark of surprise when her hind paws landed on the hot edge of the vat. With a surge of panicked strength, she pushed off with all the power in her hind legs and landed in a skid next to Hunter.

Before her heart had a chance to beat, she turned on the executioner. He stood with a silver sword in his grip, but it wasn't held in an attack position. It was pointed at the ground in disbelief. His wide eyes and opened mouth gape stared at something behind her. She turned towards the council, and understood his shocked expression.

Her last lunge for safety had tipped the vat over, drenching the entire council in silver. Some stragglers behind the council screamed in pain as silver flooded into the third row of chairs before cooling enough to halt.

Metal clanged against wood, and Alessandra's gaze snapped to the executioner. His gaze was now on her, but it transferred from shock to a kind of awe she wasn't sure she deserved.

"Let my pack go," she ordered, and then realized she had shifted back to human form.

He tossed her the keys hanging from his belt. And then the man dropped to his knee and bent his head in submission. Alessandra raised an eyebrow and turned her head to look at Hunter. He was staring at her with the same wide eyes the rest of her pack gazed at her with.

"What?" she asked, suddenly self-conscious. She wrapped her arms around herself, and that was when she understood. She looked down at what was left of the front of her dress. It was in burned tatters, revealing her creamy, unscathed skin. They had seen her naked and drenched in deer blood, so the sight of her flesh shouldn't be a big deal, and yet it was. Hunter's gaze was locked on something she couldn't see, and she pressed her breasts in and gasped.

The werewolf leader symbol had formed in the ash on her stomach. No wonder the place was bathed in silence. She had wiped out the entire werewolf council and now wore the symbol of a leader, a position she had no idea how to carry. Instead of focusing on what it meant, she crossed and kneeled next to Hunter, unlocking his cuffs.

He stared up at her but didn't move, except to rub the burn marks on his wrists. He winced and did a poor job of smiling. He still had the lingering scent of death on him, and she swallowed the lump in her throat.

"I still can't move my legs," he whispered.

She palmed his cheek and leaned down, pressing her lips to his in a gentle expression of everything swirling inside her. "You need rest to heal properly," she said when their lips parted.

His eyes moved to the sky behind her and after a moment, he nodded. "Yeah," he whispered, and his eyelids slid closed. Hunter's breath remained steady, and she glanced up at the crowd gathering around her.

"He needs help," she said. Her pack, newly freed from their cages, picked him up and carried him down the ladder. The only vehicle that still had working tires was the original truck they had tied him to. Alessandra had him laid out on the backseat with his head in her lap.

Nathan, one of the older pack members, climbed into the driver's seat and started the car. "Where do you want to go?"

"The nearest hospital. He needs stitches and we need to find out just how serious his back injury is."

She met his gaze in the rearview mirror. "And it will give you time to talk about what's eating you," she added.

He pulled out and skirted around the silver puddle. "Thank you."

"For?"

"For freeing us. You didn't have to return."

"We had no idea that you were imprisoned. If we had known, we would have come sooner." She brushed the hair off Hunter's forehead. "He would have come sooner," she clarified.

"You wouldn't have?"

She kept her eyes averted. "One of you turned us in," she said.

"None of us said a thing, Ally."

Her gaze snapped up to his. "Then... how come they plastered our faces everywhere for what we did?"

He let out a sarcastic laugh. "I've been listening carefully to the council member conversations. They tried to get us to talk, but even sweet Charity didn't tell them what happened. As horrific as it was to watch, those beasts deserved what you and Hunter did."

"I still don't understand how they knew we killed humans." If the pack hadn't turned them in, why were they being held? It didn't make any sense. She kept running her fingers through Hunter's hair. It was as soothing to her as she imagined it was to him.

"The council sanctioned it. They grossly underestimated our pack. We were supposed to kill you in that field, and die ourselves."

The animal blood had been used to mask her scent long enough for the pack to bite her. Even so, the thought of them killing her wasn't anything she entertained, despite what Jeremy had said. "Well, they tried to hide my scent with the deer blood."

"Actually, they expected us to kill you because you were dying."

"What?" She wasn't sure she heard him right. "Why the hell would they think that?"

He chuckled. "I guess it's the norm in other packs. When one becomes too sick, the pack turns on them to thin the herd." He visibly shivered. "I guess that's what they were hoping for."

"What the hell kind of wolf pack does that?"

He shrugged. "Apparently, a lot of them."

"That's so fucked up," she muttered. She may have been as self-centered as Hunter indicated, but she would never intentionally hurt her pack, and Nathan obviously was of the same mind. The pack was her family, and she could never intentionally hurt them. She turned her attention to Nathan. "Why would they want the pack dead?"

Nathan's gaze dropped to Hunter and then returned to the road. "You need to ask Hunter about that when he wakes up."

Alessandra looked down at Hunter's unconscious form before glancing back at Nathan. "I'm sorry we didn't come sooner."

He handed her something from the front seat. She took the fabric and unfolded it. With a soft laugh, she slid the chambray work shirt over her shoulders, threading her arms into the sleeves and buttoning it up before the heat reached her cheeks.

"Thank you."

"You are welcome," he said.

Silence settled over the cab while he drove through the woods. The jostling of the truck pulled a grimace to Hunter's face, but he didn't wake. She let out a sigh of relief when they finally hit the blacktop.

WOLF MOON
Chapter 10

THE STEADY BEEP INFRINGED on his dream, and he went to roll, but couldn't move away from the sound. Hunter's eyelids flew open to the white floor tiles below him.

"Hold still, Mr. Blaez," a voice said.

He moved his gaze until white shoes came into view.

"Where am I?" he asked.

"The hospital. We had to fuse one of your vertebrae together and need you to remain still for another couple of days. You had significant injury to your spinal column, but with the traction you underwent prior to arriving at the hospital, and the fusion of your broken bone, we are hoping to reverse some of the damage to your spinal cord, but you must not resist the position we have you in, okay?

His eyes closed as it all came flooding back. The car accident, the clearing, everything. "Okay," he said, ignoring the reference to traction. That was actually an attempt to tear him in half, but if it somehow helped, he would not correct the nurse. Instead, he relaxed. "Is Leigh here?"

"Your girlfriend?" the nurse asked.

"Yes," he said, refraining from moving his head.

"She went to grab a bite to eat and to tell the rest of your friends how the operation went."

Coolness passed into his hand, burning through his blood, and he sucked air between his teeth.

"That should help you relax. I will be back in a little while to check on you." Her feet disappeared from view.

The burn altered, sending heat through every muscle, turning him into a giant mass of putty. His eyelids drooped. The soft patter of feet brought his fuzzy brain back to the moment instead of somewhere out in space.

Her scent filled his world. Warm cinnamon and spice, with a pinch of underlying power that was undeniable.

"Leigh," he whispered, intoxicated by her.

"Jake."

Her breath tickled his ear, sending cooling heat through him that tingled all the way to his toes. His eyes snapped wide. His toes tingled, and he jerked in the restraints.

"Easy, there." Her painted toes appeared, clad in flip-flops. Alessandra's hand caressed the back of his head. "You need to stay still for another twelve hours."

"My toes tingled."

Her hair came into view and then her beautiful face. A face he didn't think he'd ever see again; and he blinked back the sudden mist that blurred his vision.

"The only way to heal is to stay still, even if you're starting to get some feeling back. This puts the least pressure on your spine, so just chill, okay?" She put her drink on the floor and stretched out underneath him. The way her hair fanned out on the white tile stirred a need in his core and she smiled up at him. "You definitely can't do anything related to that," she whispered.

Hunter raised an eyebrow. "What's that?" he asked, toying with her.

She reached up and gently patted his cheek. "Were you aware your scent changes just a little whenever you're aroused?"

"Really?" Hunter had no idea. He was familiar with the fact that women had different pheromones when they were horny, but he never really detected a change in the male scent.

"Yes. It reminds me of salted caramel," she said.

He stared into her eyes. "Why didn't you run like I ordered you to?"

Her fingers slid away from his skin, and she sighed. "I couldn't let you take the fall for what I did. Besides, I saved your ass, so, no harm, no foul."

"You have no idea what Winters had planned. If you hadn't gotten lucky..." He couldn't finish the sentence. Winters had told him that his trophy room would be a fitting place for Alessandra, especially with Hunter's silver-cast body forever witnessing her suffering. He had promised that what those fraternity boys had done would be mild foreplay compared to what he and his pack would do to Alessandra. Winters' foul words still clouded his thoughts.

"He would have marched us all to our death," she said, thinking she was accurately finishing his sentence.

Hunter laughed. "Not all of us. The rest of the pack and I would have died in that field. But you, no, he wasn't going to kill you." His stomach turned sour at the thought, and he chose his next words carefully. "You would have served his pack."

Her head cocked for a minute and then her eyes widened as the color drained from her face. Hunter didn't break her gaze.

"He had some very graphic descriptions for me, between his announcements to the crowd," he added. The coil of anger burned in his stomach and he drew a slow breath, calming his tightening muscles.

"Let it go, Jake," she whispered. Some of the color returned to her cheeks. "We made it out alive."

Hunter nodded but didn't comment. He wasn't sure what kind of life he would have going forward, but he didn't want to lay that on her right now. That would have to wait until she wasn't lying on the floor looking up at him. That was more of a sit-on-the-side-of-the-bed type of conversation.

"Nathan said I needed to ask you why the council wanted our pack dead."

Hunter closed his eyes and pressed his lips together for a moment. "Because I wouldn't give

Winters the evidence my father had against him." Silence filled the space, and he opened his eyes. "He warned me he'd tear down everything I cared about if I didn't do as he commanded." He wished he could reach out and caress her cheek. "I should have known he'd use you against me. Especially with the shit my dad had on him."

They stared at each other for a moment.

"Why didn't you give the evidence to authorities?"

Hunter laughed. "Because the bastard has greased palms all the way up to the White House, and the justice system is equally as corrupt. I had no idea who to give it to."

The shuffle of feet and a throat clearing pulled Alessandra's gaze from his to her right. Hunter couldn't see anything, but from the sudden tension in her jaw, he could tell it wasn't someone she wanted to see.

"Ms. Tate?" the voice inquired, and relief flooded Hunter. He didn't want to discuss this anymore.

Alessandra put her finger to her lips and Hunter grinned. He raised an eyebrow.

"Ms. Tate. I know you are in here."

Alessandra rolled her eyes and sighed.

"What, Hans?" she said without moving.

Hans? He mouthed at her, and she gave him a single shoulder shrug. The pop of knees pulled his gaze to the side, and an older gentleman peered under the bed.

"As I told you earlier, we need to sort out some... issues," Hans said.

"What items are you referring to?" Hunter asked.

The man's tiger-like eyes swiveled in his direction. "Council business," he nearly barked.

Hunter narrowed his eyes, glaring at the intruder.

"Jake *is* the council," Alessandra said, leveling an equally intimidating glare.

Hunter jolted in place as if his entire body had been plugged into a socket. His gaze bounced to Alessandra, and she gave him a small smile of condolence.

The man straightened out of his sight, and Alessandra sighed. "We'll talk later," she whispered, and slid out from under the bed.

He stared at the spot she had vacated, his mind circling around the conversation and her last statement. The medicine fogged his brain, and his vision blurred. He let the high take him into a sedated stupor.

WOLF MOON
Chapter 11

HANS BROUGHT ALESSANDRA TO Winters' old house where the local police had converged. Nathan stood next to the entrance, along with an officer, who was scribbling in a notebook as Nathan spoke.

For a second, Alessandra had the urge to flee. Her muscles burned with it, but she forced herself to cross the snow-covered lawn to the front door. Nathan gave her a quick forward tilt of his head, but there was no warmth in it.

"Nathan," she said as she approached. The officer closed his notebook and retreated, leaving Alessandra, Hans and Nathan alone.

"Ally," he replied, but even his tone was frosty. His gazed moved to behind her. "You didn't need to bring her here."

Alessandra cocked her head, but Nathan just gave her an almost imperceptible shake of his head.

"She is the head of the council. She deserves to know," Hans said from behind her.

"What the hell is going on?"

Nathan traded a glance with Hans and then met Alessandra's gaze. She couldn't read anything beyond his poker face. He didn't speak, just waved her inside the house. The house crawled with police. They lined the hallways, filled the office spaces studying files from open cabinets. But it wasn't the police or the rooms on the main floor that caught her attention.

The scent of death and decay made her nose wrinkle. She didn't want to see the source of that stink, but it seemed that was exactly where Nathan was leading her. As they approached the far end of the house, doors leading to what she could only surmise as hell leaned open on broken hinges.

"You don't have to go down there," Nathan said from behind her.

"What am I going to find?" she asked, numb from the deep-seated fear spreading through her. She turned and met his gaze.

Nathan inhaled before he licked his lips. "Ally," he started, and shifted his feet. His gaze dropped to the ground before moving to Hans and back.

"What—"

"—Your parents," Hans blurted.

The numbness encompassing her turned to a burning fire, and her feet moved faster than her mind. She skidded to a stop at the bottom of at least two stories of stairs. Her hand shot to her mouth at the display of silver-coated death posed for Winters' entertainment. Mounted heads covered the walls and figures littered the floor. In the middle of the room lay empty chains, but the videos the police were cataloging showed enough.

Hunter's earlier comment about servicing the pack wasn't exaggerated. His choice of words seemed tame compared to what was flowing on the screens. She shivered and rubbed the gooseflesh on her arms, trying to return the heat that had fled from her the moment she stepped into this hellish trophy display.

The silver coat preserving the dead did nothing to quell the decomposing flesh underneath. At least not for her. The humans in the room didn't seem to take notice of the vile stench, but perhaps they had been trained to ignore it.

She scanned a room almost the size of a football field. "Where?" she asked, when Nathan stepped next to her.

"They all have plaques," he said, with a tone laced in the same disgust accosting her. "Winters was a narcissistic sociopath."

Alessandra forced her feet to move through the cluster of statues, her eyes glued to the plaques near the bottom of every posed effigy, instead of the mask of pain and horror forever preserved in silver.

The men were all posed in some subservient manner, kneeling with their gaze forced towards the ground. Some women were in the same pose, but there were also more disturbing poses, ones that reminded her of the whore of Babylon, making their screams look like ecstasy instead of suffering. As she got closer to the center, a pattern appeared. The few male statues looking straight ahead from their kneeling position held expressions of righteous anger instead of pain, and they all faced a woman posed in a lewd position.

Her gaze caught the name Blaez on one of the righteous statues. Alessandra stopped and stared at the angry and pained face of Hunter's father. She had seen that expression before on Hunter's face the moment Winters appeared. Her heart dropped to her stomach. She was reluctant to turn, but she couldn't help it, and sure enough, a woman positioned in an X-rated pose held another plaque with the last name Blaez.

She closed her eyes and turned away. She didn't want to see the plaques labeled Tate. Not now, but when her eyes opened, her gaze fell on another set of silver statues that pulled her breath from her body.

Her mother and father kneeled with their foreheads touching. The sorrow and pain etched in their expressions created agony inside Alessandra. It was as if they were both alive when Winters coated them with silver. Her gaze moved to the screens showering the room with the sounds of abuse. Her throat closed and she couldn't draw a breath. Her mother had 'died' years ago. The insinuation of life in their statue pose broke something inside her. The primal pain formed a scream that transitioned to a howl as the shift took over. The haunting sound echoed off the concrete and silver.

All her father's over-protectiveness now made sense. Especially if her mother's death had actually been a disappearance. There seemed to be only one path for the missing of her kind, and it all led to this horrifying room.

Alessandra turned and ran without regard to her surroundings. Her powerful shoulders knocked over at least a dozen statues, and more than a few of the police officers she passed had pulled their guns at the sight of a giant wolf plowing towards them.

"Don't shoot!" Nathan and Hans yelled as they followed her on foot.

Some force beyond her control gripped her, and she ended up in Winters' sparse bedroom. With teeth and claw, she tore the bedding to pieces between her wailing howls of loss. With feathers and pieces of cloth spread from wall to wall, Alessandra shifted and fell to the ground, covering her face with her hands.

"Holy..." a voice behind her made her stiffen, and she glanced over her shoulder at the cop standing in the doorway with Nathan and Hans.

"What? You've never seen a shifter before?" Alessandra snapped and sniffled as she wiped her face with dusty hands.

"It's not that." He pointed. Within the frame of the bed lay ledgers, along with neatly stacked one hundred-dollar bills. There must have been at least fifty stacks visible.

Perhaps this was what the police were after. Winters' private stash, and who knows what those ledgers held. Alessandra climbed to her feet.

She didn't give a damn about the money.

She didn't give a damn about anything except Hunter right now.

She turned and walked out of the house of horrors.

WOLF MOON
Chapter 12

EVER SINCE SHE HAD been taken to deal with the council issues, Alessandra had been distant in his company. Hunter stared at her from his reclined position on the bed. The nurses had moved him out of the inverted position after another round of x-rays showed alignment in his vertebrae.

He hadn't had any sensations since that first tingle when Alessandra whispered in his ear. And the prognosis was still the same. According to the doctors, he would never walk again.

But that wasn't his greatest concern at the moment.

"Leigh?" he asked, and she turned her gaze from the world outside his window to him. The haunting look in her eyes left him hollow. The last time he saw that expression had been after they'd rescued her from that field. "What happened yesterday?"

Her eyes glossed over, and her lips pulled at the corners. The fast blinking didn't stop a tear from escaping, and his chest constricted. He couldn't fathom what had caused the heart-wrenching pain in her eyes.

She glanced at the ceiling before she met his gaze and crossed to the chair next to him. "I know what happened to your parents."

He inhaled. "You found the documents in the jeep?" he asked, still wondering what caused her to look like she had seen a ghost.

Her eyebrows shot up. "What documents?"

He blinked. His mind was still fuzzy from all the pain meds, but even with that disadvantage, he caught her surprise. "The proof that Winters was killing innocents. That's what he wanted me to give up. If you didn't find the papers, then how do you know what happened to my father?"

She cocked her head and took a deep breath. "They were a part of his trophy display."

Hunter's brain slowly processed the information. Rumors, along with Winters' taunting, gave him a clue of what the trophy room encompassed. While he knew Winters killed his father, the fact Alessandra had said 'they' sank in. "My mother was there?" he asked, still trying to wrap his mind around that. The papers he had proved Winters was a twisted serial killer, but he never connected the dots as to why his father was so hell-bent on bringing the man down.

"Jesus," he whispered. According to his father, his mother had died in a car crash. That was just before he had turned twelve. Just before his father moved them to the northeast and started investigating Winters. "Winters had her?"

Alessandra nodded and wetness pooled in the corner of her eyes. "And he had my parents."

All the air in his chest blew out with those words. He still couldn't wrap his mind around his mother being part of Winters' collection. He blinked as Alessandra's words sank in.

"Parents? Both of them?"

Alessandra's tears spilled over. "The way they were posed... I think my mom was alive when they died."

A chill ran through him. Her mother had died when she was a teenager. Thinking about the possibility that she might have been at Winter's mercy for more years than he cared to calculate left him shivering. Christ almighty.

"Winters might have posed them that way to screw with you," he said, hoping it sounded as logical to her as it did to him.

Her chin trembled.

Hunter patted the mattress next to him and she moved to the spot and into his waiting arms. His eyes burned with unshed tears, and his stomach cramped at the thought of his mother having to do all the vile things Winters had insinuated he was going to do to Alessandra. The impact of what Winters had done to everyone he cared about tightened his throat, but the shake of Alessandra's body against his kept his own emotions at bay.

"I'm so sorry. This is all my fault," he whispered in her ear. He brushed his lips against the edge of her cheek and she pulled away. Her tear-stained gaze met his.

"Why is it your fault?" she asked again, wiping the tears from her cheeks.

"If I had just given him the papers..."

"He still would have done all this. He was a sick fuck." Anger laced her voice. He would have still attempted to kill us just because you knew about his psychosis.

"Maybe. And maybe he would have paid me off and left us alone," Hunter said, owning part of the blame for all that happened.

Her brow smoothed, and she sighed. "I saw the malice in the way he looked at you. He never would have let you live." She sniffled and met his gaze.

He didn't disagree, but they might have had a few years of bliss before the gauntlet fell.

"Did the doctors say when you're walking out of here?" she asked.

His heart plummeted at the change of subject, and he took a deep breath. "Here's the thing," he started, and shifted, unsure of how to summarize his condition on the heels of such bad news. "I'm never going to walk again."

She blinked and leaned back, staring at him like she was waiting for the punch line. It took a few moments, and then sadness filtered into her irises, and he cursed himself for blurting it out so callously.

"Ever?" she finally asked.

He shook his head, pressing his lips together, trying to push off the memories of running with the pack, of running alongside her. That wasn't in the cards. And neither was having the alpha dote on him for the rest of his life.

"No. And I don't expect you to stick around," he said, forcing the words to come out steady, without the pain that crushed his insides.

Her gaze hardened, and her lips thinned. The bloom of red in her cheeks spread until it encompassed her nose. "I'm not leaving you," she said through clenched teeth. "How dare you even suggest that!"

"Ally," he started, and her fingers covered his mouth.

"No."

He pulled her hand away from his lips. "You've got your whole life ahead of you. You don't need to be saddled with a paraplegic werewolf in a wheelchair."

"You don't want me?" she asked, her voice as small as he felt.

Hunter closed his eyes. "What I want isn't part of this discussion. This is about what you need."

"I need you."

Hunter opened his eyes and met her gaze. "You do not get it. I can never run with the pack. I'm not going to be able to go for walks with you or dance with you. I'm going to be stuck in a goddamned wheelchair." His voice rose to a pitch he recognized as much as the tightening of all his muscles. Anger had finally burned to the surface. "I'll never be able to fuck like a normal man," he said through clenched teeth as everything blasted through.

He didn't know who he was angry with. Alessandra. Winters. His father. The doctors. Right now they all were on his shit list, and the news of so many dead didn't help.

"Why are you yelling?" Alessandra asked, with a voice so calm he wanted to scream. The hurt in her eyes just fanned the inferno further.

"Because I'm fucking paralyzed, and that royally screws up all of my plans. Why..." He stopped himself from asking her why she saved him. Even through his current state of fury, he was aware that if the tables had been turned, he would have done the same damned thing.

They studied each other in silence.

"I think you need some time alone."

Alessandra stood, and he grabbed her wrist, kicking himself for letting his aggravation cloud his thinking. "I'm not angry with you," he said, forcing his voice into a calm cadence that belied the tornado inside.

"Then why push me away?"

"Because you deserve better than this." He waved at his useless legs.

She cocked her head. "What are you afraid of?"

He narrowed his gaze. "Stop trying to psychoanalyze me."

Her lips tilted into a whisper of a smile. "Sucks when someone does that, doesn't it?"

"Fuck you, Leigh," he said, under his breath.

"Back at you, Jake," she replied and twisted her wrist from his grip. He expected her to turn and leave. Instead, she leaned in and pressed her lips to his.

His mind stalled when her tongue swiped his lips. The kiss turned sweet and sultry, melting his resolve. He didn't want to give her up, but he didn't see any other way for her to be happy.

"I don't really give a damn if you're sequestered to a wheelchair. I'm going to be there for you like you have been for me. And if you don't cut it out, I'll order you to do as I say," she said, after she pulled away with eyes full of hellfire.

"Order me?" His voice cracked.

"Yep. I'll pull the alpha card."

Her hands landed on her hips, and if he could have jumped to his feet and stared her down, he would have, but glaring from a bed was the only thing he could do. It was less than ideal and had nowhere near the same results. In fact, he was the first one to break eye contact. Hunter huffed in frustration.

"Where do you want to go when you get out of here?"

"I want to go home," he said. He wanted familiarity and comfort. Hell, he wanted his bed.

"Do you think our houses are still there?" she asked.

"I'm talking about our place in Maine. The one I bought outright, and we lived in for a little over two months with no interruptions?" He challenged her with his tone. He hadn't even thought of their hometown, nor had he thought about the pack at all. He just wanted a quiet setting with no complications.

"We'll have to actually get phone and internet service," she said.

He'd thought she'd put up some sort of argument and raised an eyebrow.

"Nathan's taking the lead with the pack," she said. "He knows I need to take care of you for a bit. Besides, I nominated you as the council lead."

Hunter leaned back into the pillow. "Why?"

"You are the most level-headed werewolf I know, and there's a lot of shit to sift through. There was no way I was taking that on without you by my side. Besides, you're the better leader, despite the spooky ash marks on my stomach."

"Did you just admit I'm a better alpha than you?" This time, his eyebrows rose all the way to his hairline.

"No one, not even my parents could give me an order I had to follow. No one. Until *you* ordered me to leave that ditch. So, maybe I am."

He chuckled under his breath. "Shit got crazy," he said.

"It certainly did." She settled back into the chair. "I'm ready to sleep through the rest of the winter," she added with a yawn.

He said nothing, just watched over her as she leaned her head back on the padding and closed her eyes. That familiar tingle settled over him and she opened a single eye before she closed it again, this time with a hint of a smile on her sweet lips.

WOLF MOON
Chapter 13

THE COLD MARCH WIND howled around the house and the fire crackled in the fireplace, sending warmth all the way over to where he sat on the couch. The internet was spotty again, and he slammed the laptop closed, setting it on the coffee table before he ran his hands through his hair.

The lights flickered, and Hunter glanced towards the kitchen. "How close is dinner?" he called and peered at the mountains of papers spread across the kitchen table. To say the council was a mess was an understatement. Winters had been cooking the books and skimming off the top for years, which explained his stash in his bedroom. So, not only was the prick a serial killer, but he was also a thief.

The committee had paid for the rest of his physical therapy down in Virginia, and sent him home with Alessandra, an architect, and what had to be some of the fastest builders on the planet. It had only taken them a month to renovate the first floor with a master suite, so he didn't have to navigate the stairs.

They also sent them with all the shit that needed sorting, from valid crimes that needed to be addressed, to the nitty-gritty requests that flooded in daily. He had only been home for two weeks and he was ready for a vacation. On top of that, the bitter cold had settled over central Maine, which made the Florida Keys sound better and better.

Alessandra came out of the kitchen with two plates and took a seat at the other end of the couch, handing him one like a sacrificial offering.

"We might be eating by firelight," Hunter said, taking the plate. The meatloaf weighed the china down and he took the offered silverware before setting his dinner on his lap desk. As if on cue, the lights flickered again.

Alessandra was quiet and focused on her food, which was unusual. She was normally the one to pull the conversation out of him, not the other way around. He studied her profile and the tension in her posture.

"What's wrong?" he asked around his first bite of the thick meat.

"Six months, today," she whispered.

His gaze flicked to the calendar, and his appetite vanished. Their life had taken a turn into hell six months ago. All at the bidding of Ken Winters. Hunter had uncovered all the documentation in emails and the money trail leading to Alessandra's rape while they had sequestered him in the hospital in Virginia. The sick fuck even had the video those monsters took inside the van. Hunter could only stomach a few minutes of the brutality, but the video, along with the evidence he supplied the newly formed council, absolved both Alessandra and him from what they did to those boys.

But that event didn't take away the nightmares; although they had evolved for both of them. Now the nights were filled with ripping flesh, silver, and other horrors he would rather not focus on.

He slid his plate onto the table, and dropped his lap-desk on the floor, before spreading his arms wide for her. He signaled with his head for her to come to him, and she crawled into his grasp. After all this time, she still shuddered when he wrapped his arms around her, but he understood it was because of this particular date and the unwanted memories, and he couldn't blame her one bit.

Hunter kissed her forehead, keeping silent because there were no words that would wipe out what she'd lived through. Only time would heal her wounds. Time and his infinite patience. She hadn't actually been in his arms since the night in the hotel, and the physical sensation of her body against his stirred something deep within him.

She inhaled. "Salted caramel," she said, and he shrugged in response. "I haven't caught that scent since the hospital."

"I'm sorry," he started, but she stopped him, planting a kiss that sizzled. Every muscle in his body tensed with the intensity, and his arms tightened around her. Her tongue explored his mouth, teasing at first, but it soon escalated into a burning need. He groaned under it.

The lights finally succumbed to the weather, flickering out, leaving them with only the fire casting shadows. She pulled away and straddled his lap as she stared into his eyes. "I honestly thought..."

Her gaze moved away from his, but he hooked her chin, forcing her to look at him. "I've been a little busy trying to figure things out."

"Including me?" she asked, her eyes wide with the fear he sensed radiating from her.

"No. You're the only thing that's right in my life at the moment." He cupped her cheek and the fear in her eyes abated, turning into a fiery storm of desire.

She blessed him with a beaming smile and then leaned in for another soul-searing kiss. Again, that tingle spread through his entire form, as if kissing her was a reprieve to the numbness. Her tongue twirled with his in a magnificent dance that sucked the air from his lungs. Her hands skimmed over his shoulders and before he had any awareness, her fingers had already unbuttoned his shirt. The sensation of her palms on his chest nearly drove him mad.

Alessandra pulled away from his lips, and trailed kisses over his cheek to his earlobe before her teeth nipped, creating another shock of tingles. He closed his eyes and leaned his head back, enjoying the sensations of her hands and mouth moving down his body. "When you touch me like this, I can almost feel tingling in my toes," he whispered and opened his eyes. "It happened in the hospital when you whispered in my ear, too."

She looked up from his chest. "Really?"

He met her gaze. "Yes. So, don't stop. I like that tingly feeling. It makes me think their diagnosis was wrong." He had studied the x-rays. He acknowledged that it was wishful thinking, but there was still a slight chance of the impossible, especially with the wolf's blood in him.

She ran her fingers down the center of his chest, down to the elastic waistband of his sweatpants. "How much of that theory do you want to test?"

It wasn't so much the words as the sultry tone of her voice that stalled his brain. His legs were a shadow of what they used to be, with almost two months of non-use, and that played with his confidence. She hadn't seen how much his lower half had wasted away. The desire that swept through him moments ago disappeared. It was his turn to look away.

"Jake?" she asked, pulling his attention back to her.

"I'm not sure what I can…do," he said, meeting her gaze. This level of vulnerability seemed unnatural to him. It was as if the tables had turned, and he was the one afraid to explore this attraction. "I mean, I know what I can do with my hands and mouth," he added, with a twist of a his lips as he wiggled his fingers. "But as far as anything else…" He shrugged.

"And if I said I wanted to make love to you?"

"I'd be flattered, and I'd wonder what you had been drinking in the kitchen," he answered, and his gaze moved to her hands, now gripping his pants. "But I'm not sure if I have the ability to follow through." Heat filled his cheeks, and he met her gaze.

"Then let's just view this as relationship experiment number two."

"What was number one?" he asked, stalling as a measure of panic bit at his skin.

"The hotel," she said, and pulled his pants clear to his ankles, freeing one foot and leaving the rest bundled around his other ankle. She took off her shirt and pants, leaving on only her sheer underwear.

The flames of desire returned, turning his heart into an aching throb that echoed through every cell. Her hands slowly slid up his legs. The sensation was lost on him, but even in the dim light he could see her progression, and when she dipped down and kissed the inside of his knee, he cursed the gods for not allowing him to feel this. She didn't turn away from the atrophy in his muscles, nor the non-response from his body. Instead, it just seemed to fuel her.

She moved her gaze to his. "Any tingling?" she asked.

He slowly shook his head.

She dragged her tongue from his knee to the middle of his thigh, and while his breath quickened at the visual, his legs didn't bother sending the right signals to his brain. He thought his mind would crack when she took the tip of his cock in her mouth. His wildest dream of having Alessandra Tate giving him head was happening, and he couldn't feel anything but a distant tingle.

She looked up at him. "Now?"

He lifted a single shoulder and licked his lips. "Maybe," he whispered with a voice like sandpaper.

"Well, somewhere there's a reaction," she chuckled, and her mouth covered the tip of his growing cock.

Hunter thanked the gods that something was working. They had told him it was a slim chance and to catalogue what triggered an erection if he was able to get one. Alessandra's mouth. Check. He'd keep that catalogued for a very long time. Her slow head bob sent another wave of tingles through him as did the hollowness in her cheeks as she sucked.

What he wouldn't give to feel her lips sliding up and down his shaft. His heartbeat picked up, and he gently ran his fingers through her hair. "Leigh," he whispered, and she pulled away, meeting his gaze. He cupped her cheeks and pulled her to his lips. He needed to experience her mouth, her breasts... her pussy. God, he wanted to taste her, but before she allowed his mouth to cover hers, she slid her underwear off and positioned herself over his hard shaft.

His gaze remained glued to the space between them as she guided his cock into the folds of her pussy. She moved down his shaft with a moan. Her eyelids were at half mast, her mouth opened in a sexy pout. She took his hands and placed them on her hips.

Her slow rock turned his breathing into something akin to a pant. The flush of her skin and the hardness of her nipples pulled a smile to his lips. She was enjoying herself. He slid his thumb to her clit, circling at the same speed her hips moved. Alessandra nearly purred and despite not being able to actually feel the sensations of her pussy milking him, the simple fact that Alessandra had given herself to him completely, especially on the anniversary of her attack, brought him closer to his own release.

He leaned forward and took her breast in his mouth, sucking the hard nub while he still massaged her clit. He moved to her mouth, capturing her tongue in a frantic dance. His entire form tingled as she rode him. Heat pooled in the center of his abdomen and then exploded, yanking a groan from his lips. She pulled away from his mouth, arching her body as she let out a howl that sent a shiver through him.

Her body shook with her release and finally her breathing slowed and she relaxed into him.

He stared at the ceiling as she nestled on his chest. "I think I came," he whispered, astonished by that mere fact. That was something the doctors were sure wouldn't happen.

Alessandra started to giggle. "I think you did, too."

He pushed her away from his chest. "I wasn't supposed to be able to do that," he said, and her giggles subsided a fraction.

"Well, you did. I clearly felt it."

He started laughing. There was only one other explanation, but he didn't smell urine, so it clearly was an orgasm. His toes were still tingling from the power of it, and he wrapped his arms around her, pulling her into a bear hug.

"I love you, Alessandra Tate," he said through his laughter.

"I love you, too, Jacob Blaez." She kissed the curve of his neck, and another rash of tingles flowed through him.

"Marry me?" he blurted. His eyes widened as much as hers at the sudden question, and then he dropped his forehead to her shoulder, cursing himself for such an awkward proposal. It certainly wasn't how he'd ever envisioned asking her. He had exchanged the idea of him kneeling in the center of a bunch of rose petals for hiding the ring in a dessert. Never had he imagined he'd just blurt out the question after sex. She deserved so much better. Jesus, he didn't even have her ring yet.

"Did you just ask me to marry you?" She pushed him away so he would have to look at her.

He glanced up at her with his cheeks on fire. "Yeah, well, it just kind of...," he stumbled.

She threw her arms around him and squealed. "Yes! Yes, I'll marry you!"

Stunned didn't begin to describe it, and when she pulled away, he asked, "Really?"

"Hell, yes."

"You realize that was the lamest proposal in this hemisphere, right?" He raised an eyebrow.

She laughed. "True..." She leaned in and kissed his nose. "Do you want a do-over?"

It only took a moment for him to think it over, and then he shook his head. "No. I got the answer I wanted. Besides, if I had to make it big and fancy, it might take years."

"I'm not waiting years to marry you," she said, and yanked on the collar of his shirt, pulling him to her lips.

As their tongues intertwined, his heart sang in response.

THE END

J.E. Taylor

If you enjoyed WOLF MOON, turn the page to start book 2 HUNTER'S MOON.

MOONLIGHT DUET
Book 2
HUNTER'S MOON

A werewolf family saga.

Life handed me a real shitty deal. I'm now bound to a wheelchair for the rest of my life, which sucks for a beta werewolf. Especially one who's in love with my alpha.

She deserves far more than my useless ass.

But she has other ideas. And I can't walk away from her.

Instead of letting me wallow in my misfortune, she puts me in charge of the national werewolf council.

But I can't command respect from a wheelchair.

Will I end up putting a target on our backs again?

HUNTER'S MOON
Chapter 1

I STARED OUT OVER the thick woods from our back deck, wondering how the hell I got here. A light breeze rustled the sparse spring leaves, sending a few of the smaller ones flying in the wind. Anxiety mixed with the heavy pine scent as I pondered my current situation.

Alessandra should have never insisted that I run the werewolf council. I couldn't walk. I couldn't shift without making a fucking fool out of my wolf with my useless hind quarters. How the hell was I supposed to command the respect required to enforce pack laws across the entire continent?

And now she expected me to raise a child.

I was still numb from the news of her pregnancy.

Hell, I hadn't even married her yet. I ran my hand through my hair while I tried to get my bearings. I mean, we'd only slept together a handful of times since fate handed me this shitty paraplegic card.

"Hunter?"

Her voice blanketed me with warmth and terror at the same time. Even if she wasn't my mate, as the alpha of our pack, she couldn't miss my turmoil. The sickly sweet scent of my fear slipped out of my pores.

When her hands landed on my shoulders, I stiffened under her soft touch. I refused to look up at her.

"You will make a fantastic father."

I scoffed at her and glanced up at her. She had her long, dark hair in a braid as she did any time she cooked. Her blue-eyed gaze pierced right to the depths of my soul.

"You are out of your mind." I couldn't keep the words from tumbling from my mouth. "I can't shift. I can't teach my kid to hunt." I bit down the rest of the words at the flare of hurt through our bond and its presence in the watery glaze forming over her eyes.

"Being a father takes more than just running in the woods." She turned and headed back inside in a huff.

I maneuvered my wheelchair and followed her inside. "I get that. But I can't even do the simplest things. I can't protect a child." I waved my hand at her. "I can't even protect you."

Her eyes narrowed at me. "You know how to shoot." She nodded to the hardware attached to my chair.

What the hell was she thinking? "Yeah, and having a gun within reach of a child is reasonable." I couldn't help the sarcasm dripping from every word.

"Well, I'm not getting rid of it." She crossed her arms, and her tight-lipped expression filled with her fiery, stubborn resolve.

That was the look I couldn't fight. The one that shut me down. I had no chance in hell of swaying my alpha, and as her beta, I had to come to heel. The growl forming in her throat challenged me to say otherwise.

I lowered my gaze and nodded once. There was so much more I wanted to say, but it would just push her buttons, and I couldn't defend against her hormonal wolf.

"I guess we should get married," I mumbled under my breath.

"Don't sound so excited about it."

I snapped my gaze up to hers as my hackles rose in aggravation. I could feel my teeth elongating and I clenched my mouth closed before I shifted into my wolf out of sheer exasperation. "This is not what I envisioned."

"You've had enough time to design the perfect proposal."

"I've had six weeks. That isn't enough time." I knew it was just an excuse. I didn't believe an alpha should be subjected to a life with a cripple. Especially one as hot and smart as Alessandra.

"Do you even love me?" she shouted.

"I've killed for you. I've run from the law for you. I've nearly died for you. I fucking love you more than anything, and that's why I haven't asked."

Her eyes widened.

"You don't need to be saddled with someone like me for the rest of your days." I rolled past her toward my office, but she swung me back so I was facing her.

Her eyes shined with tears and raged with anger at the same time. "Jacob Randall Blaez, I don't care that you are in a wheelchair. It doesn't change who you are."

Oh, she pulled out the big guns by using my given name, not the nickname everyone else called me for as long as I could remember. "That's easy for you to say. You can still let your wolf out to run. I can't. I'm damaged!" I yelled in her face, fisting my hands and slamming them on the twigs of my legs. "I'm useless."

She grabbed a fistful of my hair and yanked my head back. "Don't you ever say that."

Her command wrapped around me. "You deserve more," I snarled through my clenched teeth.

She closed her eyes and tilted her head back, taking a deep breath, before she returned her gaze to mine. "Jake," she started, and the use of the nickname she used while we were on the run stole my ability to breathe. "You are the only one there is for me. And I don't care about your disability. It's you I love." She poked my chest with her free hand before covering whatever words I was going to hurl at her with her mouth.

Her tongue tangled with mine as she slid onto my lap, and I forgot every point of argument. Even though I've loved her forever, I still didn't think she should settle for me. But I was her beta, and I would serve her until the day I died.

HUNTER'S MOON
Chapter 2

ALESSANDRA'S DISTRACTION DIDN'T DISSUADE me from my original thoughts. She didn't understand how unprepared to be a father I was. Hell, I took two to three hours to even be presentable in the mornings. My new humiliating reality included a fucking bowel program, so I didn't shit my pants later in the day.

I learned *that* lesson pretty quick.

Being confined to a wheelchair for the last six months had been more of a wake-up call as to what the rest of my life would be like. I wasn't sure I could saddle my alpha with this burden. There were plenty of eligible wolves in our pack, and the council had access to many more.

My routine was grueling enough without throwing a wife and child into the mix. And although Alessandra wanted to help, I could not allow it. I didn't need her to be my nursemaid.

I rolled my wheelchair into my office while she went back to preparing our dinner. I carefully inserted myself behind the desk, making sure I was in the center where the drawer was at its thinnest. I'd misaligned before and found massive bruises from the desk pressing on my legs when I undressed that night. It wasn't fun trying to explain to Alessandra that I hadn't felt the desk doing the damage she saw.

That was my existence. Bruises and cuts on my legs could kill me. And if I wasn't careful, I would develop sores on my ass from not moving for hours on end. It was obnoxious. It was a damn hazard.

And God forbid if we were ever attacked again. I'd be a liability, despite what Alessandra or the other pack members said. And that weighed heavily on me.

Which meant I had to be extra vigilant. Not only here at home, but on the council. The judgments we rendered had to fit the crimes laid before us. Anything else but just sentencing and we'd be targeted.

Sometimes, I had to make tough calls that put me on some wolf's shit list. It wasn't easy, especially with my vulnerabilities exposed for all to see.

Then there was the Monster Defense Agency. Run by Winters's brother, of all people. If Terrance Winters didn't run that agency, I would have gladly opted for a more global organization to oversee the laws of pack life. But I didn't trust him, despite his denouncements of his brother's atrocities.

If I wasn't careful with how I operated the council, the Monster Defense Agency might decide that we were within its domain, like they had done to some packs in the area around the city.

The pressure of being the leader of the werewolf council, coupled with my condition, exhausted me. And now I had to find the energy to raise a child?

I mopped my face with my hand, grumbling to myself. I leaned back and ran my fingers through my hair before I looked out into the belly of our house. If I hadn't been confined to a wheelchair for the rest of my life, the news she gave me would have made my heart soar.

I closed my eyes and opened my mind to our connection. I hadn't done it since the accident because I didn't want to know what Alessandra was feeling. I didn't want her pity at my sorry state. I clenched my teeth at the hurt that radiated from her; just below that was anger. And below that was the love she felt that kept her tied to me.

I sighed and moved away from the desk. I had been the one to pull away, and she let me because she thought I needed space to come to grips with this news. But my reaction made her miserable.

Fuck.

I reached into the drawer and took out the little box that I had bought weeks ago when I thought maybe I'd get the feeling back in my legs, and from there be able to walk again. But the tingling in my toes hadn't occurred since. The doctors said it was a ghost tingle, which happens with paraplegics and amputees.

After that news, I couldn't bring myself to give it to her.

I went in search of her and found her chopping carrots in the kitchen. Well, it looked more like massacring the carrot bits, but I would not comment while she held a fast-moving blade. I waited until she finished this round of kill the carrot and cleared my throat the minute she put the sharp kitchen utensil down.

"I'm sorry." I met her gaze and shrugged. "If it weren't for this" —I patted the arms of my wheelchair—"I would be ecstatic." I licked my lips under her sharp stare. "And I would have already married you."

Her eyes narrowed, and she grabbed the carrots, tossing them into a pan. "So, I get a raw deal because you did?" Her words came out in a snarl.

"Being saddled with me *is* a raw deal."

The muscles in her jaw jumped. "Am I not enough for you?"

I blinked and pressed back in my chair. Her words cut as effectively as the kitchen knife she had been using on the carrot. "It's not you who isn't enough, Leigh, and you damn well know that."

Tears bloomed in her eyes, and one rolled down her cheek.

Double fuck.

"What happens now?" Another tear slid down her cheek.

Defeat scraped my skin. I hated when Alessandra cried. It broke me more than this fucking chair I was chained to. And I loved her. I just didn't want her to be stuck with me for the rest of her life. I rolled to the counter and put the box on the edge across from her, and then moved back to where the kitchen turned into the living area.

"I can't sweep you off your feet." I looked at the ground, trying to find the right words. "But if this is what you want to settle for…" I glanced back at her with a wince. "I'll give you the best that I can." The entire proposal sucked. There were no rose petals leading to me with the ring box. No soft music. No candlelight. Nothing but my lame offer and a ring.

Just like the course of my life, my plans changed drastically the moment that car overturned down the embankment and the crash shattered my spine.

She looked at the box as if it might bite her, but after a moment reached over and snatched it as if I might change my mind. When she snapped the box open, her eyes widened and her gaze jumped to mine.

"I got it after…" I waved at her, and my cheeks heated. "I thought the tingling meant I might regain feeling in my legs." I let out a bitter laugh. "Then I got the news that it was a fluke. Ghost tingles, like an amputee."

She closed the box and put it on the counter before she leveled a glare at me.

My heart dropped.

J.E. Taylor

HUNTER'S MOON
Chapter 3

THE WAY HER LIPS pursed, as she considered my failed proposal, left me fidgeting in my wheelchair.

"Is this what you want?"

If she had asked me before I put the ring on the counter, I might have said something sarcastic, but with her intense stare settled on me, I chewed on my lower lip. I had already made my feelings known about what I wanted for her. But I probably would waste away to nothing if she left. I loved her enough to let her go if she didn't want this life, but I also couldn't see my life without her.

"For purely selfish reasons, yes," I whispered.

She rolled her eyes and turned back to the roast, putting it back in the oven before she wiped her hands and faced me again.

"Then ask me the proper way." She crossed her arms, waiting.

I ran my hand through my hair and sighed before I rolled the chair around the island and faced her. I couldn't reach the box where she had placed it, so I put my hand out for it, staring her down.

She slammed it in my palm and crossed her arms again, silently daring me to follow through, as if she didn't believe I actually would.

I took a slow and the inhale and blew it out in a long stream, getting the right words in place in my head before I looked up at her.

"Leah," I started with the nickname I had used for her when we were on the run. "I love you. And while I don't want to saddle you with my situation, I cannot see my life without you by my side to kick my ass into next week when I'm wallowing in self-pity."

Her lip twitched up on one side.

"As I said before, I can't sweep you off your feet or slow dance with you in my arms, but I can try to give you my best in other ways." My lips curved at the thoughts of how much she liked my mouth and my hands on her. I had gotten very good at hitting all the right spots to make her squirm and cry out my name.

Blush shaded her cheeks.

"I'd give anything to shift and run with you again, but you'll just have to settle for my endless adoration instead." I opened the box. "Will you spend the next however long we have at my side as my wife?"

This time, her hand fluttered to her lips and her eyes teared up again. And to my eternal relief, she nodded.

"Yes, Jake. I'll marry you." Her husky voice bled from behind her splayed fingers.

I took the diamond solitaire out of the box, and she stuck her left hand out. I slid it on her ring finger and leaned back in the chair. It wasn't what I had envisioned, but the teary smirk she gave me made up for my lack of finesse.

"Now, was that so hard?" She held out her hand and scrutinized the ring before smiling at me.

I gave her my *cut the crap* look and rolled backward. My emotional reaction wasn't what I expected, either. Right alongside the relief was a healthy dose of fear, as if I had sentenced her to a life of pain and anguish.

She sniffled and then blinked at me. Her head cocked to the right side and that line between her eyes creased deeper. "What are you afraid of?"

I laughed, trying to shake the certainty of pending doom. "Regrets."

Her eyebrows rose, and she shook her head. "My only regret was that I didn't realize how you felt about me sooner." She glanced down at the ring. "If I had, you'd still be able to walk."

"Or I'd be dead by Winters's hand." I wouldn't have been able to let that whole situation go. Not with the information my father left me, and she knew it.

Her face paled enough for me to sigh and move toward her. I knew where her mind drifted. I had seen those awful silver statues, too. She didn't know, but I made Nathan take me down there before those hideous things were removed. I needed to see what had been done to my parents and to let them know I'd avenged their deaths.

I wrapped my arms around her waist and pulled her down onto my lap. "My regrets have nothing to do with the past and more to do with the future. I wanted more for you than my sorry ass." Before she could argue, I pulled her lips to mine, silencing her with a kiss.

She melted into me, and the kiss lingered, warming my blood and teasing my nerves. But it only lasted for a few moments before she pulled away.

"There is no one else out there for me. Or for you." She met my gaze and poked my chest to bring home her point. And although I had fooled around before her, it never felt right. As frustratingly blind as she had been for years, the only time I felt complete was when I was near this beautiful woman.

I had never told her that, and I wasn't sure I could leave myself that vulnerable by spilling that piece of my heart. Not when she had all the rest of it laid bare. I loved the woman, but I needed that last shred of dignity to remain intact.

HUNTER'S MOON
Chapter 4

NO ONE EVER TOLD me how amazing childbirth was. I sat by Alessandra's side, alternating between holding her hand and then holding her leg behind the knee when she had to push. I stared at the crop of black hair as it crested her opening, and my heart nearly seized in my chest.

Alessandra panted and pushed until the baby's shoulders breeched, and then the doctor pulled the baby out of her womb.

"You have a boy!" the doctor announced.

I swear, my heart grew in my chest with the amount of love that filled me in that moment. I was in utter awe of my wife and the baby. Enough so when the doctor handed me the surgical scissors, I stared at him, dumbfounded.

"Would you like to cut the cord, Mr. Blaez?"

I blinked and glanced at the loop of umbilical cord he held. I took the scissors and cut where the doctor instructed me to, and then the baby was taken to be cleaned and weighed and measured.

"Do you have a name?" the delivery room nurse asked.

"Archer. Archer Henry Blaez," Alessandra said.

My heart expanded with pride. We had discussed which of our father's names would be first, and she initially wanted her father's first. But she must have changed her mind at the last minute.

I looked over at my father's namesake as he wailed on the table. I wanted to go to him, but Alessandra gripped my hand as another contraction had her gasping.

"Is this normal?" I asked the doctor.

He nodded. "The placenta." He pulled out a rubbery bloody thing that had housed my son for the last nine months. The doctor put it in an empty clear pan on the table to the side of us.

Before I gave in and poked the placenta to see whether it indeed felt as rubbery as it looked, the nurse brought Archer to Alessandra and laid him in my wife's arms. I stared at them and smiled, forgetting all my misgivings about being a father. It didn't matter because I would go feral for that child if I had to.

Alessandra looked up from our son's little face and grinned. She had never looked so exhausted or radiant. "Archer," she said to the baby in her arms and pressed a kiss to his forehead.

THE NOVELTY OF A child wore off quick once we arrived home with our little bundle of joy, and my limitations soon became glaringly apparent. Don't get me wrong. I loved the little guy. But I couldn't get him out of the damn crib from a wheelchair. The changing table was too tall and even trying to change him on the couch or the bed once he started rolling was more of a challenge than I thought it would be.

Plus, getting on the floor to play with him wasn't an option without a handful of the pack members here to pick me up and put me back in the chair. If my legs were amputated, I might be able to get myself up with no issues. But my legs were dead weight I couldn't maneuver easily.

God knows I've done it before, like the time a nightmare caused me to fling myself out of the bed. Alessandra had been out late at a pack meeting, so I had no one to help me get back to the bed. It took a bit to get into my wheelchair and then into the bed. Much longer than a parent has when dealing with a mobile infant or toddler.

But even with the less-than-ideal situation, I found there were moments with my son that I would not trade for anything in all the world. Like when he fell asleep on my shoulder or when I read to him and he pointed at the pictures when I named what they were.

And damn did he grow fast. One minute he was in diapers and the next he was eleven and coming into his wolf. Unfortunately, he didn't have the mark of the alpha like his mother, but that didn't keep him from dreaming.

ARCHER RAN AROUND THE backyard with the girl from down the street before the school bus came to pick them up. Alessandra stepped next to me at the sliding doors and handed me a cold beer. She sighed, and I glanced up at her. Melancholy etched into her features.

"We used to run around like that." She nodded at the kids outside.

"Yeah, well, you married my sorry ass." I turned my attention to my son and his girlfriend.

"I know. But I was talking about Archer and me. Not us." She whacked my arm lightly with the back of her hand.

I just grunted, acknowledging her statement. But I would have given my left nut to do that now.

"I miss running in the woods with you. It was the highlight of my youth."

I raised my eyebrow at her. "You could have fooled me. You tried to get out of every pack run possible," I teased. After all, once she went off to college, she nearly cut us all off just to find herself. And look what that cost us.

She smirked. "Yeah, well…" Color crept into her cheeks. "I was kind of a brat back then, wasn't I?"

"Don't make me answer that." I smiled up at her and poked her in the side. Archer's friend was cute with dark hair like Archer, but her eyes were a different color blue. Archer had Alessandra's eyes but seemed like he was going to have my build. Well, my former build. Anyway, Alessandra said he looked like I did when I was his age.

She was studying the two wolves in the backyard, playing as if there wasn't a care in the world. "I hope he ends up with an alpha by his side."

I agreed. Even with Alessandra training him to be a leader, she couldn't give him the alpha position. In other packs, the alpha position was passed down within the family unless a challenge was made. Then there would be a fight to the death for the position. Being the child of an alpha didn't make it a given in our pack. Only the member with the leader symbol was viewed as the alpha. And it only appeared on those who were worthy of the position.

Alessandra had been magically branded with the stamp of a leader the day she saved me from a vat of silver.

Her father had the same mystical tattoo on his forearm, but his had appeared early on. Hers only appeared after defeating the council. And the next alpha in our pack would be branded the same way. She had deferred leading the council to me because she felt she had zero political savvy.

And somehow, I kept us out of the oversight of the Monster Defense Agency. Although they visited once a year to compare notes. Until recently, I had dealt with Terrance Winters. Every time I got near that man; I had to lock down my wolf. Terrance's brother's actions had put me in this wheelchair, and as much as I wanted to peg Terrance as the same, he didn't seem to be.

He couldn't shift, so he wasn't as critical of a threat as his brother had been. Even so, I was sure he was keeping secrets of his own. Secrets that would turn the council against him if they ever came to light.

The last couple of years, he came with a sullen wolf who had haunted eyes that reminded me of my own. This past year, Terrance told us that Robert Young of the Allegany pack would represent him in these annual reviews of pack laws.

And Robert Young called to ask for a private meeting with me, without the council and without my pack's alpha. Easier said than done considering I was married to the alpha, but his request scratched at my curiosity enough that I agreed.

Thankfully, I still had my driver's license and a car made specifically for paraplegics. I wasn't housebound, but I'd have to figure out a reason to go off on my own, which was rare.

I glanced at my watch and then at the kids outside. "I need to run out for a few." I rolled away from the back slider.

Alessandra raised her eyebrow. "Where are you going?"

"I will be back before dinner." I just smiled and left it at that.

Thankfully, the Allegany pack alpha had requested a meeting near Alessandra's birthday, and where I suggested the meeting was in the middle of a shopping mall far enough away from most of the pack that the likelihood of being seen was low. So, I could pick out a gift she wouldn't find delivered on the doorstep.

The cryptic way he had sounded on the phone didn't fill me with warm and fuzzies, but he insisted I meet him. I just hoped going alone wasn't a mistake.

HUNTER'S MOON
Chapter 5

I ARRIVED AT THE coffee shop early to account for the time it would take me to get out of the car and into the quaint shop. If I didn't know better, I would have thought the place was packed based on the long line of cars at the takeout window. But thankfully, there was only one table occupied inside.

I ordered a coffee at the counter and rolled to a table in the far corner, away from the counter and at the farthest point from the other person, and took the space that faced the door.

The barista was kind enough to deliver my coffee to me instead of just calling my name. The moment she stepped away, Robert Young stepped inside with another person trailing a step behind him. He handed the woman a bill and nodded toward the counter.

I sniffed, trying to detect whether she was a wolf, but all I smelled was Robert's unique hemlock scent and her human sweat aroma. I met Robert's gaze as he approached. His usually neat hair looked as if he had repeatedly raked his hand through it on the drive here. And he seemed more nervous than a groom at a shotgun wedding.

Robert Young fell into the chair across from me. "I hope like hell I've pegged you right."

A low growl came from my throat as I raised my eyebrows. "I came alone like you asked and lied to my wife in the process."

Robert ran his hand through his hair. "At least your wife is safe. Mine was killed by the agency, along with my kids."

I sat back in my chair, rolling it with the action. "Excuse me?"

"Terrance Winters is just as fucked up as his brother." His voice rumbled from his chest. "And he is in league with the vampires."

"Why haven't you brought this up with the council?" My mind couldn't wrap around the venom coming from this man. Especially with how docile and under control he seemed over the years when he accompanied Terrance to the council meetings.

He laughed. "If I had, the council would have been slaughtered." He leaned forward. "It has taken me years to earn Terrance's trust. And because I pretended to be his lackey for so long, I am in the position to figure out a plan to bring the bastard down, along with the damn agency." He looked at the coffee line where the woman he was with stood, spouting off their order. "And save some lives in the process." He turned back to me. "That's where you come in."

I pointed at my chest in surprise, still digesting his little speech.

"I need people to disappear."

My mind closed down. I crossed my arms. "I don't kill people."

His smile was sarcastic, and he leaned forward into my personal space, speaking so softly that only a wolf could hear. "No, I need them to disappear into the world. I need new identities and places where they will be safe from the retribution of the agency."

I blinked and glanced around and then back at him as everything he said processed slowly. "What exactly am I protecting them from?"

"Unjustified murder."

I pursed my lips. Being on the council taught me that justification varied from person to person. What one may feel was unjust mighty actually be valid. "Define what you feel is unjustified."

"Being sentenced to die because of a relationship with another agent. Or wanting to leave the agency. Or letting a target go because the facts don't support killing them like we are ordered." He cocked his head. "Or using boiling silver to threaten and control wolves, or to torture and kill them if they are not complying with agency rules."

Heat fled my face. Torturing werewolves with boiling silver had been outlawed in the United

States. That was the first law I put into effect, and Terrance Winters knew that.

"Shall I go on?"

"No. You've made your point." My gaze moved to the woman approaching with coffee. Her pale eyes held hope and her hands shook as she gave Robert his coffee. "But how do you know this is happening?" I couldn't just take his word. I needed more than that.

"I was promoted to the position of agency enforcer. I'm supposed to kill these people and bring proof back to Winters." Bitterness framed every word.

My insides turned. "You've killed our kind?"

"I've been able to avoid it so far. But I've been forced to witness enough gruesome deaths to want to help others." He glanced at woman still standing next to him. He waved her to the adjoining chair. "This is Stacy. She didn't follow through on an order to kill and her partner ratted her out. I'm supposed to kill her, but I want you to secure a new identity for her and help her get a new life."

I looked her over and then moved my gaze to Robert as everything hit with the force of a flying brick. Thankfully, none of our wolves ever signed on to work in the Monster Defense business.

"Witch?" I asked. It was well known that witches and wolves were paired together in the agency.

Stacy nodded as her eyes darted around the room, looking for a sign of anything wrong.

"Will you help me?" Robert asked.

I stared at him and then looked around the café. The man who had been in the far corner had left soon after Robert arrived, and it was only us and the staff serving the takeout window. Agreeing to this without really thinking it over made me uncomfortable. Although saving innocent lives was a righteous endeavor, this could paint another target on me and my family.

"I have a wife and a young son. Will this put them in danger?"

Robert closed his eyes and hung his head. "If the agency finds out what I'm doing, yes." He took a breath and opened his eyes. "If they find out, my son will die. I've come to heel to the agency to save that boy. He's all I have left. You are not the only one risking everything."

My gaze narrowed. "I thought you said the agency killed your kids."

He nodded. "My oldest and middle child were slaughtered. By dumb luck, my youngest was at a sleepover for his friend's birthday. If he had been home, he would have died, too."

"And you didn't kill Winters?" I couldn't fathom letting the man walk if he harmed my family.

"He threatened to kill my son if I didn't straighten up. So no, I didn't kill him. Besides, while he's as screwed up as Ken was, he's not the top dog running the show. The agency has vampires and other ancient beings pulling the strings." He wiped a hand down his face.

"Vampires?" Mangy beasts that drained others of blood. We were their food as much as humans were. "I thought the agency put vampires down?"

Robert laughed. "Only those that the vampires sanction. It's not black and white like the agency makes it sound. They are snowing you, appeasing you and the council, so they have a chance at recruiting more wolves. My pack isn't under the rule of your council. And there are others that aren't either. They are bound to sacrificing their members to the damned agency."

"But they honor the annual gatherings. You've been here with him and gone over the rules that werewolves are supposed to live by." I blinked, thinking about how many years we had gone through the rule book with the head of the agency in attendance. And how that bastard always had spoken down to me, as if he thought he was better than all of us. Righteous anger filled me, and I stared at Robert.

"Yeah. I was part of that ruse." He had the sense to look remorseful. "But now that I'm not under his watch all the time, I have the latitude to keep you informed of what is really going on. And if something happens to me, I'd want you to talk with my son. I don't want him to be trapped in the agency once he comes of age."

"And what of your pack?"

His jaw tightened, and he shook his head. "The new alpha would have to make that determination. But the agency has several hooks into the pack already, so I don't know that they'd be able to break free."

"Your son wouldn't be named alpha?"

Robert hung his head. "He has the ability to be a phenomenal alpha. He's a natural leader, even as a teenager, but it would put him in the direct line of fire of the agency. I might not have a say in his future, but I'd like some assurances that if I die, someone with values and honor outside of my pack will step in and take care of my boy."

That was an enormous sacrifice. One which made me understand the true magnitude of what was going on. Everything up to this point had warning bells clanging in my head, but asking another pack to take in your child if something happened made me take all this seriously. That just wasn't done.

"Just so I am clear. If something happens to you, you want Alessandra and me to raise him?" He'd likely never be an alpha in our pack unless the magic surrounding the mark made that decision.

Robert did not hesitate. "Yes."

I slowly nodded. Alessandra would take him into our pack if disaster struck, and we still had control of the council, so we had the power of most of the packs in the nation behind us to make that happen.

"So, about Stacy?" Robert asked.

I licked my lips and sighed. I couldn't in good conscience let her die now that I'd looked into her eyes and smelled her fear. "Where do you want to go?"

She blinked at me, and her mouth popped open. "You are going to help?"

My lips tilted into a smile. Hope flared in her features, brightening her eyes. "Yes. Robert makes a very compelling argument. So, where do you want to go?"

"Go?"

"You can't stay with my pack. That's too dangerous. But I can help you with a new identity and at least get you to a destination of your choosing. Then it is up to you." I had some questionable people that my father had connected me with before he disappeared, and I had kept contact with them over the years. I had an exit plan in place if our lives ever went to shit again. They had the ability to create identities for me at the drop of a hat. And they were discreet enough that word would not get out.

"Anywhere but New York," Stacy said.

I swiveled my gaze to Robert. "This will not be a weekly thing, right?"

He shook his head. "No. I might not get the chance to do this again, but Stacy has been a friend of mine since the academy. I think Terrance did this to test me again. Anyway." He turned to Stacy. "I'll need your wallet and your agency ID." He put his hand out.

Stacy handed both items over. "What are you going to do?"

Robert stared at her and then turned to me. "Thanks," he said before he stood and left the shop.

I glanced at Stacy. "Why did you ask that?"

"Because there has to be a body."

"Meaning?"

"He's going to have to kill someone and make the authorities think the body is mine." She stared at the door and shivered. "But at least he'll find someone who deserves it. He doesn't kill innocents. Ever."

I had killed before, so I knew the price that exacted on a soul. I just hoped he'd make it happen as far from our pack lands as possible. "I need to pick out a gift for my wife for her birthday." I rolled back from the table. "And then I have to figure out what to do with you."

She remained seated until I stopped and spun toward her. "Are you coming?"

"Oh. You want me to come along with you?"

"Yeah. I'm not just going to leave you in a coffee shop." I gave her my best "duh" expression and then rolled out onto the sidewalk with her at my side. "What kind of magic do you have?" I asked as we rolled toward a jewelry store.

"I have scouring magic."

I glanced at her. "That really means nothing to me."

"The easiest way to explain it is I can scour a room of grime just as easily as I can wipe a mind clean."

I slowed to a stop as a fantastic idea came to mind. One that would give me time to get her a new identity and give Alessandra a gift that I know she'd appreciate, even if it was only for a couple of months.

Stacy side-eyed me. "What?" she asked, as if she saw the wheels in motion in my head.

"Look, I was going to get my wife some jewelry for her birthday, but I still would have to explain you. So, how do you feel about cleaning our house for the next month while I work on getting you that new identity?"

"I thought you didn't want me staying with your pack."

I sighed. "I don't, but I can't exactly leave you somewhere on your own where you could draw attention and get yourself killed. My home is secluded enough to be off the agency's radar. Besides, I have a finished apartment over our garage for visiting alphas and their families. No one is scheduled to be there for a while."

"Rob said you had a run-in with Winters's brother?" She shifted her stance, studying me.

I snorted a laugh and nodded. "You could say that. Ken Winters killed my parents and put me in this damn wheelchair." I started rolling toward the stores again. "Do I need to pick out a necklace for my wife, or would you be our new house cleaner for a short time?"

"They can track my magic."

I sighed and rubbed my face. "Okay, then how about doing it for real instead of with your magic?"

Her eyebrows rose.

"I know. You're a big, bad Monster Defense agent. But it buys me time to get what I need to get you a new identity and gives my wife a break. As you can see, I'm not very helpful around the house." I waved at the chair. "I try, but I just irritate the shit out of her."

For the first time since she walked into the coffee shop, Stacy smiled. Her freckled cheeks pitted with dimples, and she swept her honey-blonde hair over her shoulder. "Fine. But you might want to get your wife that necklace. My manual cleaning skills are rusty as hell."

HUNTER'S MOON
Chapter 6

WE ROLLED INTO THE driveway as the school bus pulled away. Archer stood at the front door and even from here, I could see the cock of his eyebrow as Stacy stepped out of the passenger seat.

She waited for me to get in my chair and roll to the front door.

Alessandra stood at the door with her arms crossed and her gaze drifting between us.

"Happy birthday a little early," I said as I made up a new identity for Stacy on the fly. "Rosie Beeswich, this is my wife Alessandra and my son Archer." I waved between the group as I tucked the jewelry bag into the side of the chair. I turned to my wife. "Rosie is our new maid. She'll stay in the apartment above the garage for the time that I hired her for."

Alessandra stared at me. I shifted in the seat and kept her gaze, hoping she would buy this.

"It's nice to meet you, Mrs. Blaez." Stacy stuck her hand out without missing a beat. "Mr. Blaez said you'd be able to show me to the apartment?"

I was impressed. She must have seen the stairway in the garage. Stairs I couldn't climb in a wheelchair.

"Sure, just as soon as we finish dinner. I made enough for an army, so you're welcome to join us." Alessandra waved her inside and then gave me a *what the fuck* look.

I held out the car keys to Archer. "Her suitcase is in the backseat of the car. Can you bring it up to the garage apartment?"

Archer grumbled but went and did what I asked.

"So, where did my husband find you?"

"Through Holly Maid. It's a national maid service that matches maids with households in need." She smiled. "I was looking for a live-in opportunity since rent has gone insane the last few years. And this will give me a chance to get back on my feet."

I wanted to ask how she knew that, but I guess her using my phone for web searches on the ride back had a point. She must have been studying up on a cover story for the ride home.

My wife glanced at me. "Get back on your feet?"

Stacy licked her lips and glanced at me before she looked at Alessandra. "I recently got out of an abusive relationship." She looked at the ground and then back up. "I've been living in shelters and working locally, but I needed a change of scenery, and this job offered the perfect opportunity to start over."

Based on what Robert had said about the agency, this really wasn't that much of a lie.

"Well, I'm glad my husband found you. We could use the extra hand around here." She glanced around the house. The only thing out of place were the magazines on the coffee table. Everything else here was neat enough, but that's only because she took pristine care of the place.

She led us into the kitchen and put another place setting on the table.

I excused myself and rolled into the bedroom to hide the necklace I had gotten. If Stacy was that lame in cleaning, I'd need to have something to appease Alessandra. I still didn't know whether to clue her into the truth, but I certainly wouldn't broach that subject until we were alone and Archer was fast asleep.

I wasn't sure whether Alessandra would slap me or hug me for taking this on. But I knew damned well she'd want to take out Winters. That condescending bastard was breaking the rules and being such a barbaric dick.

I'd have to tell her, eventually. But until then, she'd have a little less work to do around the house. I just hoped all this wouldn't backfire.

HUNTER'S MOON
Chapter 7

I T WAS WELL PAST midnight, and the possible consequences of helping Stacy kept me awake. I studied the ceiling as if it would give me magical answers, but it was just paint and spackle and imparted zero knowledge.

"What's bothering you?" Alessandra asked, pulling my attention to her.

I wiped my face and then glanced at her, weighing my options. I decided to come clean because my brain couldn't work fast enough at this hour to provide a convincing lie. "Robert Young asked for a private meeting today."

Her sleepy eyes widened, and she propped up on her elbow. She had never been comfortable with the idea of the Monster Defense Agency. And although she knew it was required of them to attend the annual standing meeting with the council, she never really felt comfortable in Terrance's presence. But she had been curious about the alpha he dragged around with him over the years.

"Why didn't he come to me?" she asked as that crease of irritation formed between her eyes.

Protocol for visiting alphas made it clear they should meet with the head of the pack before coming into pack territory. Otherwise, it could be seen as encroachment.

Her irritation raked over my skin. I glanced at her and sighed. "I know Robert didn't follow protocol. But he wasn't here to challenge your territory."

"Then why did he ask for a meeting?" The clip in her voice and the way her eyes went to a darker shade of blue announced her aggravation.

"It seems Terrance didn't fall far from his brother, after all."

She blanched and her exposed skin broke out into goose flesh. Her gaze narrowed, and her lips thinned. Anger radiated from her, brushing my skin with its heat. "What's he doing?"

I didn't want to explain the particulars and send her into a frenzy. "So many unscrupulous things. Enough for Robert to ask for our help smuggling people out of the agency."

Her eyebrows rose. "Why don't they just quit?"

I pinched the bridge of my nose, wondering whether he was actually playing me. They knew torture and death by liquid silver were outlawed. That was the first pack law I put in place when I took over as the council head. And Robert was versed in our history with Ken Winters enough to play that card, knowing I would react the way I did.

"According to Robert, once you're in, that's it. There's no getting out."

In the wee hours of the night, my acceptance of the situation seemed just as ludicrous as his story. I glanced at Alessandra. She blinked, and I knew all the pieces were falling into place.

"Rosie?"

"Her name is Stacy, but we're going to get her a full identity matching the name I came up with on the fly." I chewed my bottom lip, waiting for Alessandra to lose her cool with me.

"Why isn't Robert doing something about it?"

The snap in hcr voicc tugged at my core.

"He can't. It seems the agency has some powerful benefactors calling the shots and when he stepped out of line and disobeyed the rules, they killed his wife and two of his three kids."

She sucked in a breath and her fingers fluttered over her mouth as her wide eyes stared at me.

That in itself was a reason to go after the bastards, but we did not have the power to take on an army of supernaturals. Not even if we had all the packs in the werewolf council backing us.

"And if he doesn't play the faithful employee, they'll go after his remaining son," I added as my first comment settled in.

She covered her eyes with her arm and flopped back on the pillow. Anger and sorrow leaked through our bond.

I'm sure her mind went where mine did on hearing all this. I would do anything to keep my son safe. "He asked if we'd take his son in if anything happens to him."

Her gaze whipped to mine. "Wouldn't his son be the alpha of their pack?"

I nodded. "But that would damn him to be under the control of the agency." He sighed. "And if they find out we are involved in helping the agents get new identities, we'll likely be targets again." I met her gaze.

She studied the ceiling the same way I had been doing for most of the night.

I expected an argument. We had lost so much to Ken Winters and his quest for power. Both our parents, and my ability to walk, were stolen from us by that bastard.

"Is there anything else we can do?" she asked softly, surprising the hell out of me.

"Not without putting our family in danger."

She scoffed at me, and her fierce glare moved to me. Her unsettled itch to exact justice filled every pore. If I didn't lay this out in a way that she could grasp, she was likely to go after Winters without backup. And although she had won the last war we had with that family, it had cost us a lot more than just a few scratches.

"He doesn't want us in the crosshairs of the agency. He asked that we just shield and save those he funnels to us. If we get involved beyond being *'the wizard behind the curtain,'* we'll be screwed, and Robert will lose his son and likely his own life." I framed the wizard saying in finger quotes. "The agency's allies include vampires. They aren't things I want to tango with. Especially not in my condition." I waved at my useless lower half. "Robert wants to keep our involvement at a minimum, so he has a haven for his son. But he can't save these people alone."

She moved her gaze to the ceiling again as she digested the situation. Her turmoil bled through our bond, but the scrunch of her forehead and then the long sigh announced her acceptance of the situation more than the soft "Okay" she whispered before she rolled toward me and fluffed her pillow up under her cheek.

It was my turn to blink at her. I expected more of a fight, especially considering I put us in the middle of this mess. "You're not mad?"

She palmed my cheek. "Your heart's in the right place."

I waited for more. When it didn't come, I said, "But...?"

"No buts. I would have done the same. But where are you going to find the right contacts to get fake IDs?" She searched my gaze.

I grinned. I had quite a few reliable—if questionable—alliances that I could tap into to help. She just didn't know about them. My father had connected me to a lot of different sources in the event I had to go on the run. I just hadn't had the chance to reach out when we were on the run, but I had kept in contact over the years.

"I do." I didn't expand further. She didn't need to know how fully prepared I was for another catastrophic event. I would not leave us in the dark and on the run without a plan again.

"We also need to build stronger alliances with all the packs who are not involved in the agency, so we are all protected from their insidiousness. Once they get their foot in the door, they own the pack. And I don't want them anywhere near any of ours."

HUNTER'S MOON
Chapter 8

STACY STAYED WITH US for a couple of months while I sorted out her documentation. She wasn't the best maid in the world, but she helped Alessandra a lot, lifting her home burdens much more than I could. She also helped Archer with some of his more difficult math and science homework while I worked my ass off on setting up a solid network to tap into whenever I needed.

Archer was the only person in the house who did not truly know where she came from. And we had agreed to keep it that way.

Alessandra kept the secret from the pack as well. This was not something that should be broadcast widely. It needed to be conducted in secrecy, so our wards survived. If anyone slipped, it would put the pack at the Monster Defense Agency's mercy. And she reached out to the other alphas, building more powerful alliances, just like I asked her to do. She also influenced several of them to avoid giving in to the pressure of the agency.

Archer delivered an express mail package to me in my office after school. I put it with the stack of mail I hadn't had time to address due to some sketchy cases on my desk that needed my attention more than the mail.

Stacy had yet to grace us with her presence today, which wasn't unusual. She preferred late nights, which resulted in her arriving in the late mornings or early afternoons to vacuum and dust the house. And today, Alessandra had a meeting at the pack clubhouse, so I was alone with Archer for the afternoon.

The sound of a car outside didn't fully register until Archer knocked on the door and stepped into the office again.

"Um, Dad, you have company."

I glanced up and looked beyond Archer.

My heart dropped, and I quickly schooled my features, letting only the surprise at seeing Terrance Winters through. My mouth dried as he strolled into my office with an air about him that set my teeth on edge. I turned my attention to Archer.

"Weren't you heading to your friends after you got the mail?" I didn't want him here just in case things went south.

"I think he should stay. I'm here to see if your young ones are interested in a career in the Monster Defense Agency." He smiled, but there was tension behind it.

I leaned back in my wheelchair and studied Terrance. "Why aren't you discussing this with my wife? She is the alpha of this pack."

"What does the agency do?" Archer lingered by the door. He wasn't even a teenager yet, and I did not want him having ideas about working for this man. Not after everything Robert had told me.

I shot a sharp glare in his direction. "You've kept your friend long enough." I didn't mean for it to come out in a snap, but I also didn't want him hanging around. I glanced at the clock. "While you're at it, let the housekeeper know we have company, and she doesn't need to come by today."

His eyes widened a fraction, but not enough for anyone who didn't know the kid to suspect anything. Even though he didn't know Rosie's background, the mere fact I didn't want him to hang back for this conversation or her to barge in on it conveyed the need for privacy.

"Sure," he said after a beat.

I waved him away and then turned back to Terrance. "Now, I should call Alessandra."

"I think we can have this conversation without your wife."

I detected the condescending nature of his tone. As if a woman couldn't be an alpha. It irked me. "If it has to do with the pack…"

Terrance lifted his hand, stopping me. "It's more about the council rather than the pack." He took a seat in the chair facing my desk.

I waited in silence, unnerved by this visit already.

"I'd like to see if any of the packs would be interested in agency jobs."

"The council is not your recruiter." I stared him down. He couldn't shift, so I was in no danger of that type of attack, but I had my hand on the gun attached to my wheelchair.

He leaned forward. "I always thought an alliance between the werewolf council and the agency would be mutually beneficial." He studied his clasped fingers before raising his gaze, and my bullshit meter went into overdrive.

"If there had been an alliance, I don't think my brother would have strayed so far from doing what's right."

I narrowed my eyes at him, letting my skepticism bleed through. "And why didn't you have an alliance with your brother?"

His smile wasn't the least bit pleasant. It looked as if he had bitten into a sour lemon. "My brother wanted control of everything and that would have pushed me to the back of the pack. The agency is my domain, and I did not wish to give that up."

I cocked an eyebrow. "Then you will understand why I must decline."

He slowly sat back, perhaps realizing how much of his hand he just showed me in that little admission. "You don't trust me."

It wasn't a question. I stared him down. "You have the same blood in your veins as your brother, and he was a monster."

"Yes, he was. But I am not Ken. Besides, haven't I proved that over the last eleven years?" He held his hands out in faux innocence.

I sighed and wondered if I hadn't had a conversation with Robert, would I be considering this offer right now?

"I don't know that I'll ever fully trust anyone in your family." I kept his gaze and took a breath. "But that isn't why I would prefer to keep the organizations separate."

His eyebrow cocked as he waited for the rest of my explanation.

"We have our pack rules and, from what I understand, the agency is intertwined with our government. I'd prefer not to have government oversight on pack life. Humans don't understand our hierarchies or our laws." I gave him a tight smile. "Perhaps in another fifteen or twenty years, when there is more global acceptance of shifters, I may feel differently. But at this juncture, I really must decline your offer of access to the packs associated directly with the council."

His neck reddened, as if the bite of anger lived in his blood. I couldn't smell it, but he was always good at hiding his emotions. "Perhaps we can talk again when the pains of the past are truly put behind us."

I inclined my head in a slow nod, not really committing to anything that would put my constituents in danger. "Will I see you at the summit this year?"

"I may make an appearance if my schedule allows. Otherwise, I'll send Robert Young in my stead like I have for the past couple of years."

I pushed away from the desk and rolled out to the side of it. "I can show you out." I waved toward the door, waiting for him to step in front of me. I did not want this man at my back.

I followed him to the front door.

"Until the summit." He nodded and walked out the door to the waiting car. A driver opened the back door for Terrance and then hurried into the front seat.

I lifted my hand in a wave and watched until they were out of sight. The tightness in my chest abated enough for me to take a deep breath. And it was only then that I looked toward the garage.

The curtain twitched, and I saw a glimpse of Stacy staring out of the small crack. Our eyes met, and I gave her a thumbs-up, even though I wasn't settled at all by the visit.

Then I rolled back into my office and just stared at the paperwork in front of me without seeing what it was.

Terrance Winters had never set foot in this house before. The summit was always held at the town hall, where there was more than enough room to house all the alphas for all the packs who had a vote for the legislation we put forth. So, how did he get our private address? A shiver stalked down my spine.

A clearing of a throat made me jump, and I reached for my gun. At the sight of Stacy at the door, I exhaled long and loud and slouched in the chair.

"The agency?" she said with a voice drenched in dread. It matched the shaking in her hands and the fearful frown etched into her lips.

"Yes. But I'm not sure if this was a fishing expedition or some unspoken warning." I dropped my gaze to the express pouch. The source address registered and I snagged it out of the mail pile. With a rip of the seal, I dumped the contents on my desk.

"Is that what I think it is?" Her eyes filled with hope.

I nearly laughed at how damn thorough my contact was. Not only did he have a license in Rosie Beeswich's name, he had a passport with stamps in it, a birth certificate, and a Social Security number, along with a few wallet-size photos of her as a college graduate. Then there was a professional photo and dossier along with a work history list...even a couple of actual written recommendations for her maid work. And every one of the work history numbers would result in a glowing review of her work.

I gathered the documents and stretched my hand out. "Miss. Rosie Beeswich, it looks like you are free to go home to—" I glanced at the license on the top of the pile. "New Orleans whenever you'd like."

The smile she shined on me as she plucked the documents from my hand radiated through the room. She shuffled through the papers. When she looked up at me, the reality of the situation hit.

"It's been nice having a clean house," I said.

Her smile faded. "I owe you my life."

I laughed. "No, you paid your dues already. Cleaning up after Archer and me can't have been easy."

"You paid me for that. You hid me from that monster, gave me a roof and a job, and now this." She waved the papers. "I don't know if I'll ever be able to repay you and your wife."

My lips twitched into what I hoped was a smile. "Pay it forward. Help someone in need when you can, and that will be enough."

She pressed her new legal documents to her chest. "I will, Mr. Blaez. I promise I will never forget you."

"Will that be far enough away to mask your magical signature?" The after thought dropped before I could catch it.

"If it isn't, I can always go on a cruise around the world and just disappear on the other side of the globe." She smiled. "Besides, New Orleans is a hotbed of supernatural activity. It's one of the few places in the world that magic is so intertwined that the agency cannot differentiate, even with boots on the ground."

I had hoped that was the case, especially when my contact asked if that would be acceptable.

"I'll just pack up and be on my way."

"Do you have enough money?" I reached for the side drawer of my desk.

"I've kept most of the pay you've given me. It's more than enough for a bus ticket."

I reached into the metal cash container and pulled out a few bills, offering them to her, but she shook her head.

"You've done enough. Once I get there, I can find work easily with these recommendations." She waved at the documents.

"Take care." I didn't offer any other platitudes. This was always meant to be temporary.

She gave me a curt nod and spun on her heel, but not before I caught the sheen in her eyes.

I was going to miss her presence and her help around the house just as much as Alessandra. I might actually have to look into the maid service and hire one now that we'd had a taste of it for the last couple of months.

At least until I got another meeting request from Robert Young.

HUNTER'S MOON
Chapter 9

MY PHONE DINGED, AND I glanced at the text from an unknown number. The same meeting place as before, with a date and time, blinked on the screen. I glanced across the dinner table at Alessandra and put my silverware down. I had just enough time to get there if I left right now.

"It seems a council member wants to discuss our latest case," I said.

Alessandra cocked her head with a look that screamed *'really?'*. The council never bothered me after work hours. It was an unwritten rule we all had. Unless it was a dire life-and-death emergency, it wasn't done during what we all considered family time.

"They want me to meet them down at the coffee shop near the strip mall with that jewelry store you like." I waved the screen at her, then pocketed my phone and rolled out from the table.

I moved toward the door and stopped by Alessandra's chair. I showed her the text, and her brow creased. It had been over a year since Stacy had left and I hadn't heard a thing from Robert. It looked like we were going to have another house guest, but this time, at least I had the network in place to get documentation much quicker than before.

"Be careful," she whispered.

Archer looked up from his phone and stared at the two of us. "Why would Dad need to be careful?"

"He's driving at night," Alessandra said without missing a beat.

I adored her quick thinking under the gun. Her ability to create a believable statement under duress was probably as sharp as mine.

"Oh." He went back to whatever game he was playing on his phone.

Alessandra gave me a peck on the cheek, and I rolled out of the house. From the ask on the text, I had a feeling this was another rescue operation. We hadn't talked since he dropped Stacy off, and he did not know that Terrance had swung by before Stacy left us.

I needed to let him know that happened. Terrance had never set foot in our territory without a formal invitation, and he certainly had never been to my house before. I pulled into the parking lot next to the coffee shop, but before I could get my wheelchair out of the car, the back passenger door opened, and Robert dropped into the seat.

"Drive," he said as he lay huffing on the seat.

I swung the wheelchair back into the car and closed my door before I backed out. "Where am I going?" I asked, trying to ignore the scent of blood coming from the back seat.

Fabric tore, and then the familiar pant of a wolf came from the space. A low whine escaped.

I sighed. "I wish like hell I could shift and heal my back, but my spine severed, and no shift will fix that. Believe me, I've tried." Werewolf shifting usually helped heal wounds. But in my case, with the severed spine from my accident, along with being stretched to almost being torn in half, even shifting, could not repair that catastrophic damage. I glanced in the rearview mirror and caught Robert's blue eyes surrounded by jet-black fur. "I know it hurts, but by the time you shift back, you'll be whole again."

His slow nod acknowledged my ramblings.

"Do you want me to take you to my house?"

He growled.

"A no then. Okay. So, I'll just drive around until you shift back and are ready to talk." I let the silence fill the car. I flipped on the radio and tuned into a rock station. I sang along while I drove in circles, watching behind me to make sure we weren't being followed.

Finally, a groan came from the back seat.

I shut off the music and pulled over in a quiet cul-de-sac. "What the fuck?" I turned toward the back of the car.

Robert slumped against the passenger door. "I was double-crossed."

My chest constricted, and Terrance's meeting jumped to the forefront of my mind. "Do they know I'm your contact?"

"No. And I killed him before he could report on his location. Thankfully, I destroyed his tracking before I left the city." He wiped his face. "And now I'm going to have to sacrifice my son to the organization in order to throw off suspicion." He closed his eyes and leaned against the window.

I blinked and swallowed hard. "What do you mean, sacrifice?"

"I'm going to have to insist he go to the Monster Defense Academy and follow the same path to damnation that I've had to walk."

The devastation in his voice cut to my soul. "Did you know Terrance swung by just before Stacy took off?"

His eyes darkened. "I found out after the fact. Terrance wants control of the council, but he's not foolish enough to make a move that will put the agency at risk. Plus, I discouraged him from pushing further."

I didn't want to know how, but I was relieved he discouraged that maniac. "Thank you."

He nodded. "I've had to do some seriously shitty things to my kid over the years, but what's coming next is going to fuck up any chance of a relationship with him. But I will do anything I have to, so he survives."

"Why are you telling me this?"

"Because someone has to tell him I loved him if all this blows up in my face. I'm running a tightrope here, and it could fray under my feet at any moment."

I couldn't imagine alienating my child to keep them safe. It had to be a living nightmare. I laid back against the seat and rubbed my face, looking at him in the rearview mirror. "Where do we fall in this tightrope act?"

"You're my son's safety net." His eyes closed.

"How do I know you aren't playing me?" I challenged him. As much as I didn't want to entertain the thought, I had to be sure. After all, the organization he worked for wanted our council to offer our young to their agency. They wanted their hooks in us. If anything this wolf said was close to the truth, I had to protect our packs.

His eyes opened, and he stared at the rearview mirror. He didn't say anything for a few minutes. Then he whispered, "You don't. There isn't anything I can offer as proof that I'm not."

The fact he didn't press his alpha dominance on me said a lot. I knew he was just as powerful as Alessandra. If not more. And he could very well exercise that on me to coerce me, but he hadn't.

He rubbed his face. "I need to figure out a viable story about Greg. He was from another pack and Terrance asked me to get rid of him, since he screwed up an important job. So, Terrance might suspect I'm compromised."

"Did Greg know you had saved someone from the same fate?"

Robert shook his head. "I just asked him to go for a ride. No explanations, just like the others I've had to kill for valid reasons."

"You've embraced the job of assassination for the agency?"

Robert's sharp stare caught mine. "Yes. My hands are far from clean. I am very particular about who I choose to save. If I saved everyone who the agency put a hit on, I would have been in a grave a long time ago."

I shivered and wished I had my firearm. That was tucked safely in my chair at home in the garage. "And what if Terrance sends you on a job to take me out?"

"He wouldn't go after you. He'd go after your wife. The alpha of the pack. She's the one who appointed you to run the council." He cocked his head. "And you better make sure that if your son has the alpha mark, it isn't announced until he is out of school and on his way to a solid career."

I blinked, and my mouth dropped open before I could recover.

Robert chuckled from the back seat. "The agency knows how your pack alpha is chosen. It's something almost mystical and, from what I understand, centuries old. It has everything to do with the original, and the fact your wife is from the original line hasn't been a secret."

My eyebrows rose. They didn't know whether Archer had the mark or not. I kept that to myself. This entire encounter seemed more of a threat than anything amicable.

"Are you threatening me?"

"No." The answer came quicker than expected. "You are the only ally I have. It behooves me to tell you what the agency knows about your family.

Besides, the seer I went to told me I had one true ally in this mess and that he was bound to a mechanical chair." He waved at me.

Now my eyebrows felt as if they rose all the way to my hairline. "A seer?"

"Yeah. I found one outside the agency, and she gave me a private reading. I didn't want to believe a thing she said, but so far, she has been dead on. And if I don't somehow prevent my son from claiming his fated mate, I'll never get to see vengeance for my family. Apparently, she is the key, and I have to keep them apart. Otherwise, this entire world is fucking doomed."

Bitterness as thick as poisoned fog filled the car.

"And he has no choice but to join the agency." Robert's chin dropped to his chest. "So, whenever my time is up, I expect you to relay all this to my son. Hopefully, by that time, I am able to make amends with him."

I put the car in gear and drove toward the coffee shop. "I assume you have the means to get out of our pack lands without an issue, correct?"

"Yes. And I apologize for the mess in your back seat. You'll have to think of something to tell your wife that won't alarm her."

"My wife knows about our deal."

His gaze shot to mine. "You told her?"

"I won't ever lie to her. She's my wife, and she's my alpha. She owns my ass, as feeble as it is these days."

"You may be in a wheelchair, but you aren't feeble. You're probably the most damned honorable son of a bitch I know."

I snorted. "You know I killed humans out of vengeance, right?" I glanced back at him. "It's why Leigh and I were wanted by the council."

"The way I hear it, they had it coming."

"It's still against the law." I wasn't particularly proud of it, but after what they had done to Alessandra, there wasn't a person on this green earth that could have stopped me from tearing their throats out.

"I would have tortured them slowly and reveled in their screams before I killed them."

Well, okay then. "Once I got over my rage, I knew I had to hide her until it all blew over. But I hadn't had a clue it was an actual trap. One way or another, the council wanted us dead, either by poison or by a farce trial." I flicked my gaze at him in the mirror.

Robert nodded. "Just be glad Terrance hadn't weaseled his way onto the council. Otherwise, it would have been the agency gunning for you."

I shivered as I pulled into the parking lot. I wouldn't have wanted the agency hunting us. The council was bad enough, but the agency trained for that kind of shit. "Was Stacy the only one you got out?"

"No. I got my partner out years ago. And I was able to help a couple of wolves, but not nearly as many as I wanted." He opened the door once I came to a stop. "I'll be in touch. I have a feeling there will be more to save in the coming years while the agency culls those who aren't militant about their rules."

"I'll be available any time you need me. And I'll see you at the next annual council meeting."

He nodded and shifted and then used his front paws to close the door. He was gone in an instant, and I prayed I would hear from him again. I didn't like being in the dark about the agency, even if I had to make a deal with the devil himself.

HUNTER'S MOON
Chapter 10

HE HAD BEEN TRUE to his word. The next several years were packed with agency escapees. And Alessandra was just as invested in saving as many as possible. Wolves and witches made up most refugees, but occasionally we would get some other type of supernatural. My contacts became efficient in getting documentation for me and the longest time frame that they stayed with us was a month before I could send them on their way.

During those occasions, Robert and I had little time to chat. It was more of a handoff and then he'd be gone, as if he had never stepped into the shop. The only other time I saw him was at the annual council meetings, but there was no real chance to talk with so many ears around.

It was almost six years to the day from when I received that first text from Robert Young when I called a special annual meeting of the packs. This meeting had to do with the widespread use of silver by packs. Most just used it to lock up dangerous characters, but there were a few who needed to be called out for using it to keep members in line.

I knew this meeting would be a nightmare, but we had an important piece of legislation that needed to be voted on now, before things got more out of hand.

I rolled into the town hall with Alessandra by my side. Archer wasn't quite seventeen, so although we had talked with him about this new law, we didn't feel this was the right time to bring him into the fold of the council. Besides, he still didn't have that infamous mark of the leader of our pack.

Members milled about, and we took our places behind the council table. Minutes later, Robert walked in the door with a younger version of himself. Tension filled the air between the two of them, palatable enough to notice. Alessandra and I traded a glance as they strode across the floor toward us.

Robert smiled, but it didn't reach his eyes. He stopped in front of us, keeping my gaze for a second as if reminding me that no one else at the agency knew of his actions. Including his son. Then he said, "Chairman Blaez, Alpha Blaez, this is my son. Robert

Young Jr." He waved at his look-alike. "Robby, this is Hunter and Alessandra Blaez."

Robby stuck his hand out, and his grip was firm.

"Robby has taken over as the alpha of the Allegany pack," Robert said.

Both our gazes jumped to him and then to his son. This news took me by surprise. We hadn't even received the notice of alpha change. Even though their pack was not one with the council's direct oversight, it usually was customary to notify us of the change.

"It was time for me to focus on the agency and make sure my pack had a good leader." Robert smiled and this time, it reached his eyes. "But I will still represent the agency at these meetings, while Robby represents the Allegany pack."

"Welcome." Alessandra hooked her arm into Robby's. "Let me introduce you to the other alphas." She steered him away, leaving me with his father without me having to suggest it to her.

Robert stepped around the table and stood next to me as we watched Alessandra lead him away. "He knows nothing," he said very softly.

"I got that."

"And he won't unless I am dead."

"Got that, too."

"He hates me."

I huffed. I could have told him that just from the animosity radiating from his son. But the pain in Robert's tone hit home. I wouldn't be able to deal with that kind of animosity aimed at me from Archer. "He'll understand someday."

"I hope so." He was quiet for a moment. "Terrance wants me to force Robby to marry his niece."

"And what of his fated mate?" I looked up at Robert, and his expression soured.

"She's his partner. If they cross the line, she dies, according to company policy."

"That's fucking barbaric," I muttered.

"The agency is fucking barbaric." He glanced around and cleared his throat.

Werewolves were known for their exceptional hearing, and even though we were speaking in hushed tones, anyone close by could make out what we were saying if they were tried.

"Have you read the newest bylaws up for vote today?" I asked in my normal tone and turned my attention to him fully. I had made certain that the use of silver in any manner with werewolves as a point of torture or containment was not allowed.

"Yes. The agency has some reservations but will comply with the majority vote." He gave me a look that told me they'd do whatever they damn well pleased despite whatever law was written today.

I wasn't sure the law would stand as it was spelled out, and I expected some modifications in this meeting, especially considering I had already received written notification against it.

It had the makings of a very spirited debate indeed. By the time we settled in our seats, the rumblings had begun. I grabbed the gavel that had been set out on the table and cleared my throat before I pounded it to get everyone's attention.

An unsettled silence fell over the room. I glanced to either side of me and the six alphas representing the council, including Alessandra. We had come to a consensus on the wording of the new law, but even that had taken longer than I had hoped. But as I looked out at the floor at the near hundred other

Hunter's Moon

packs represented, the animosity was louder than the hush.

"You all are aware of the prior council's legacy of torture and killing with silver." Rumblings continued among the alphas. "I witnessed one of our pack members dunked into a vat of boiling silver." Shudders ran through me as that vision surfaced again. I wasn't the only one in the room who reacted to that statement, either. Most of the alphas frowned, and some even bared their teeth. "I was supposed to be next, but my wife saved me." I glanced at Alessandra before launching into the meat of this gathering. "I have worked diligently with the alphas at this table to come up with a law regarding the use of silver for years. And you were all sent the final agreed-upon version."

"And if we don't agree with that version?" The voice in the back came from the alpha of one of the southwestern packs.

"Then we discuss the points you have contention with, Jared." I called him out. Jared Thurman hadn't accepted my appointment to the council and had been contentious ever since. And any time a council member stepped down, he threw his name in the ring. Thankfully, he could never get enough votes to back him. He was just as twisted as Winters had been and wanted the power of a council seat.

He weaved his way through the crowd, emitting a low growl as he approached the table where we sat. "You are purposely sabotaging our ability to keep our pack in line." He leaned on the table, staring down at me.

If only I could stand, I would have towered over him. Alessandra let out a growl, and I shot my hand out for her to stop. I wasn't an alpha like the rest of the room, but I had to stand my ground in order to gain their continued respect.

I let out a warning growl and leaned forward. "You use silver to keep your pack in line?"

The mood in the room instantly turned as I twisted his words against him. Snarls erupted behind Jared. No alpha here needed outside torture instruments to do that. I knew the core of their argument against the law as written was based on being able to cage those who perpetrated more serious crimes rather than the clause for keeping members in line.

He blinked as if he realized what had just come out of his mouth. And then his glare pinned on me. His shift was quick, but my draw was faster. I pointed my gun at the wolf snarling at me from the other side of the table. If he had launched, he would already be dead.

"I pack silver bullets in this gun." Thankfully, my hand remained steady as I stared down the alpha. Even if the bullets weren't silver, a headshot would still kill. But this way, if I missed a major organ, the silver poisoning would do the job, except it would be a hell of a lot more painful.

"Stand down." The order settled over the room, and most of the alphas actually lowered their heads in obedience under the power of the order.

The only alpha in the room who wasn't impacted by the decree was my wife. She kept her gaze on the alpha who had issued the order. I fought against the command and nearly lowered the gun, but I only obeyed *my* alpha's orders. When she used her alpha influence in these meetings, it had the same effect on the others.

Robby Young stepped away from his father's side. The alpha energy coming from him was just as powerful as my wife's. I'd wager it was more powerful than his father's, as well.

Jared cowered under the command.

I slowly lowered my gun to the table but kept my hand on it just in case Jared decided he wanted to kill me despite the Allegany alpha's show of dominance.

"Explain," Robby demanded of Jared as he towered over him. The fury in his eyes matched a majority of the wolves in the room.

I didn't interrupt, either. I wanted to see what this alpha was made of.

Jared shifted and turned on Robby Young. "Who the fuck are you?"

Robby Young smiled in a way that unsettled me. "I'm the alpha of the Allegany pack and an agent for the Monster Defense Agency."

I traded a glance with his father from across the room, but Robert Senior didn't flinch. He just crossed his arms and watched the show like the rest of the alphas in the room.

Jared spit on his shoes.

Robby's reaction was instantaneous. His hand shot out and clasped around Jared's neck, surprising all of us. When he pulled him close to his face, the growl in his throat was on the edge of deadly.

Jared clawed at his arm, but Robby held fast.

"Anyone using silver to punish pack members should be sentenced to death. It's one thing to lock up dangerous wolves in a cell made of silver, but that's not the same as what you are insinuating."

I respected Robby Young even more than I did his father. He held the righteousness that a protective alpha should. I glanced at Alessandra, and she gave me a sideways look, confirming her approval as well.

"Stand down," she commanded.

Robby slid his glare in her direction.

"This council will investigate and render judgment if need be. But thank you for your support." She smiled in a way that announced her agreement.

Robby tossed Jared away and made his way back to stand by his father. But his interruption did not ease the tensions in the room.

"Council, if I may approach," the alpha from the northwestern pack asked.

I nodded. This alpha was blonde and built like a bombshell. "Clara." I bowed my head to her as she stepped a respectable distance from the table.

"Hunter." She used the nickname everyone had called me since I was little. Only Alessandra called me by my real name. "Council." She showed her respect with the same tilt of her head. "I think I speak for a majority here when I state we do not have an issue with the torture and terrorizing piece of your legislation. What we have issue with is not being able to imprison felons and dangers to our society in silver cells."

I leaned back in my chair. This was the one thing we internally fought over, but eventually, my logical argument won. "Define cell."

"A standard jail cell, similar to the size of those found in human jails."

My lip twitched, and I glanced at the council surrounding me. Clara had just confirmed the definition I was hoping for, because just saying a cell was not enough. Some would consider a six-by-six cell enough, but most werewolves could be taller than six feet, thus a six-by-six cell wouldn't be enough to be comfortable without the threat of burning skin on the silver.

"I would concede to amending the legislation to include jail cells of no less than eighty square feet that have bars of silver to imprison those who commit serious crimes and are dangerous to the pack and society. But there must be proof of the crimes enough to convict in a court of law in order for you to jail any offender."

The room exploded in conversation. I waited to hear the consensus. I already knew what the council alphas at the table thought. This was what we had dared to hope for. We knew it would be more readily accepted if the alphas thought they put it on the table instead of us dictating the rules, but I wasn't about to leave the torture clause to the committee. I wouldn't bend on that one despite the heated debates we had on the matter.

Clara turned to the rest of the alphas and engaged in their conversation. After a few minutes, she turned back to us. "We accept those changes."

I nodded and glanced at the alphas surrounding me. "Council members, all in favor of adding the language to the legislation?"

"Aye." Every one of them raised their hand.

I looked at the room. "With a unanimous vote from the council, I turn it to you to vote. All in favor?"

Everyone but Jared raised their hands.

"Opposed?"

Jared slowly raised his hand.

I glanced at the lone hand raised. "Let the record show one opposed. Majority rules. As such, this legislation passes." I hit the gavel on the table and stowed my gun back in the holster on the inside of my chair armrest. "Is there any new business that we'd like to discuss?"

All eyes turned to Jared.

Alessandra cleared her throat. "What are you doing with silver to keep your pack in line?" she asked Jared directly.

His growl filled the space. "None of your fucking business."

I sighed and nodded to Kyle, the alpha from western Texas who had been on the council as long as we had. He was one of our first allies after the original council perished. He rose and crossed to the side door. He stopped and faced us with his hand on the knob.

"Last chance to come clean, Jared." I turned my stare in his direction.

"I should have torn your throat out the first time we met," he growled at me.

Alessandra's menacing growl filled the space, and she launched over the table, shifting in mid-flight. Her powerful jaws clamped down on his human throat, snapping closed. Jared's head hit the floor and rolled to the middle of the room. His death was as swift and violent as I had ever seen her deliver.

She shifted back and stood tall in all her naked glory. The tattoo on her abdomen glowed with her power. But in case the group had any qualms about Jared's death, I gave Kyle the signal, and he opened the door.

Three men and one woman stepped in the room. All of them had silver burns on their cheeks and their arms. The brand on the woman's shoulder actually made my stomach roll.

Jared's execution was warranted. Although I wish I had shot him with a silver bullet instead of having my wife kill him in such a vicious display. But I suppose her actions reinstated her post as the head of all of us in the room. She even made Robby's cheeks dull, and he was probably the only alpha in this room who could challenge her.

Sharon, the alpha next to Alessandra, handed her a bathrobe as I concluded the meeting. With Jared's body still marring the floor, we skirted around the blood and gore and headed toward the door and the fresh evening air.

At least it was the bastard I had been researching who bit it. This entire meeting was more about posturing than legislation. And we pulled it off with no one else being harmed.

I was glad that my goal for this meeting had been addressed before blood flew. That didn't always happen at these things. Too many alphas in a room were bound to launch tensions beyond the brink.

That was one of the few reasons I hated being on the council. It put a target on our backs.

HUNTER'S MOON
Chapter 11

THE YEAR WENT BY with no tensions, but we had a few transient refugees from Robert. Archer had just started his senior year in the pack high school and was doing well in all his classes, and we had visited a few prospective colleges over the summer months.

On this cool fall afternoon, I sat in my office, going over the latest documents for the next annual council meeting. Archer slid inside and took the seat across from the desk. He rarely bothered me in my office after school, but right now, his anxiety pelted me hard enough that I stopped reading in the middle of the case instead of finishing before I gave him my attention.

"Everything okay?" I closed the case folder I had been reading.

He laughed and looked at his hands. "Well, it depends on your viewpoint."

I raised an eyebrow. "What is it?"

"Well, Cheryl's pregnant."

My brain stalled. I blinked at him. I wasn't sure I heard right. "What?"

"I didn't want to tell Mom."

He had the sense to look uncomfortable, but it wasn't enough to dull my building anger. "Why are you sleeping with her? You aren't even eighteen!"

He rolled his eyes at me. "We've been together since freshman year."

"Do her parents know?" My entire mind went into damage control mode. Hopefully, the due date would be after graduation, but it still meant their futures were now limited. The idea of my son's potential being shot down because of an act of stupidity nearly made me lose my shit.

"Not yet. She's afraid to tell them." He picked at a hangnail.

"So, what? You expect us to tell them?" My question was filled with angry snark, and the fury just escalated when he raised a shoulder and dropped it in a half-assed shrug.

I sent out a silent request for my wife to come to my office because I mentally couldn't deal with this alone. Thankfully, the connection we had was stronger than most mates. She probably already knew I was pissed, but she usually assumed my aggravation was council related.

"What's up?" she asked from the doorway.

Archer glared at me. "You called Mom?"

"Yes." I waved at her while staring him down. "Go ahead."

Alessandra stepped into the office, and her concern radiated from her. She looked between the two of us as Archer shifted in the seat and stared at the ground. "What's going on?"

"Your son has something to say."

My phrasing caught her by surprise, and her eyebrows darted up. Normally, I referred to him as our son, unless I was furious. She crossed and took the seat next to him and covered his hand. "What is it, honey?"

He pinched his lips together and inhaled loudly. "Cheryl's pregnant."

She pulled her hands away and leaned back in the chair. Disappointment etched into her face, pulling her lips down, and the sickly sweet scent of it drifted around her. "Do they not teach you about protection in school?" The edge in her voice matched the anger rubbing my skin raw.

"It was only one time," he protested with a whine.

"That's all it takes." I would not fall for this *pitiful me* act.

Alessandra nodded. "What are you going to do about it?" She crossed her arms.

"I-I don't know," he stuttered, looking between the two of us.

"This isn't our mess to clean up, Archer," I said.

He looked utterly lost, and his eyes darted around in panic. I remembered feeling overwhelmed by the thought of a child, and Alessandra and I had been living together at the time. We were not in high school, although she had been in college when our lives turned upside down because of Winters and his schemes.

"Well, you better start figuring out a plan," Alessandra said.

Archer wasn't reacting well to our less than compassionate response. His frantic blinking nearly made me laugh, but the subject at hand was as far from funny as it got in parenting. When Alessandra told me I was going to be a father, I had literally freaked out. Just putting myself back in those shoes humbled me. It also quieted the anger rioting in my blood a fraction.

"What does Cheryl want to do?" I tried to keep all the frustration still present from leaking into my voice.

His wide eyes caught mine. "She doesn't want an abortion." He swallowed hard. "And neither do I."

I should have expected that from our child. We believed life was a gift and fought diligently to make sure everyone else had fair treatment. Of course, we had limits and laws that forfeit life when broken. But we believed in the sanctity of life, so his decision to not abort a child made sense.

"Okay," Alessandra said, stretching the word out.

"So, we are back to the question of what are you going to do?" I piped in when he didn't take Alessandra's baited question.

He picked at his hangnail. "I was thinking of that Monster Defense Academy."

"Absolutely not," I said at the same time as Alessandra's snarling, "No."

Archer's eyes widened as he stared at me. "Why not?"

"First of all, the academy does not pay. Second, the agency is a deplorable institution, and I will not have you under their thumb." I leaned forward. "Plus, it isn't something that you bring a child into. Not when your life is in danger, and you could drag that shit home with you."

He made some disrespectful noise, as if I didn't know what I was talking about.

"What happens to you if a vampire you're hunting finds your home and kills everyone you love? Huh?"

"That doesn't happen," he scoffed at me.

"Yes. It does. I know at least a half a dozen people who have suffered that fate." I bit my tongue on telling him he'd met a few as well. I heard some of their stories while he was off at school and I was getting their fake identifications in place. "Vampires, rogues, soul eaters, ghouls. You name it, once you hunt it, you become a target. Is that what you want for your family?"

"But I thought..." He trailed off.

"You thought what?" I stared him down, and Alessandra let me lead this conversation. "That the agency protects their people?" I laughed, but there was no trace of humor in it.

"Well, yeah. That's what they said at school."

Alessandra growled in her seat. "The Monster Defense Agency has been in your school?"

"Yeah." He glanced at her and then back at me. "On career day."

"Shifters have been on our pack lands?" Her clipped question agreed with the red now filling her face.

He shook his head. "They were human, not shifters."

"Choose something else," I said through clenched teeth.

"You can't stop me!" he yelled and stood.

"Sit down," Alessandra snarled in her alpha tone.

Archer sat so quickly, I almost smirked.

"You cannot ever consider the Monster Defense Agency as a prospective future. That is a direct order from your alpha." Her power even made me want to curl in on myself.

Archer's shoulders rounded, and he stared at the ground. "Then make me alpha."

Alessandra stared at him for at least three solid beats of my heart. "I can't. You do not carry the mark."

It wasn't something she could pass down from generation to generation, like Robert could do with his son. Our pack required the mark of the alpha to be present. Alessandra contained the authority of the alpha, and after her father disappeared, we assumed she was the proper alpha just by her incredible power. However, it wasn't until that mark appeared that she was recognized by the elders in the pack.

Unfortunately, Archer did not develop that power in puberty like we had hoped.

"Then what the hell am I going to do?"

His outburst set my teeth on edge, and I clenched my jaw.

"Get a real job, marry that girl, and raise that child the best you can. Understand?" My wolf shot to the surface, and I closed my eyes, stuffing him back in the cage that was my broken body.

"But she's expecting me to become the alpha," he whined.

"You are going to need to manage her expectations." Alessandra stared him down.

"But Mom…"

"I love you with everything I am, but you do not have the mark. I cannot hand the pack to someone without the mark. It just isn't the way our pack works."

At least she didn't tell him he didn't have the authority of an alpha. That's a confidence killer.

"Fine." He chewed on his lip for a moment. "She wants me with her when we tell her parents."

"Good luck with that," Alessandra said under her breath.

"Can you be there with us?" He wasn't looking at his mother.

I pointed to my chest, and Archer nodded. "Why, so you can hide behind the cripple when her father launches to kill you?"

"N-n-no."

His stuttering reaction gave me pause. "Then why?"

"Because you're the calmest wolf in the pack. And Mom will just issue an order to sit and deal with it. I don't want to piss them off more than they will already be."

"If he takes a swing at you, I can't stop him."

His gaze dropped to my sidearm.

I huffed. "I only pull that if I intend to use it. Besides, you deserve a punch for sleeping with her with no protection or thought of either of your futures."

"You really don't want me there?" Alessandra asked.

Archer shook his head. "I love you, Mom. But you can be scary if someone even looks at us wrong."

He wasn't incorrect. And when Alessandra turned her attention to me, I shrugged. My mind went to the last council meeting where blood was spilled. Alessandra had been the one to react.

If Cheryl's father launched at Archer while she was in the room, she wouldn't be able to sit and allow him harm. It just was not in her to allow either of us to get hurt. Not since I nearly died at the hands of our enemies.

HUNTER'S MOON
Chapter 12

THE CARSON'S WERE MID-LEVEL pack members; the moment I rolled into the local pub with Archer, they stood as if I were some visiting dignitary. It made me uncomfortable, as if they were expecting great things from the relationship between our son and their daughter.

"George, Tabitha," I said as I rolled to the table they sat at. I had chosen this place because it was rather empty for the afternoon, plus it had a handicap ramp. I did not want to raise this issue in either of our homes.

I didn't expect violence, but I still had my side arm on the chair. I never went anywhere without it because it was my best bet at surviving an attack.

"Hunter," they both said and dipped their heads.

"To what do we owe this pleasure?" Tabitha added as they sat down.

I pulled to the head of the table. Archer and Cheryl sat to my right while George and Tabitha were to my left. I took a breath and glanced at the two kids. Neither of them would meet my gaze. From their lack of speaking up, it seemed they were letting me lead this conversation. I was not willing to let them off the hook.

"Our children have something to say," I said.

Archer sent me a sideways glare. Cheryl didn't even look up from the menu that sat before her, but she stiffened in the seat next to Archer.

Archer cleared his throat and took Cheryl's hand in his. "I'd like to marry your daughter."

My eyebrow rose, and I kept my reaction neutral, while the excited gasps from the Carsons made my center tighten in frustration.

Archer peeked up at Mr. and Mrs. Carson, and then his gaze darted to me.

"Oh, we can plan such a grand affair for the spring after graduation." Tabitha almost bounced out of her seat at the thought.

"Well, we'd like to do it as soon as possible," Archer said. "Right, hon?" he asked Cheryl.

Hunter's Moon

"Yes. I'd like to marry Archer next weekend." She looked up and straightened her spine.

The Carsons traded a glance before they looked at me. The gears in their head were spinning, and I wasn't giving them any indication of my dark mood. I hadn't been privy to this plan, either, and the fact I wasn't smiling also must have been a factor, because finally George's eyes narrowed at my son.

"Why the hurry?" he asked, but it came out in more of a growl.

"Because I'm pregnant with Archer's child." Cheryl's voice seemed steady, the bead of sweat at her temple belied her nerves.

Tabitha just stared at the two teenagers with her mouth open. All her dreams of a grand wedding fizzled into palpable anger.

George shot to his feet. "Why you..." he started and then launched over the table, shifting in the air. He slammed into Archer and both of them toppled over onto the ground.

This wasn't what I expected. Although I thought Archer needed to be punched for his lapse of judgment, I did not agree with a full-on beating, or worse. And the fury radiating in the small space was on par with murder. He was going to kill my son right in front of me, despite his wife's and daughter's frantic pleas.

The cock of my gun caught everyone's attention. George's wolf growled at Archer, but his eyes were now on me.

"If you so much as scratch my son with your damned teeth, I will shoot you." My words came out in a feral growl, accompanied by a deadly glare.

Silence filled the entire place. No one moved.

"Back off slowly and then take a seat, George." My voice carried my beta power. It wasn't as powerful as Alessandra's alpha, but I carried my own level of deterrent in order to keep the peace. I waited until he moved away, shifted back into human form, and took a seat in the buff.

A staff member ran over with a bathrobe for him. Most bars within pack lands had one or two on hand if things got out of control in the establishment. I gave her a nod and put my gun away. If my spine hadn't been severed, I would have shifted and stopped him before he even reached Archer.

I once had been a scary son of a bitch. Several elder pack members assumed I might actually be the one to get the mark, but I was never as strong as Alessandra. Even so, no one messed with me before the accident. Hell, this would have never happened had I not been in a wheelchair.

Once he was covered up, his gaze snapped at me. "You condone this?" He waved at the two teenagers now huddled together on the opposite side of the table, rattled by what had occurred.

"No. I do not condone this at all. What they did was stupid and reckless. But they did it all the same. It takes two people to make a child and from what I understand, this was a mutual screwup." I looked at Cheryl and got a nod in response before I met George's angry glare.

"I can't believe you put any blame on my daughter," Tabitha finally said after she recovered from the last few tense minutes.

"Mom, I wasn't forced into anything. Archer and I made the mutual decision. I wanted him just as much as he wanted me, so don't make this into more of an issue than it is." She took a breath. "We've known forever that this was it for us." She shrugged and then took a sip of her water. "It just means we'll be together earlier than planned."

I blinked at her calm demeanor in the face of her father's outburst.

"I love your daughter, Mr. Carson." He inspected his ripped shirt and the welts left in his chest before he met his future father-in-law's gaze. "We didn't intend for this to happen. And yes, it was reckless for us not to have had any protections in place—"

"You shouldn't be sleeping with my daughter!" His growl was back as he spoke over Archer.

"You two slept together before you were married." Cheryl fluttered her hand at her parents. "So do not judge us."

"We were not in high school," Tabitha scolded.

I watched this train wreck unfold and kept my comments to myself. I wasn't happy with the situation, but I understood their point of view.

How long had I pined for Alessandra?

I was a couple of years older than she was, so approaching her while she was in high school wouldn't have been cool. But Archer and Cheryl were the same age and basically had been together for their entire high school tenure.

"But where will you live? What will you do about school? How will you afford a child?" Her mother fired questions without giving them a break to answer.

Archer finally lifted his hand, stopping the questions from continuing to barrel at him. "First, I get it. You're as pissed as my parents were, but we have a plan. We'd like to live in the apartment above the garage at my folks' for now."

He glanced at me, but I didn't confirm or deny that as an option. I wasn't sure that was available, especially considering that was my hiding place for Robert's agency refugees. I would have to think about what we'd do in the event we had any more before the kid could get on his feet and get out of our house.

"The baby isn't due until June, so we'll graduate before the baby comes." He glanced at Cheryl, and she gave him a nervous smile. "We'll get jobs. One of us first shift and the other either second or third depending on if there is a crossover of hours, and we'll see if we can find online degrees in the subjects that interest us. It might take us longer to get a degree, but we'll be able to do it while taking care of the baby."

My eyebrow rose at his semi-thorough explanation. He had just told me about this yesterday, so either he came up with this plan pretty damn fast, or he and Cheryl had talked about what to do before he told me and was waiting for an audience to share their plan.

Both their gazes jumped from her parents to me and back. I kept my emotions in check and did not show that I was surprised. Her father's anger still stunk up the air like a batch of burned toast, but at least he was no longer assaulting my kid.

"So, will you give us permission to marry next weekend?" Cheryl asked her parents.

They looked at me for an answer, but it wasn't my decision. I had already given my son an ultimatum when he told me, and it looked like he had taken it to heart. "It's not my decision," I said after too long a silence.

"We'd like you to be at the wedding." Cheryl's voice was nearly a whisper, but it caught her father's entire attention.

"You should have thought of that before you opened your legs. You are a disgrace. Consider yourself disowned," George snapped and grabbed his wife's hand, pulling her to her feet along with him as he stood. He looked at me. "She's your problem now."

They marched out of the restaurant like a pair of angry toddlers, leaving me with my son and his pregnant girlfriend.

"Maybe we should have brought your mother," I muttered under my breath and focused on the teenagers. Archer's eyes were almost as wide as his slack mouth. Cheryl's chin trembled as the door closed behind her parents. Her gaze jumped to mine, and her panic soiled the air with a bitter tinge.

Archer put his arm around Cheryl, pulling her close and then met my gaze. "What now?"

I sighed. "It looks like we need to get the guest room ready."

"What about the apartment over the garage?"

"We built that for visiting dignitaries. Not for you to shack up in while you both are in high school." Besides, I had to talk to Alessandra before I made that kind of decision. "We need to get your mother to go to Cheryl's house to grab whatever she needs in the way of clothing, along with her schoolbooks."

They nodded.

Before I rolled away from the table, I pulled out a twenty and left it under the saltshaker for the trouble we caused, even though we hadn't ordered anything yet. The staff had kept their distance while the discussion occurred. They probably read the emotions of all parties and made the wise decision not to interfere with the conversation. Other than delivering the bathrobe, they had been scarce.

"Come on, you two. You have to deliver the news of how this went to your mother. And I expect she will be pissed."

HUNTER'S MOON
Chapter 13

"**W**HAT HAPPENED?" ALESSANDRA ASKED the moment she got a look at who was walking through the door.

I rolled into the house after Archer and Cheryl. "It looks like we will have a long-term houseguest." I cut my gaze to Cheryl to give her a chance to digest that. "Archer, set Cheryl up in the guest room while I talk to your mother."

Archer opened his mouth and then shut it before he nodded.

I am glad he didn't argue with me. I wasn't in the mood to deal with his attitude right now. And I did not want to talk to Alessandra where he could hear. I rolled into my soundproof office. A moment later, she followed and closed the door.

"What happened?"

I rubbed my face. "Her father attacked him. It wasn't a punch. He shifted and went for Archer's throat. I had to pull my gun and threaten to shoot his ass if he harmed my son."

Her mouth dropped open.

"I'm actually glad I can't shift into a functioning wolf. If I could, her father would have died on the spot." I met her gaze. "And it is good you weren't there for the same reason."

"But what is she doing here?"

"They disowned her and said she's our problem now." I shook my head as I tapped my fingers on the arms of the chair. It was my nervous tendency since I couldn't pace the room. "And apparently, they are getting married this coming weekend."

Alessandra made a noise like a squeak.

"And he thinks they can stay in the apartment over the garage."

Her mouth popped closed. "That's for..."

"No shit. I couldn't very well say that out loud, either. So, it looks like either we have Robert's refugees stay in the house with us, or we have Archer and Cheryl in here along with a baby."

She chewed her bottom lip. "Both have their drawbacks. I'm not all that thrilled about waking throughout the night, but I'd rather have my son under our roof than a stranger."

I exhaled a breath I hadn't realized I was holding. She nailed my discomfort. Although I had become less wary of the refugees fed through this channel, I still wasn't comfortable sharing space with them on a regular basis.

"What do we tell Archer?"

"I will talk to him," Alessandra said. "And don't worry, I'll explain that the space over the garage is for traveling dignitaries from other packs and for those in transition who need a roof over their head. It isn't a big enough space for a child. There isn't a second bedroom over there. But they can take over the guest room once they are married and we can turn Archer's room into a nursery."

I tilted my head at the excitement finding its way into her tone. "Are you going soft on me?"

She laughed. "She's carrying our grandchild, Jake."

"I know." And despite being angry at my son and his hormones, I found myself just as enamored with the idea of a grandchild as my wife.

"We need to make it crystal clear that we" —she pointed between us—"are not raising their children for them."

I couldn't have agreed more with her statement. I just grinned instead of commenting.

HUNTER'S MOON
Chapter 14

SPRING STROLLED IN LIKE a hurricane and with it came another meeting with Robert. I arrived at the coffee shop and settled at a table with my drink, just waiting for Robert. I glanced at my watch. He was late, and I wondered whether he had another incident. Instead of heading outside, I sipped the hot drink and pondered what lies I would have to tell my son and daughter-in-law. At least they still had school for another couple of months.

My nerves prickled, and then the bell over the shop door jangled. A man that I could only describe as cagey preceded Robert into the shop. He looked jumpier than a junkie shooting up on the street. They crossed to the counter and put in their order while I continued to study them. All my internal alarms clanged like a tornado siren.

Thankfully, this coffeehouse was run by humans and not pack members.

When they sat down at the table with me, I had to fight not to recoil. Not only were my nerves on edge, but this close, my senses stung, making my hackles rise. If I were in wolf form, everyone would have known I was fighting going on the attack. Robert didn't look affected by this man's scent. I stared him down and cocked my head.

Usually, I greeted him with a smile. Not this time.

"I have a pregnant teenager in my home, and you want me to bring this into my house?" I hissed and waved at the stranger. "Alessandra will attack on instinct alone."

Robert hung his head. "John has done nothing against the law, yet the agency saw fit to eliminate him." He met my gaze. "I don't condone that. Even if he is a hybrid witch with a mix of demon blood."

"How did he get on your radar?" I crossed my arms.

"They killed my son, and I foolishly resurrected him, thinking it would be okay," John breathed.

"A necromancer," I hissed under my breath and visibly shivered. Necromancers were abominations, and the things they brought back were worse.

"I had to try," he added. "Even though I logically knew what came back to life would never be my son, I thought…" John wiped his face. "I put him down right before my house was raided by the agency."

I closed my eyes and pinched the bridge of my nose.

"I found him with the remains of his son." Robert's gaze met mine. We both knew what we would do for our children. "I hid him and then cleared the house. I got him in my trunk with no one noticing and then burned the house to the ground."

The explanation didn't help. I couldn't hide his stench or the danger response it evoked. Thankfully, this shop was on the outskirts of pack lands; otherwise, there would have been a bloodbath the moment John stepped out of Robert's car. "If I wasn't chained to this wheelchair, I would have attacked the moment he walked in the door. I cannot see Leigh being any different."

"Robert assured me I wouldn't be put in danger." John looked between the two of us.

"Your smell set me off. Can you mask it?"

"Not without using magic, and from what Robert told me, my magical signature is unique."

"Fuck." I pulled out my phone and dialed Alessandra. I put my finger up, silencing them both. "Hey, babe. Can you come down to the coffee shop?"

"What's wrong?"

I laughed a little. "I need your opinion before I agree."

Silence met my comment and then an exhale. "I'll be there in a half hour."

I disconnected the call and nodded toward the counter. "We might as well get some food because not only will Leigh be pissed off at having to come down here, she's likely to be hangry on top of that." I went to roll away from the table.

"I've got it. What will she want?" Robert stood and glanced at the menu.

I didn't need to look at the menu. I knew it by heart after all the visits here over the years. "The Philly cheesesteak. Make that two orders. I expected to eat at home, too."

Robert glanced at John.

"Make that three." He gave me a smile of commiseration.

"Four cheesesteaks." With a nod, he moved to the counter.

"My wife had a pretty volatile temper," John said as Robert put in the orders.

"What happened to her?" Usually, Robert's refugees had the same sad story. I really didn't want to hear another one, but we had to kill some time.

John tilted his head and stared at the table for a moment. His silver hair blocked my view of his face. "She turned me in, and I've been running ever since." He let out a sarcastic laugh. "Black magic is frowned upon in the agency, especially for an agent's spouse."

Robert slid into the seat across from me, and I gave him a pointed look. This person didn't seem innocent like the rest. I was about as comfortable with black magic as I was with necromancy.

"Your wife is no longer breathing." His statement hung on the air, and John slowly nodded. Robert pinned me with his gaze. "The black magic he is talking about was for me. It blocks seers in the agency from seeing anything beyond what I want them to."

My eyes widened, and Robert's protective instincts all fell into place. This man had sacrificed his relationship and his freedom for Robert.

"She set off the alarm, but didn't know what the magic was for. And John was bound to keep my secret." He glanced at John. "Which ended his relationship and nearly got him killed. Unfortunately, his son wasn't so lucky."

I wiped my face and shook off the feeling of emotional whiplash. I still wasn't comfortable with either of these men, but I would honor the agreement. I just needed Alessandra to not react to the stench and come up with some sort of story to tell our son and his wife. They could be just as triggered as I was.

And teenagers talk.

The server interrupted us by placing the four plates on the table. "Can I get you anything to drink?"

"Water would be good." I smiled up at her, hiding my discomfort.

As if on cue, the jangle of the door hitting the bell rang across the tiny space.

Alessandra froze on the spot and trembled. I met her gaze as she fought her wolf, and the alarm blazing in her eyes quirked the edge of my lips. My smile did nothing to quell her alpha vibe filling the shop.

Robert stiffened in the chair, and the fine hairs on his arms rose. He didn't even turn to acknowledge Alessandra; however, he waved his hand to the empty seat with the untouched plate in front of it.

Alessandra walked to the table as if her legs were made of wood and not flesh. The low growl in her throat got more pronounced the closer she got, and

I already knew this probably would go to hell very quickly.

She stared at John across the table as she slowly lowered to the seat. The smell of her sandwich had her gaze dropping for a split second.

"I'm John. Your husband said I don't smell very appealing." He offered an apology smile and a shrug. "I mean no harm," he added before he took a bite of his food.

The high-pitched laugh that came from Alessandra made Robert twitch in his seat.

I took a bite of my food to stall whatever might fall out of my mouth.

"How am I supposed to hide him?" She stared at Robert. "No amount of air fresheners will dull that." She waved at John. "And it's not like we are on the outskirts of town like this place is. We are in the heart of our pack."

"He can't use his magic, and I don't know of any witches who can do that kind of wizardry without throwing up all manner of red flags," Robert said. "It's not ideal, but he needs to get out of the country as soon as possible." He turned his gaze on me. "Preferably a place that accepts more pagan-like religions where he could blend in."

Alessandra looked John up and down. "That would be fine if he was dark-skinned, but he's as white as my Irish uncle. He will stick out on most of the islands."

Robert and John snorted laughter.

"I'd prefer going somewhere that the agency has no reach," John said. "Somewhere easy to get lost."

"And where magic, particularly dark magic, is in abundance. I'd suggest Haiti, but there are so many issues happening there that I'd be concerned—"

"Haiti would be perfect," John interjected. "There's a lot of magic layering over that country, enough so that my wife mentioned more than once that the island has more power than most places, but nothing the agency could pinpoint."

I took a breath. "I can get you to New Orleans—"

Robert put his hand up and shook his head. "He needs to leave the country."

"Why?" Alessandra asked.

"Because there wasn't a body, and my boss has made it clear that the agency needs to find him and put him down before he disappears. New Orleans was one of the first places he tasked agents to look."

"That's all well and good, but it will take time to arrange." I took another bite. "And short of dousing him from head to toe in peppermint essential oil, I don't know that he will survive being near a pack of wolves."

Alessandra stared at me for a moment before rummaging in her pocketbook. She pulled out a little vial and set it on the table. "Let's see if it dulls the stench any."

John finished his sandwich, wiped his hands and mouth with a napkin, and then picked up the vial.

"It's undiluted, so hopefully you don't have a reaction."

"I usually use a carrier oil, but I have put this directly on achy joints." He poured at least ten drops on his hands, rubbed them together and then wiped his hands on his arms, neck and head, but stayed away from his face.

Peppermint penetrated the air, dulling his vile smell to the point it wasn't triggering the attack response.

Robert even seemed to relax.

Alessandra nodded and glanced at me. "I can work with this. Plus, it gives us an easier alibi with Archer. We can tell him John is sick and the undertones he's smelling are the disease. John combats some of the more painful symptoms with peppermint oil. And he's only staying with us until his surgery is approved and scheduled. Plus, we can tell Archer that the more contact we have with John, the more his condition flares up."

Okay. My wife can spin one hell of a tall tale—it was believable and ensured that John would stay in the apartment until he got the call.

HUNTER'S MOON
Chapter 15

ALESSANDRA BOUGHT A METRIC fuckton of peppermint essential oil on our way home so John would have it on hand. She also bought some extra-virgin olive oil in the event he had any reaction from using the oil directly on his skin. And she was the one to get him settled into the apartment.

I rolled into the house to Archer pacing the living room floor, biting a hangnail.

"What's up?"

He lifted a shoulder and glanced toward the hall where their bedroom and nursery were set up. "She's talking on the phone with her parents."

Surprise raked over my skin. Her parents hadn't reached out at all, even over the holidays. "Really?"

He nodded. "She wanted to see if they wanted to come to graduation." He cocked his head. "Why do you smell like peppermint? And where's Mom?"

Leveraging Alessandra's story, I answered, "She's getting a sick guest settled. He needed a place to wait for surgery. He uses peppermint to help with the pains of his disease." Archer's eyes widened, and I knew exactly where his mind went. "And no, it's not anything transmittable, so you and Cheryl are safe. But interactions with him makes his pain worse, so we shouldn't be visiting if we can help it."

"Oh. Okay." He went back to chewing his nails.

Cheryl came out of the bedroom, her face scrunched in annoyance. Her belly protruded enough to announce her late stage of pregnancy to anyone looking at her. Her face was a rash of red, and her dark hair looked as if she was pulling at it in aggravation.

Archer's eyebrows rose.

"My parents are assholes. Remind me of that if they decide they want to be a part of our child's life."

Archer went to her and gave her a hug. "Don't worry. I won't let them anywhere near our kids."

His fierce response brought a smile to my face. "I'm sorry your parents haven't come around." I couldn't imagine cutting my child off. Being disappointed, oh yeah. But walking away? Nope. Not me, and certainly not Alessandra. After seven months under my roof, I even considered Cheryl my daughter and not just through marriage.

"At least I have you and Leigh," she said, using my nickname for Alessandra.

"Always." I headed toward my spot across from the television. I needed something to take my mind off the fact we had a witch who practiced dark magic on the premises.

GRADUATION CAME AND WENT, and Cheryl's parents ignored her accomplishment. And John was still with us, layering peppermint on himself to avoid being attacked. The kids had a handful of interactions with him over the last month and a half, but thankfully nothing raised flags.

John's new identification was due within the next couple of days, and I was just as antsy to have him gone as Alessandra. The one benefit he provided during his stay was he painted runes on the apartment walls, so whatever magic he practiced inside those walls was suppressed. The agency couldn't detect a thing. I asked him to do that with the house, too. Having that kind of protection was essential for any of the supernaturals staying with us. We now had less of a chance of being detected. Even so, any time the doorbell rang, I stiffened, thinking that perhaps the agency had sniffed us out.

The file on my desk irked me as I browsed the list of infractions. It was bad enough that the complaints came from our pack, but the kicker of the issue was it involved Cheryl's parents.

The knock on my doorframe lifted my gaze. Alessandra leaned against the wood. She had been the one to give me the file and had been patient with me while I read through the many situations.

I leaned back in my seat. "I don't know what to do with this."

"Do I have the authority to exile them from the pack?"

I blew air out between my lips. They were using silver to keep their nephew in line. They apparently didn't want a repeat of what happened with Cheryl in the family, and their nephew was orphaned earlier this year. They had threatened neighbors and anyone else who found out what they were doing, and even threatened bodily harm to those who they suspected might know of their actions if word got to Alessandra.

All of it was unacceptable. I guess they must have forgotten that Alessandra had the pulse of the pack at her disposal. She felt the unsettled air and reached out to those who were emitting downright frightened vibes. She usually could tell the difference between family squabbles and an authentic problem. And this was a mother of a problem.

Based on the laws the council had passed, their transgression of using silver to control their nephew was a capital crime. As alpha, Alessandra had the right to tear them apart. And as the head of the council, I had the right to bury a bullet in their brains.

"They are committing a capital offense." I couldn't go easy on them because they were Cheryl's parents.

Alessandra's jaw dropped. "But…"

"But what? I cannot let personal connections impact my judgment. I need to bring this to the council."

She crossed her arms. "It's a situation within our pack."

"You brought it to the council." I waved at the folder on my desk.

She closed the door behind her. "I brought it to my husband." She crossed and leaned on the desk, glaring at me.

I pointed at her. "Don't even…"

"You will not bring this to the council." Her alpha command rolled over me, and I gritted my teeth. I had the power to ignore her order. I had done it a thousand times over the years, when I knew she was wrong, but it still goaded me to no end.

I slammed my palm on the desk. "Fucking hell, Leigh. I cannot be compromised like this. It puts my integrity on the line."

"And offering it up to the council undermines my alpha authority."

She wasn't budging on this, and I could see her point. But it still didn't help the slew of questions I'd have to answer for not bringing this immediately to the other council members.

"What about their nephew?" I tossed out. Because if she exiled them, they might insist on bringing him along and continue to torture the poor kid.

She straightened. "I'll give him the option of staying if he chooses." She closed her eyes and sighed. "I'll call a meeting of the elders and will have Hans and Nathan bring them in with their nephew. I will do it here so you, Archer, and Cheryl can witness the outcome."

I nodded curtly, still very unhappy with my wife's choice to attempt to use her alpha commands on me.

HUNTER'S MOON
Chapter 16

I WAS THE LAST one to enter our great room. Alessandra had the furniture pushed against the walls and the elders sitting around the outer space of the room. In the center, Hans and Nathan stood behind George and Tabitha. Their low growls seemed to keep the Carsons from bolting.

Archer and Cheryl were behind Alessandra, sitting on the couch together, looking just as confused as most of the faces in the room.

I rolled up next to them, waiting for all hell to break loose.

Alessandra held the file in her hand and opened it while silence descended. Her fury blanketed the room, nearly drawing everyone into a hunch from the weight of it.

"Why are we here?" George ground out the words between his clenched teeth.

The front door opened and a group of George's neighbors, followed by John, shuffled into the space. Peppermint swept through the room, mixing with Alessandra's fury. I hadn't expected John to be present. Nor did I expect he'd have a basket with vials filled with clear liquid.

Alessandra gave him a nod, and he handed the vials to the people who entered with him, leaving only three left in the basket.

"This is a friend of ours who is staying until he gets called in for surgery. He has experience with truth serums." She nodded at the vials in the pack member's hands.

John crossed and handed her the last three before retreating to a chair near where I sat.

Alessandra stared George down. "Will you drink this willingly?"

"You bitch." George lunged forward, but Nathan grabbed his arms, holding him in place. Hans still held one of Tabitha's arms, but she didn't seem to be a flight risk or an outright danger the way George seemed to be.

"I guess that's a no." She looked at their nephew. "Kane, will you?"

Hunter's Moon

He hunched over as if in constant pain. His face was pinched as he looked at his aunt and uncle with trepidation. But he nodded. His light hair lay limp on his pimpled forehead. The young teenager shuffled forward.

"Don't—"

"Shut it." Alessandra's command shut down George.

"What's going on?" Cheryl whispered to Archer as Kane downed the liquid, along with the others who had come in with John.

"No idea." Archer glanced at me.

I just shook my head. They'd hear the damning evidence soon enough.

Alessandra kept her gaze on George. "Kane, can you tell us what has been going on at your uncle's home?"

He grimaced. "After my parents died in that car crash, they took me in. And I was happy at first, but the minute I took an interest in a girl down the road, he got unreasonably irate." He seemed to pick his words so he could be within the truth parameters of the serum. And he kept his gaze on the ground.

"Define unreasonably irate." Alessandra stepped closer and tilted his chin up so he could see her. "There will be no retribution for telling us the truth."

His chin quivered, and his gaze fluttered from Alessandra to Cheryl and then back. "They didn't want me to be like his disowned daughter, and they made sure that wouldn't happen."

So far, there was no evidence as to the notes in the file. Only that a parental figure was stricter than most. But there was so much more to this than he had been drilled into saying. The story he told was spun well, but we all could smell the swell of fear in the room.

"How did he make sure, Kane?"

"Silver," Kane hissed and cowered at the growl from his uncle.

"He threatened you with silver?" Cheryl asked, now on her feet. Her anger nearly matched Alessandra's.

A tear dropped from Kane's eye. "Not threatened." His answer was just a whisper.

"Show me." The command from Alessandra rang through the room.

Kane's face turned beet red, but he couldn't refuse his alpha's command.

When Kane reached for his belt, my stomach clenched. The file had just said they used silver to keep him in line. The kid's eyes pleaded for the order to stop, but Alessandra just looked on without flinching, until the boy dropped his pants.

A gasp went through the room at the silver cock ring around the base of the teenager's member. The blackened skin visible around the silver had me nearly drawing my gun and killing George.

"What the fuck?" Cheryl blurted, and her gaze jumped to her father.

Alessandra put her hand out, silencing Cheryl and anyone else from speaking. She turned to the only non-werewolf in the room. "Can you remove that?"

John waved his hand and the silver ring split in two, falling to the ground at the boy's feet. His nonchalant manner impressed me, but the magic that fell over the room had my nostrils flaring.

All eyes turned in his direction.

"He's harmless," Alessandra said, pushing the command out and bringing eyes back to her. "Do you have a healing salve or elixir?" she asked John.

His lips twitched, and he pulled out a small vial from his pocket, handing it to her. She held it out to Kane, and he took it without question.

"That should help you heal faster." She waited until he pulled his pants back into place before turning her icy stare at George and Tabitha. "Do you have anything to say? Or should I continue with the testimony of your neighbors and acquaintances who you threatened?"

"We didn't want another disgrace."

"And you believe you had the right to do what you did?"

"We are his guardians. We have the right to oversee his life as we see fit."

"Bullshit." Cheryl was on her feet. "You used silver. That leaves a permanent burn." Her belly protruded before her, and the way she stood showed just how close to term her pregnancy was. "You have no right to be a parent when you so easily discarded your only daughter. And then you abuse your guardianship of Kane in this manner? You are the disgrace."

"You do realize using silver to torture a werewolf is a capital offense, right?" Archer stepped next to Cheryl and put his hand on her lower back in a show of support.

"Pft. It wasn't torture, it was prevention."

"I beg to differ." Kane glared at his guardian and uncorked the vial, downing it as if his action were more of a rebellion. Then he crossed to Cheryl and slung his arm over her shoulders. "And she is not a disgrace."

Archer traded a nod of acknowledgment with Kane.

George and Tabitha let out growls as their faces turned almost beet red with anger. If the elders hadn't been present, they surely would have turned into their wolves and attacked.

Alessandra glanced at me before she looked at the rest of the elders. "I am seeking your verdict, since I have a personal connection with the accused beyond being the alpha of the pack."

They nodded and Samuel, the eldest of the elders, asked, "May we step away for a moment?"

"Yes." Alessandra nodded toward the door to my study. "You can use Hunter's study."

My soundproof office was a necessity. Cases discussed between council members were not fit for public consumption, especially sensitive ones that required confidentiality. And the pack was aware of the arrangements and accommodations made in this house, since some of them helped with the modifications.

The moment the elders left, the tension in the room increased. One glare from George had the witnesses quaking. Even the muscle of Hans and Nathan keeping them in place couldn't wipe their fear away from those the Carsons threatened.

And Cheryl's anger seemed to add to the unease. Especially with her parents now aiming their gaze her way. They stared at her as if she were a diseased bug.

Everything about this was unacceptable, and all I wanted to do was empty my revolver in their hides. Their lack of compassion for their own child astounded me, and now this heinous treatment of their charge just added to my anger. I hated to think

Hunter's Moon

what they would do to my grandchild if given the chance.

My back tensed against a shiver. I couldn't allow them to continue glaring that way at my daughter-in-law.

I rolled in front of Cheryl, giving them another target to glower at. Despite being confined to a wheelchair, I could make my presence and my disdain just as loud as Alessandra's. After all, I was the beta of this pack.

Alessandra put her hand on my shoulder as if reading my volatile emotions accurately. I wanted control of the meeting, and I craved justice being served. And these two needed to be taken down. But I wasn't in charge right now.

The door to my office opened after what seemed much longer than I thought it would take, and the pack elders filed back into the room, all with stern expressions on their faces. As soon as they gathered outside my office, Samuel gave Alessandra a nod.

"While the council's law states that this infraction is a capital offense, we will leave the punishment to you, Alpha."

I glanced at Alessandra as she nodded at Samuel and the elders. With a deep breath, she moved her gaze to George and Tabitha.

"As Samuel pointed out, this type of abuse is a capital offense. And while I'd like nothing more than to tear you to pieces for what you have done, I will show mercy because you are related to my daughter-in-law."

George's face broke out in a smug smile.

"So, I give you your life, but I exile you from the pack. I will give you an hour to get off pack lands. If you ever set foot within our boundaries, you will be executed."

The air in the room buzzed as Alessandra severed George and Tabitha from the pack bond.

It took George a moment to realize what Alessandra said, and then his growl became feral. He broke away from Nathan and lunged forward with a knife in his hand. The blade whistled close to Alessandra, but she ducked out of the way.

I rolled forward, intercepting him before he could recover from missing her. I grabbed his hand and pulled to the side while I drew my gun and squeezed the trigger. The bullet exploded out his back and wedged into the ceiling. George fell over my lap.

Tabitha gripped her hair and screamed as I shoved George's dead body off me.

I pointed the gun at her. "You did nothing to stop this."

"I-I," she stuttered, unable to deny my accusation. "I didn't know," she finally whispered.

Kane scoffed from behind me. "This was your idea, not his."

Her frightened gaze turned sharp as it jumped to Kane.

"Um, Hunter?" Alessandra said.

"What?" I didn't take my gaze off Tabitha.

"You need a doctor."

I didn't dare look at whatever Alessandra was looking at. Instead, I said to Tabitha, "Exile or death?"

The smile that twerked her lips as she looked at my lap nearly made me look down, but she didn't utter a word beyond the satisfied grin that appeared.

Her choice was made for her when a wolf launched past me and ripped her throat to shreds in seconds.

That wolf was not Alessandra. She was at my side with John. My brain went fuzzy as the wolf shifted and the image of Archer standing next to Tabitha's dead body with blood smeared on his face came into focus.

"Get everyone out and I'll fix him," John whispered.

The wolves in the room were too stunned at the quick turnaround. Plus, their ears were still ringing from the gunshot, so thankfully, John's statement was lost on them.

"Everybody but my family out!" Alessandra commanded.

The room cleared quickly, although the smell of blood and feces nearly made me gag. When John lifted me out of the chair and laid me on the floor, I still wasn't aware of my damage.

"What are you doing?" Archer nearly threw John off me.

"He's a powerful witch. Let him help." Alessandra glanced at Cheryl and then back at Archer. "You might need to tend to your wife."

He glanced at her, then at Cheryl, and stepped away.

John chanted under his breath with his hands over my abdomen. Heat enveloped me. I lifted my head enough to look, and I immediately wished I hadn't. George had ripped through my abdomen and left the damn knife embedded in my flesh. Flesh blackened by silver. The asshole had used a fucking silver knife.

I dropped my head back on the carpet.

Alessandra took my hand and squeezed as she kneeled at my side, watching John do his thing. She winced when John pulled the blade out. But he was still chanting and light cascaded from his hands.

Instead of watching his magic, I stared at the awe filling Alessandra's face. Her eyes widened and her lips opened in a way that had me wanting to kiss her instead of coping with being on death's door.

"It's no wonder Robert wanted to hide you." The words were out before she could stop them, and her gaze slashed to mine. Her eyes widened, and she turned to Archer and Cheryl.

Archer stared at us with Cheryl in his arms, but the puzzlement line between his eyes announced he had heard his mother. But at least he had the sense to not make a big deal of it. His hands were full with Cheryl as the reality that both her parents were dead left her a sobbing mess.

John reached into his pocket and handed Alessandra a vial that looked like the one Kane had taken. "Make him drink." And then he began chanting again.

Alessandra dumped the contents down my throat without hesitation.

I only had a fleeting taste of citrus before it hit my stomach. A bomb of heat spread through me, making my toes actually tingle. I hadn't had that type of reaction since the night Archer had been conceived. I blinked and tried to wiggle my toes, but nothing happened.

When John finished chanting, I asked, "You don't have any more of that elixir left, do you?"

"Sorry. No. I had made two batches as a failsafe." He wiped his forehead and glanced at the state of our living room. "Why?"

"Because I thought my toes tingled."

Silence fell over the room. Even Cheryl's whimpering stopped.

"You what?" Alessandra asked.

Before I could speak, John raised his hand to stop her. "A tingling sensation is normal when the magic works. While I can mend cuts and suck out silver poisoning from the blood, I cannot heal a broken spine. If I had that kind of angelic magic, I would have fixed you on my first week here."

I closed my eyes and turned my head. When I opened them, my gaze landed on the dead littering our living room, along with all the bits and pieces splattered on the ceiling and walls.

"We are going to need this professionally cleaned." I wiped my face and sighed.

"Why are you here?" Archer asked, pulling all our attention to him.

"Your mother asked me if I could make some truth serum and a healing elixir for her, and if I knew how to reverse the effects of silver poisoning."

"No. I mean living over our garage?"

"I'm waiting for an operation." He used the agreed-upon story.

Archer shook his head. "Then why would you need to be hidden?"

John chewed on his bottom lip and traded a glance with me. "Well, you've smelled the disease, right?" He twirled his finger. "Even with the peppermint, it can leak out and it apparently causes wolves to get hostile."

He was good. That was just enough of the truth to settle Archer.

"If I don't get in for surgery soon, even the peppermint won't help and then I'm as good as dead.

So, considering I'm a witch who has been around supernaturals all my life, this affliction makes it so I need to be in a safe place until the call comes in." He glanced at me and then Alessandra. "Your parents have a reputation in the community, and I reached out for help."

"Oh." Archer seemed satisfied with the answer, and it looked like the stress of this situation was behind us.

And then Cheryl cried out as a river of water gushed from between her legs.

HUNTER'S MOON
Chapter 17

"**D**ID YOU JUST PEE on the floor?" Archer asked.

Alessandra burst out laughing.

I just stared at the mess from my prone position and laid my head back down. "You should take her to the hospital."

Archer's face blanched. "Why?"

Cheryl cried out and doubled over.

John muttered under his breath, and magic filled the air. His eyes widened. "No time for that." He dumped me back into my chair, leaving me to my own devices. "She needs to be in a clean environment, though."

Alessandra grabbed his arm as he headed toward Archer and Cheryl.

"I've delivered dozens of babies. It will be fine. Just help your husband clean himself up and then meet us in their bedroom." He turned back to the kids.

Archer's eyes were much wider than they had been. "Labor?"

"It's too early," Cheryl said, through another gasp.

"Well, he's coming out within the half hour." John glanced at Archer. "You need to clean off quickly, but before you do, bring me towels."

He escorted Archer and Cheryl back to their room, and Alessandra pushed me to our shower.

"Clean up and I'll get your chair done."

I moved myself to my shower chair and stripped as fast as I could, which for a paraplegic isn't quick, especially with pants from a sitting position. I ended up just shredding the material to get it off and turned on the water, scrubbing the blood from my abdomen and legs until the water ran clear. I had not realized just how much blood I had lost. It gave me a new appreciation for John and the level of magic he held.

Alessandra wheeled my clean chair to me and handed me the towel hanging over the bar. It wasn't quite dry, but I didn't care.

She helped me pull on underwear and my sweatpants and then towel dried my hair before rolling me shirtless to the other side of the house in nearly a sprint. It took me less than twenty minutes to clean up. Which was a new record for me, and I only got there because Alessandra helped. She was motivated and just as eager to see our grandchild enter the world as I was.

We rolled into the room just as Cheryl pushed out a head. The next push, the entire body shot into a towel that John held.

John picked up a plastic chip-clip from the fold-up table Archer must have gotten while we were cleaning up. A pair of scissors, a bowl of clean water, and a clean washcloth sat on the table as well. John clamped the cord with the clip and then handed Archer the sharp shears. "You do the honors." He held a piece of the umbilical cord out for Archer to cut.

Archer stilled the shakes in his hand and cut through the cord.

John dipped the washcloth into the clean water and cleaned the baby before swaddling it in another clean towel. He laid the child on Cheryl's chest. "You have a beautiful baby boy."

The placenta came next and then it was over, and John piled all the soiled towels on the ground and sighed. "Next time you do this, make sure you have a midwife on the premises when you are within a month of delivery. You won't make it to the hospital then, either."

I just sat in the doorway and stared at that little boy on my daughter-in-law's chest. If they had attempted to drive to the hospital, that child would have been born in the car.

John stepped over to the desk and scribbled on a piece of paper the date and time. He also wrote the weight and length of the baby as well.

I cocked an eyebrow at him.

"I used magic to get the measurements and weight." He smirked at me and glanced at the kids. "What's his name?"

"Kyle Jacob Blaez." Cheryl smiled.

My heart just about exploded with pride in my chest.

John wrote that on the paper as well. "You'll need this for a birth certificate." He handed the paper to Archer. "Whenever you decide to head to the hospital to have them checked out."

"How can we repay you for this?" Alessandra asked.

"No need. This is my pleasure. There is nothing more gratifying than delivering a baby." He looked around the room. "And this is my gift to you for all you have done for me." He looked at her and then waved his hands. Magic swelled in the room. The blood and other liquids soaked into the towels and bed trailed off, leaving only pristinely clean fabric. He turned and walked with the mess rolling in front of him like a living thing.

I watched from the door as he did the same with the living room, rolling all the blood and gore into a single mound of grossness that he pushed into the fireplace, along with the bodies of George and Tabitha. With another wave of his hand, they ignited. Burning fast and furious until nothing was left in the fireplace but ash and soot.

That was a damn powerful witch, and I was glad he was on our side.

"I'm going to go get some rest." He gave me a nod and left the house just as pristine as when he had walked in the door.

I turned my focus back to the bedroom. "Well, we don't need cleaners anymore." I rolled to the side of the bed and smiled at the baby.

"Do you want to hold him?" Archer asked.

I glanced at Alessandra. She wanted to get her hands on the child, too. "Let your mother have first dibs on holding our grandchild." I could wait. Besides, I was still recovering some from my near-death experience.

HUNTER'S MOON
Chapter 18

"WHAT IS THIS?" CHERYL asked as she un-swaddled Kyle to put him in a diaper before he soiled her or the nice clean bed John had left behind.

Alessandra and Archer looked over her shoulder. Their mouths dropped open for a fraction of a second. Archer's clamped shut and a line of irritation wedged itself between his eyes. Alessandra glanced back at me with a smile.

"It looks like Kyle is the next alpha of our pack," she said.

Archer's reaction made much more sense. Until this moment, he believed he might still be given the mark. What he failed to understand was that he never had the alpha authority.

As for my new grandson, I could feel the authority radiating from Kyle. It was much the same with Alessandra as a child. As a wolf in the pack, you wanted to follow her and protect her. That was the same instinct that flared in me when I rolled forward and saw the mark on the baby on the changing table.

"He's so young." I glanced up at her. After all, her mark didn't come until she was in college.

"My dad had the mark at birth." She beamed.

I nodded. I remembered our prior alpha. He had given his daughter a litany of warnings she had never heeded. I always wondered whether that was why the mark hadn't shown up earlier.

I glanced up at Archer and Cheryl. They both wore the same look: fierce pride and a bit of melancholy. They would never be at the head of the pack.

THE PAPERS FOR JOHN came a couple of days later. I sent Alessandra over to retrieve him.

"Hey." John walked into the office and closed the door behind him. "How are you feeling?"

"I'm good. After all the excitement, I got enough sleep to be back to my old self again."

He grinned. "Plus, I imagine having a little one sleeping on your shoulder is a source of peace and tranquility." He nodded toward Kyle curled up on my shoulder.

I rubbed his little back and nodded. "I was terrified to be a father when Archer came, but with this one, I have zero tension. I love being a grandfather."

John's smile soured, and he gave me a noncommittal nod. Unless he found someone and had another kid, he'd never know this pure joy.

I picked up the envelope in front of me and held it out to him. "You are all set. Your flight leaves tonight."

He took a seat in the chair and looked through the documents I handed him. Once he examined everything, he said, "This is impressive."

"No. What you did the other day was impressive. This is just creating a fictitious person and their life circumstances on paper tight enough to dupe everyone. It isn't magic." My lip twitched at the edges.

"Never sell yourself short like that. What you are doing here is saving lives, but in a different way. This is impressive as hell to me, and I've been out there, looking at fake documentation for years. I would pass this as real." He fanned the envelope. "Robert said you were a rare soul. I agree. Thank you for giving me a new lease on life."

I hated this part. I always felt humbled by the acknowledgment of my part in this routine. Especially because I didn't feel like a savior of souls.

"I'll get you to the airport."

"It's okay. I can get there on my own."

I appreciated that, but it still left me on edge. I wanted to be sure he got out of this country with his life intact. If he died on our soil, I would have failed in my job to keep him safe. "If it's all the same to you, I'd still like to take you for my peace of mind. Especially after you saved my life."

He glanced at the package in his hand. "No. You enjoy your grandson. I assure you, I am no longer in danger. Besides, if the agency is still scanning for facial recognition, I don't want you to be tagged as the one to drop me at the airport. That would bring on an entirely different scrutiny that your family cannot afford." His eyes lowered to my grandson.

"Point taken," I conceded. "Just text me a note when you are settled, then."

"That I can do." He stood and extended his hand. "It has been a pleasure." His handshake was firm, and then he dropped my hand and headed toward the door. "Tell your son not to forget what I said about timing if they ever decide on a second child." And then he was gone.

I never saw John again. But a few days later, I got a random text with a picture of a beach and the turquoise water beyond.

HUNTER'S MOON
Chapter 19

TIME SLIPPED AWAY FROM us all. Before we knew it, Kyle was getting ready for nursery school, the house we built for Archer and Cheryl on the acre next to ours was almost ready to move into, and Cheryl was pregnant again.

I was certainly going to miss the constant chaos once they moved out, but Alessandra and I craved the quiet we had when Archer was in high school.

We needed a little alone time, especially considering I had been experiencing more health issues related to my condition. Alessandra had pack responsibilities, and I still had the council. Plus, we'd had a few more of Robert's refugees come through. At least the last couple had been witches or wolves, and none of them had a stench like John.

And we all remembered John's warning about Cheryl and her pregnancies. So once the word was out, we hired Lina, the pack midwife, to take care of Cheryl. As soon as Cheryl hit eight and a half months, Lina moved into the garage apartment so she could be close by in the event of a repeat.

That turned out to be a blessing because once Cheryl hit the ninth month, she started having contractions. This time, she knew what they were and gave Archer a heads-up.

I don't think I've ever seen him sprint across the driveway at that pace in human form before. If we weren't so on edge about another delivery, I would have laughed. But we were busy prepping the bedroom, so it was a quick cleanup rather than a scrub fest. A large plastic tarp was laid out over the bed and stretched out on the floor. A clean fitted sheet we were planning on getting rid of covered the plastic, so Cheryl had something more comfortable against her skin.

Basins of water and older towels were also spread about the room. A table with a clean blanket to swaddle the little one was also set out. When Cheryl walked back in the room with a handful of towels, she glanced at the setup and raised an eyebrow.

"John's not around to magically clean this place up," I answered as Alessandra left the room to go

Hunter's Moon

grab the rest of the items on the list that Lina had given her.

Her smile faded. "Do you know if he survived the surgery?"

I thought back to that text I received and nodded. He survived the trip and now had a new identity. I didn't know whether he stayed in Haiti or not, but I imagined he'd have a nice quiet beach cabana and was enjoying the hell out of life.

Cheryl hissed through her teeth and nearly doubled over.

I blinked away a flashback of the last time this happened. Water gushed down her legs, but this time, she was on the tarp. I threw a towel down to soak up the fluid before it reached the wood floor, and my heart jumpstarted into overdrive because I was the only one in the room with her.

"Why don't you get comfortable? I'm going to see what's taking Archer." I rolled backward toward the door.

"Don't go," she said.

"Okay." I rolled to the side of the bed and waited for her to get situated.

Alessandra stepped into the room, looking more harried than usual. She tried to smile, but it was forced. "Um. Hunter. You have a guest in your office."

I stared at her as if she had grown another head. "Where's Archer and Lina?"

"They're coming. But you need to go." She pointed toward my office, and I rolled away, but she had already switched into nurse mode with Cheryl.

I rolled down the hall just as Archer and Lina jogged by. Neither one of them acknowledged me; they just slid by my wheelchair like I wasn't even there. I couldn't blame them. Cheryl's last delivery was in the forefront of all our minds.

All thoughts of the new baby blew out of my mind as I opened my office door. Robert Young paced in front of my desk. His hand ran through his hair, spiking it. His eyes were so bloodshot that even the blue of his irises looked like blood vessels had popped. I had never seen him so disheveled. Even the time he was attacked, he was in total control of his emotions.

"What happened?" I closed the door behind me and turned my wheelchair in his direction.

He shook his head, dropped into one of the chairs in front of my desk, and covered his face with his hand. "I got him killed."

His muttered response sent a cold chill through me. "Who?" I rolled closer.

"My son." Pain laced those words.

I couldn't fathom that kind of loss. And Robert had had more than his share of devastating cards dealt to him already. I rolled to his side and placed my hand on his shoulder, offering what little I could.

"I didn't get to tell him I was proud of him." Robert lifted his tear-stained face and stared at me as if I could bring the kid back from the dead.

I squeezed his shoulder and then rolled back, giving him some room. "Would you like to tell me about it?"

At first, he just shook his head until he had a little more control. Then he took a deep breath and launched into it. "Another fucking vampire." He wiped his face. "You want to know the kicker?"

I nodded.

"His fated mate, you know, the one I was supposed to keep him from? Well, that bitch killed him." A dry, humorless laugh rasped out of his mouth. "Her new master told me he died by her hand."

"Fuck." The word slipped out before I could stop it. Robby had been at the council meetings religiously since he took over as alpha. I actually respected Robert's son. That alpha was one of the best I had met outside of Alessandra. His pack came first, and although there were a few disagreements as to how to handle some items over the years, he treated me with respect.

If he hadn't worked for the agency, he would have been offered a spot on the council a few years back when we lost one of the aging members. And the alphas would have unanimously voted him onto the board. Not only was that a loss to his pack, it was a loss to the council.

His gaze hardened. "Yup. If I ever get my hands on that bitch, I am going to kill her slowly."

I had no doubt about that. Murderous vibes flowed off Robert. Enough to make me want to get away from him before he decided to exact that wrath on the closest person.

After a few deep breaths, he reined in his fury and gave me an apologetic smile. "Sorry."

"You have nothing to apologize to me for."

He didn't reply. Instead, he slipped a piece of paper from his pocket and handed it to me. "I need this person to be accepted by the council as the new alpha. He was Robby's beta and an extremely loyal soul. He loved my son like a brother and did his damnedest to keep Robby safe."

I glanced at the name and nodded. I had met Robby's beta a few times at the annual meetings. "Done." I took a breath. "What else do you need?"

His lip quirked up on one side. "I might need your services if my plans to take down this fucking agency go awry."

"I'll be here if you need me."

Robert looked at the ceiling and wiped the grief off his face, replacing it with a steel resolve that worried me.

Before I could ask him what he was planning, power sizzled through the house. Both our gazes darted to the door. I rolled toward it, unsure of what I might find on the other side. The minute the door opened, another blast of alpha power rang through the house, followed by the wail of a newborn baby.

I let out a surprised laugh. It looked like Cheryl delivered another alpha, and this one was strong. He couldn't possibly have a mark, could he?

"Damn. New grandchild?" Robert asked as he stood.

"Sounds like it." Kyle hadn't gotten home from school yet, so that cry could only be from their newborn.

"That alpha signature is as strong as Robby's was when he was born," Robert said in a voice rough with emotion. He passed by me and headed toward the front door. "I'll be in touch."

He slipped out before I could process his comment. Robby was an exceptionally powerful alpha. If the new baby was that strong, they would need their own pack someday. He or she wouldn't be able to stay and be subservient to another wolf, even if that wolf was their brother.

HUNTER'S MOON
Chapter 20

I ROLLED INTO THE bedroom as Lina was cleaning the baby. In my brief visit with Robert, the baby and placenta were delivered, and Alessandra and Archer were in the midst of cleaning the localized mess up and depositing it into a bucket bound for the garbage.

Cheryl stepped out of the bathroom with a fresh set of clothing, looking tired, but not as exhausted as she had been after Kyle's birth. But then again, this delivery took half the time and there wasn't the emotional punch of losing her parents moments before labor started.

"Another boy," Archer announced with a grin. "Logan." He looked at the bassinet. "It seems he's got quite a demanding presence, too."

Alessandra met my gaze, and she gave me the kind of look that silenced me. She had to have felt this little guy's power, but for some reason, she didn't want me saying anything about it.

"Is that so?" I rolled to where Lina was just finishing up and looked down into the bright-blue eyes of the newborn. "Hi there, Logan."

His gaze darted to me, and a flare of protectiveness sped through my form. He was even cuter than Kyle had been and so much more attentive. I'd have to be the one to educate this one on how an alpha should act because I had a feeling he was destined for something more than just being a shadow.

Alessandra would be busy grooming Kyle, and neither Archer nor Cheryl knew the first thing about being an alpha, so the responsibility fell on my shoulders to teach him the proper way to be an alpha. And that had nothing to do with being a bully and everything with being a leader.

Cheryl crawled into the clean bed and put her arms out for the baby. Lina promptly deposited the newborn in her arms.

"I'll go get this filed for you." Lina waved the birth certificate and then grabbed the bucket of garbage and left the room.

As soon as Logan was nestled into Cheryl's arms, Alessandra crossed and stepped behind me. "I'll give you two some quiet time with Logan before Kyle gets home from school."

I would have liked a little more time with my grandson, but I didn't argue with my wife as she pushed me back to my office and closed the door.

"Did you feel it?" she asked quietly.

"Yes. Both Robert and I felt the blast of his power." I turned toward her.

"I don't know what Archer and Cheryl felt, but as the alpha of this pack, I recognized a threat to my station within my territory." She exhaled. "It was so much stronger than Kyle's alpha presence. But no mark. I'm not sure how that's going to go within our pack."

I nodded. "Are you sure that feeling wasn't because Robert was here?" He was an alpha, after all.

"Yes. I was uneasy with him in the house, but it wasn't the same."

"Logan will be fine," I said, but wasn't as sure as I sounded. Especially if Kyle viewed him as a threat. Alphas were territorial to a fault. It amazed me that Alessandra never got antsy with all the alphas in town for the annual meeting. I'm not sure I would be as calm and commanding as she was, but then again, I didn't have the mark, either.

"What did Robert want, anyway?"

"His son died, and he gave me the name of the next alpha and asked me to clear it with the council."

Pain flashed through our bond. "Oh, no. He was such a role model for the other alphas." Her eyes filled with tears, but she blinked them back. "Is Robert taking over again?"

"No. It's Robby's beta. Rick Johnson. We've met him during at least one council meeting. I told him it's cleared."

"Jake." She sighed.

"I know. It's a requirement to vote on it, but considering the circumstances and the fact that their pack is still under the agency and not the council, I think I have the latitude to make this call."

She gave me that disappointed look.

"I will talk to the council. I doubt there will be any dissention. Besides, there's no one for Johnson to challenge for the position."

Alessandra shuddered. A challenge meant a fight to the death and the victor would take the alpha position in the pack. There had been a few of those over the years, but usually a death sentence was something that deterred challenges.

We stared at each other.

Someday, Logan would throw a challenge out. I just prayed it wasn't for the alpha position in our pack.

HUNTER'S MOON
Chapter 21

WE STARED AT THE news on television in shock. I reached out for Alessandra's hand, and she squeezed as we scanned the destruction. The Monster Defense Agency building in New York City was literally ashes. Robert flashed in my mind and then, in the corner of the screen, I saw him arrive on scene.

My heart thundered as he appeared to be arguing with someone behind the reporter.

I glanced at Alessandra. She had seen the same thing, and we both exhaled in relief. He hadn't perished in that building.

"You think this was him?" she asked quietly, trying not to wake Logan, who slept on the couch by her. I knew exactly who she was referring to. We hadn't seen him since the day Logan was born.

"I'd bet money on it. Especially after the slaughter of the vampires a few days ago. But damned if I know how the hell he pulled it all off."

My phone started to buzz, and I scanned the messages from the other council members. They wanted me to call an emergency meeting right now. I texted back asking that we wait until more information came out before we panicked. I really wanted time to hear from Robert and get an update from the source before we held a meeting, but I couldn't say that. Instead, I agreed to meet a week from today.

I sent out the request for a mandatory council meeting to all the alphas and included Robert's personal email as a blind copy. It came back as undeliverable. I would just have to wait until all the alphas and the agency representatives arrived at the meeting to find out what the hell was going on.

AS THE ALPHAS FILTERED into the town hall for the mandatory meeting, Alessandra and I kept our game faces on. My chest constricted each time the door opened. The room was nearly full when Rick Johnson stepped in, followed by a face that stole the breath from my chest.

Robert's son followed the Allegany pack alpha into the room, and a hush fell over the space.

Robby Young had the look of a prisoner of war. He was thinner than the last time he graced us with his presence, but it was his haunted gaze that made me swallow hard. His eyes darted around until they landed on me.

I looked beyond him, expecting his father to step in behind him, but the door shut. The click sent my stomach tumbling, and I cleared my throat, glancing at the other members of the council. I received nods to open the meeting.

"It seems all the alphas are present." I glanced directly at Robby Young as I spoke wondering whether he might have the answers we sought. "The reason we called you all here is because of the destruction in New York City. With the recent extinction of vampires, I know there is a worry that our species will be targeted next. But before we jump to any conclusions, I'd like to open the floor to any reports on the chaos we saw reported from the city."

Rick Johnson stepped forward and nodded for Robby to join him. The former alpha stepped close, but not in an equal line. It was an obvious display of respect for his alpha.

"The agency is no more," Rick said. "Robby's mate took out the head of the organization. The one pulling the strings and trapping our kind into a life of servitude."

I cocked my head as if I didn't know the ugly truth about the agency. "Servitude?" I sent a sideways glance at Alessandra. And then looked behind her at

Archer. His presence at these meetings had increased since he graduated from high school. Although he'd never be an alpha, he could step in and replace me when the time came.

Robby snorted a laugh, pulling my attention back to him.

"My father said you knew about the agency," he said. "Which is why not one of you got roped into joining." He glanced around the room. "Your council head saved your lives and your packs."

"Excuse me?" Roland, the member to my right looked pointedly at me.

"Where is your father?" I asked, ignoring the accolades.

"He died at their fucking hands."

That gut twist I felt when the door clicked closed increased, and sorrow formed in the pit of my stomach. Although I had been wary of Robert over the years, he had grown on both Alessandra and me to the point I considered him a friend. I wiped my face. "There are more offices than just New York City."

"But without the head calling the shots and the vampires backing them, they don't have any muscle to push back into dominance. All the major heads were annihilated when the building came down," Rick said.

"So, your silence is no longer needed," Robby added. "These people need to know what kind of hero sits at the head of their council."

I let out a laugh. "Your father was the hero."

Robby just shook his head, but didn't expound further.

Alessandra stood. "Are you certain the danger has been eliminated?"

"Yes," both Robby and Rick said at the same time.

Alessandra looked at the other members of the council and then at the other alphas in the room. "We have always suspected the agency wasn't what it seemed. Especially with Winters running it. We knew what kind of monster Ken Winters was, and the fact he never agreed to allow the agency to poach from any of the packs associated with the council said a lot. But our suspicions were confirmed when Archer was little. Robert reached out to us to see if we would help a witch who was tagged to be killed by the agency simply because she hadn't followed through on an order."

All eyes turned to me, but it was Robby who spoke.

"The agency terminated sub-par employees. They killed anyone who questioned orders. They were monsters on a grand scale." He glanced around. "A scale sanctioned by the government. The agency had access to other monstrous beings, like vampires who they controlled. If one stepped out of line, we were called to extinguish them."

"And you just went out and killed them because you were ordered to?" Archer asked.

Robby nodded. "What do you know of vampires?"

"They are monsters that kill when they feed," Archer answered.

"So do you."

Archer blinked.

"You kill when you feed. You just don't feed on humans." He glanced around, making his point. "I agree that vampires who killed humans should be put down, just like we are if we step over that line with no valid reason. But I don't know that all the vampires we have assassinated over the years deserved it. That's a stain on my soul." He focused back on me. "But you, sir, have my utmost respect. How many people tagged for death have you saved?"

I shrugged. I didn't keep count.

"Your father was able to get dozens of people out of the agency's death sentences over the years. We housed them in our garage apartment while Hunter got them new identification." Alessandra's voice bloomed with pride.

"There were at least a hundred guests who stayed more than a couple of days over the years," Archer said.

My cheeks heated.

"And you did all that without question?" one alpha in the group asked.

"It was the right thing to do." I met his gaze.

"What if they were dangerous?" another voiced.

"What if they deserved the death sentence?" another asked.

Robby raised his hands. "No one deserves to die for who they fall in love with." Silence settled on the room. "The agency killed my family because my father broke the cardinal rule and fell in love with another one of the agents."

"Bullshit." It came from Archer.

Robby reached into his pocket and pulled out a small tape-recording device. He pressed play and a chilling conversation that happened close to thirty years ago rang out in the room. The vampire's admonishment of his father's life choices chilled my blood. When it was over, Robby clicked the recording off.

"The agency let that vampire walk. But they caged my mother for the rest of her life." Grumbles filled the room. "In a tiny cage made of silver."

"Silver cells?" Roland asked.

"Yes. They threatened us with silver all the time. Even bound us in it when restraining us. And their cages designed for werewolves had boiling silver over the cell in the event the bars were breached. I was in one of those damn things, separated from my mate, who they had across the hall."

A collective shiver went through the room. The idea of being physically separated from your mate wasn't one that any werewolf could abide.

"That's illegal," Roland said after he recovered from the shock of Robby's declarations.

"Yes. It is," I agreed with Roland.

"And were you aware of this?" His sharp gaze pierced mine.

"Not to the extent Robby just described. But I knew they employed practices we deemed illegal." I licked my lips at the rising hostility.

"If we all banded together—"

"You would have all died." Robby's interruption silenced the room. "Or did you forget the agency had witches employed and vampires to do their dirty work? They had seers as well. And they would have warned the powers that be of an attack."

"Then how did you take the agency down?" I thought his father had a hand in it. Especially because he had been charmed to not be visible to seers' predictions.

"My mate took it down."

A dozen questions popped into my head, but I kept them under wraps. I knew his mate had been his partner, which made her a witch. A powerful one, which Robert had alluded to at one point.

"So, wait, was John one of them?" Archer asked, circumventing the conversation.

I glanced at him and nodded.

"Oh." He glanced at Alessandra, and she nodded as well. He moved his open gaze to Robby, and it narrowed. "Weren't you and your partner wanted by the agency at one point?"

"Robby's mate is his partner," Rick stated.

Rumbles started throughout the room. The witch-werewolf partnerships of the agency weren't a secret.

"So, you are tainting your bloodline?" Archer crossed his arms.

I turned to him. "That's enough." I would not have any alpha speaking down to this man. From the looks of him, he had been through enough hell already, and I would not stand by and let my son ridicule him.

Alessandra glared at Archer in the same way I had. But her low growl of discontent did more to him than my snapped words. His chin fell to his chest, and he muttered an apology. But the words were out there, and the judgment was on full display in the way the other alphas viewed Robby.

"I think we are done here. We wanted to understand what happened, and Rick and Robby enlightened us." I glanced around the room and then at the council. Nods greeted me. "Go tend to your families. This matter is closed."

The alphas filtered out of the room.

"Robby, can I have a private word?" I asked before he joined the crowd.

He nodded and hung back.

"Go," I said to Alessandra and Archer.

She grabbed Archer's arm and dragged him out of the room after the last of the alphas. She closed the door to give us privacy.

Hunter's Moon

I waved at the chair she had just vacated. "Have a seat."

Robby sat and studied his hands. He was a few years older than Archer, but right now, he seemed to be more of a lost boy than a man.

"Your father was proud of you."

His gaze snapped up to mine, and his eyes glossed over. He shook his head.

"When you were younger, Robert asked us to take you in if anything happened to him. He wanted you safe from harm and knew Leigh and I would protect you."

Robby leaned back in the seat as if I had slapped him. "He never mentioned you outside of council meetings."

"Your father and I had an odd friendship. He didn't have anyone he could trust, and I guess he thought I was honorable." I laughed softly. "The guy who tore a bunch of humans to pieces because they hurt my alpha."

Robby's mouth popped open. "I thought…"

"No. That's not made up. But what the records you were privy to didn't say was they had poisoned her with belladonna, raped her, and dumped deer blood all over her, intending to kill the entire pack. One bite and we'd die with her. And Winters paid them to do it."

His face hardened in response. "Why didn't she shift and kill them before they poisoned her?"

"Our pack is unique. Besides the alpha mark situation, we also have an issue with alcohol. It prevents us from shifting, and the assholes who assaulted her knew that. They slipped alcohol in her drink at a party before abducting her."

"I would have done the same. I actually tore the vampire who turned Sarah to shreds."

That was new information, and I leaned back. "I thought when you kill the sire, it kills their offspring?"

Robby smiled. "It does, but Sarah is different in ways I do not wish to disclose."

"Robert told me she was your partner, so I know she's a witch."

Robby nodded.

"I'm sorry about your father. He wanted to make sure you knew what he sacrificed to keep you safe. You were that man's world."

Robby snorted a huff. "No, I wasn't. Revenge was his world."

"And it wasn't yours?" I cocked an eyebrow.

He pressed his lips together. "Touché." He shifted in the seat and his gaze dropped to my wheelchair and then back to my face. "Winters never thought much of you."

"Neither one of them did. Ken underestimated Leigh, and it looks as though Terrance underestimated your mate."

His smile spread slowly. "Never underestimate a woman on the warpath."

I laughed. "One of these days, I'll have to meet your warrior."

"One of these days." His smile faded. "Thank you."

"Anyone with a shred of decency would have helped."

"I wasn't referring to helping to save innocent people. I'm saying thank you for being a friend to my father. I honestly didn't think he had any genuine friends."

"I don't think he dared. He was biding his time to wage a war he wasn't sure he could win, and he didn't want to put anyone in danger. I could get a decent fake identification that passed high levels of scrutiny. So, I think it was a combination of my contacts and my discretion that he was looking for. But in the end, I think we did indeed become friends."

"And your willingness to tear anyone to pieces if they hurt your mate."

"And there's that." I nodded. I inhaled and glanced at the door. "Are you going to take back the alpha position?"

"That would require a challenge."

I nodded.

"Johnson is my best friend. I'd never challenge him for the position, especially since I am a better fighter than he is. I'll support him and try to be as good of a beta as he was to me." Robby stood and started toward the door.

"If you ever need anything, please let us know."

He paused at the door. "The same holds true for you."

"Take care of that mate of yours."

He smiled, and this time it finally reached his eyes. "Bye." He slipped out the door, leaving me with the memories of his father.

HUNTER'S MOON
Chapter 22

OUR LIFE SETTLED INTO a quiet routine. Archer and Cheryl moved into their home with the two children, but we got to watch them a couple of times a week when their work schedules conflicted.

Logan was more of a challenge than Kyle. He got into everything, and I wasn't fast enough in my wheelchair to head him off. But that kid was smart, even at four years old. And he could negotiate with the best of them.

The weekends were filled with Alessandra teaching Kyle alpha etiquette and me playing with Logan.

Some Saturdays were also used for the family to stretch their legs and test their speed in the woods. I longed for the ability to join them, but I reveled in Alessandra's joy flowing through our mate bond.

The pine scent filled my nostrils as I read the latest top thriller on my reader. The children's attempt at howling made me grin. They sounded so little and fierce. I sighed and re-read the same paragraph, wishing I was running with them.

A crack echoed, and my gaze jumped from the page to the woods. My heart thundered. There was no hunting on our property. Signs and fences prohibited it. But that definitely was a gunshot, wasn't it?

I glanced at the sky to make sure there weren't any thunder clouds around, but only the clear blue sky met my gaze. And there weren't any main roads near us for the sound of a car backfiring to be that clear.

Shock blanketed me through the bond, chilling me to the core. But at least it wasn't pain. Not at first. But when it came, a human cry followed from the woods. I didn't know who yelled out, but my heart rate went through the roof.

The need to go find out what was happening overrode logic. I shifted, falling out of the chair with a yelp as I dragged myself across the lawn using my front paws. My hind legs dragged behind me, as useless as my human legs. I let out a howl. A call for help.

Hunter's Moon

It didn't take long for half a dozen wolves to tear through our yard toward the woods. One skidded to a stop and stared at me as I struggled to drag myself forward. He shifted and started toward me. It was one of Archer's friends.

"Mr. Blaez?"

I looked up at him and whined. I wanted to get to my wife and my son and my grandchildren, but my damned body wouldn't work. I forced the shift and lay sprawled on the ground, my breath heaving.

"Go." I pointed at the woods.

"At least let me help you get back to your chair." He pointed the few dozen yards back to the porch.

I considered ordering him to leave, but I'm sure if Alessandra came back and found me in this position, she'd have another concern to deal with. I knew she didn't need more chaos, so I nodded.

He stepped closer and paused.

"Just bring me the chair." I couldn't bring myself to let him pick me up.

He grabbed it and then placed it next to me. "Can I help?"

"I got it." I reached up and locked the wheel closest to me, and then rolled onto my back and pulled myself into a sitting position, using the chair as leverage. The act of getting into the chair occupied my mind, although it did nothing to calm my heart.

Sounds in the woods reached my ears as I situated my legs into place on the pads and then leaned back, huffing with the exertion. I unlocked the wheel and slowly rolled backward with my eyes locked on the tree line.

Alessandra ran out of the woods with Logan tucked in her arms and Kyle running after her in wolf form. Her eyes were wild, and they locked on me at the edge of the porch. Without a word, she dumped my grandson's body into my lap and turned to Kyle. "Stay here." Her command hit with all her alpha power, and she shifted, bounding back into the woods.

My fingers slipped under Logan's chin, searching for a pulse. It was strong and steady, despite the blood splattered all over him. His chest rose and fell in even beats, and just looking at the front of him didn't answer the millions of questions swarming my brain.

Kyle stared at the woods with a vacant gaze.

"What happened?" I asked.

Kyle didn't respond.

I felt along Logan's body, looking for the reason he was out cold, and I found it on the back of his head. A bump the size of an egg. I removed my fingers to be sure he wasn't bleeding.

"Kyle, what happened to your brother?" I asked more forcefully.

He finally looked at me and then down at the limp body in my arms. "Mom pushed him out of the way, and he hit a tree."

"Out of the way of what?" I squeezed the words out.

"A bullet."

I turned Logan to be sure there was no entry wound. The fact he had shifted back to human form wasn't lost on me. That sometimes happened with little ones when they were surprised or injured.

My brain caught up to his words. "Logan hit his head?"

Kyle shrugged and focused back on the woods. "Dad attacked the man with the gun."

Hunter's Moon

The absence of emotion in his voice announced more than his words. I took in his pale cheeks and his near panting breath. I shifted Logan to my far shoulder and pulled Kyle into my lap, hugging him.

His young form shook as his calm demeanor shattered. He buried his face into my shoulder, and I held him as tight as I held Logan. The boy was in shock and needed a connection to hold onto.

"Shhh," I cooed in his ear as his sobs ramped up. I wasn't going to tell him it would be all right. Not with the dread stressing every muscle of mine.

Archer barreled out of the woods, holding Cheryl's limp wolf form in his arms. Tears streaked through the blood covering his cheeks and his steps became unsteady as his gaze found mine. Even from this distance, I could see the damage. Half of her head was missing.

No wonder Kyle had been numb. Not only had he seen his mother murdered, he also saw his father take out the killer.

"Where's your mother?" I asked Archer.

"She's getting rid of the bodies with the others." He fell to his knees on the grass. His voice hitched. "Fucking hunters were inside our fence."

A low growl came from deep in my throat. Pack lands had posted No Hunting signs all around the perimeter. It had been years since the last hunting incident, but that had been near the perimeter, and the hunters were not on our lands when they took the shot. And the result had not been a dead wolf.

He cradled his wife's body and rocked as his sorrow overcame him.

I held Kyle's head to my shoulder so he couldn't see and shielded Logan's eyes in case he woke up. I wished I could turn around and walk into the house with them, but the lip between the deck and the lawn was too great for me to roll backward.

An echo sounded over the woods, and Archer stiffened. His eyes widened, and he lay his wife on the ground and shot into the woods, shifting as he went.

Kyle growled in my arms. I could feel the struggle within him to break the command Alessandra gave.

No negative emotions leaked through the bond I had with Alessandra. No pain, nothing but mental anguish and a grim determination to finish the task at hand.

"Your grandmother is fine," I whispered to Kyle.

"How do you know?" He pulled away from my shoulder and met my gaze.

"I'm her mate, remember?" I lifted an eyebrow. "I don't feel the pure panic like before, just the resolve to get the job done and get home."

He settled in my lap and started to turn toward where his mother's body lay.

I turned his chin back toward me. "Nope. We are not going to look that way. But I need you to push the chair over the edge of the deck so we can get your brother inside and attended to, okay?"

Kyle nodded and slid his legs off my lap to the ground. With one push, I was on the wood and rolling backward easily. He jumped back into my lap, and I continued until I rolled over the threshold and into the house.

I headed to the couch, and Kyle helped me move Logan onto the cushions. I had him fetch me some water and some rags, and we cleaned the blood off his brother.

"Is he going to be okay?" Kyle asked when we were done.

"He hit his head pretty hard." I felt the knot again and sighed. "He's going to be dizzy for a couple of days, but he should be fine once his concussion goes away." I hoped I was right. I pulled my phone out of the side pocket of my chair and called the pack doctor, just in case. He'd need to come anyway to record Cheryl's death, so he could look at Logan to be sure there wasn't anything else ailing the child.

The doctor arrived at the house at the same time Alessandra and the rest of the pack came out of the woods. I watched from the window as he inspected Cheryl's body. When he started toward the house, Archer told him not to bother.

"Excuse me," I said from the doorway. "Logan needs to be looked at."

"It's his fault that she's dead," Archer growled, waving at Cheryl's body.

"She protected her young." Alessandra nodded for the doctor to proceed into the house.

"And she's dead because of that."

I rolled back, giving the doctor room to enter the house. I couldn't stomach Archer's reaction. I would gladly lay down my life for my grandchildren. And until this moment, I would have for Archer, but something fundamentally decent in him had broken.

"It wasn't Logan's fault," Kyle said as he looked at his little brother.

"No. It wasn't. Your father is just reacting to the situation."

When the doctor touched the knot on the back of Logan's head, the boy groaned and knocked his hand away. "That hurts."

"I bet," the doctor said. "Can you tell me your name?"

"Logan," he muttered and squinted his eyes open.

"That's right. Your grandpa will get you some ice for that bump and it should help." He stood and crossed to where I was, with Kyle by my side. "How long was he out?"

I glanced at the clock and made an educated guess based on when that first shot rang out. "No more than a half hour."

"Let him rest, but wake him up every couple of hours tonight to make sure he remembers his name. He might need darkening shades in his room. And limit his time on the electronics for a few days. He should be back to normal in a couple of weeks."

"Thanks, Doc." I shook his hand.

Kyle followed him out the back door, and I rolled into the kitchen and got one of our flexible ice packs. When I set it gently on Logan's head, he hissed at me.

"This will help." I kept my hand in place.

"I think something happened to my mom," he said in a whisper. "I don't feel her connection anymore." His pain-filled eyes met mine.

I nodded. "She saved you." I bopped his nose gently. "And I'm sure she is happy that you are okay."

His eyes misted over. "But my dad isn't happy."

"He is happy that you are okay, but he is sad and angry that your mom died. It's going to be tough going for a while." I stroked his forehead.

A tear slipped from his eye, and sadness blanketed over me. The slider closed, and I glanced over my shoulder.

Alessandra stepped inside with a blanket over her shoulders. Her puffy eyes carried the red from crying, and she sniffled.

"Go wash up. I've got this one."

"Colin said you shifted." She wiped her nose on the edge of the blanket.

I nodded. "I didn't get very far."

"He said you were almost to the wood line." She stepped away and came back with sweatpants for me.

I turned the chair away from Logan and shimmied into the pants as best I could. "Thanks. Now you need to clean up while I get some dinner going for us." I pointed toward the bedroom. "And let Archer know we'll keep watch over Logan tonight."

She didn't argue with me. She slipped into the bedroom and the shower went on.

"What would you like for dinner?" I asked Logan.

His four-year-old frown looked more like an old man's. "Nothing."

"Maybe a ginger ale and some crackers?"

He made a noncommittal noise and closed his eyes.

I retrieved some saltines and a small can of soda along with a straw, so Logan wouldn't have to move. My stomach never did well with concussions either, but a little soda and a few crackers always seemed to settle it down enough to be comfortable.

ALESSANDRA TUCKED LOGAN INTO Archer's old bed while I cleaned up and slid into our bed. We hadn't talked about what happened yet. Not with our grandson in the room. I set the alarm clock for a couple of hours to wake him like the doctor suggested and waited for my wife.

She cracked the bedroom door and slid under the sheets before moving next to me. She nuzzled into the crook of my arm. "Archer wants nothing to do with Logan."

"Doesn't he get that if she hadn't pushed him out of the way, they'd be mourning a child?"

"No. He's so wrapped up in hurt, he's lashing out at his son. He needs to blame someone, and it's easier to focus his anger on the one his wife saved than on the trespassing hunters he killed." She sighed. "Well, he killed one and left the other to die from his wounds. We put that bastard down before we dumped the bodies in the ravine."

"There will be blowback." The human world always cried foul when a human was killed, even if it was because of their own stupidity. "I'll call the council members in the morning and inform them of the situation."

"Make sure the council knows they were trespassing. And they weren't from around here. According to their licenses, they were from Kentucky. Plus, their cooler was full of empty beers, so I gather they were drunk to boot."

"Idiots," I muttered.

"It's all in the ravine, so it might take awhile to be reported."

KYLE JOINED LOGAN AT our house the next day because Archer was inconsolable and unavailable emotionally to address his children's needs.

Hunter's Moon

After a week, Logan was well enough to go back to nursery school, and I rolled down to Archer's house without Alessandra. It was time for a little tough love because he could not wallow in mourning with children.

I banged on the door and waited. As each minute passed, my frustration mounted. If I wasn't stuck in this wheelchair, I would have kicked in the door by now. "Archer?" I called and banged my fist on the door again.

Finally, the door opened, and Archer squinted out at me.

He looked like he hadn't slept or ate since Cheryl died. I got a whiff of him and added bathing to the list of things he had avoided.

"What the fuck, Archer?" I waved at him.

"My wife died," he snarled.

"I know. But you didn't die, and your children need you."

He waved his hand at me. "Like you wouldn't just crawl in a hole and die if Mom was killed."

"I would die for her or you or those kids in a second. And I know your mom would do the same for me." She risked her life to save me, but I didn't need to tell him that at this moment. "If she died, I would feel like crawling in a hole, but I wouldn't because it would spit in the face of all she is to me."

He recoiled.

"I would mourn her, no doubt about that, but I would keep moving, keep breathing, keep living in her honor. With kids, you do not have the luxury of shutting the world out, or slowly killing yourself." I waved at him. "Cheryl would be pissed at you for neglecting your kids all week, especially since she died protecting one of them." I let that settle.

Archer ran his hand through his hair and the greasy ends stuck out as if they were sprayed stiff. "I can't."

"I'm giving you another day to sleep and get your shit together before I send your mother down here to order you to function for your kids." I took a breath to calm my rising anger. "If I don't see you up at the house tomorrow, you'll get that visit." I rolled away with my heart pounding and my teeth grinding until my jaw ached.

HUNTER'S MOON
Chapter 23

THE NEXT DAY BEFORE school let out, the front door squeaked open. I looked up from the book I was reading and exhaled, letting all the tension that had built through the day go.

Archer stepped into the room, bathed and in decent clothing. He sheepishly shoved his hands into his pockets. "You were right."

"Every once in a while, that happens."

Alessandra snorted from the seat next to me.

"But I have to be honest. I'm not sure how I'm going to react to Logan."

"You are blaming him for what an illegal trespasser did? That is not okay," Alessandra snapped.

"If he had just stayed put—" Archer started.

Alessandra was on her feet and in his face in a blink. "We all wanted to run. It wasn't just Logan, so don't you dare blame that boy." She poked him in the chest. "We run all the time."

"But—"

"No buts allowed on this. If you want to put blame anywhere, it's on those dead assholes who trespassed on our lands and ignored all the posted signs just to get a wolf pelt. And you already had your vengeance on them."

"And the council absolved you of any wrongdoing where those trespassers were concerned," I added, just so he knew he was in the right in the council's eyes. If they had passed any other judgment on my son, I would have pulled favors to hide him while I got him a new identification so he wouldn't have to face a death sentence.

Alessandra shot me a glare. She had been grilled by the council members about what had happened before they rendered judgment.

"If he hadn't begged—"

"He's four."

"He's going to challenge Kyle someday, and I'm going to lose him, too!" Archer blew up.

"It doesn't work that way in our pack." Alessandra crossed her arms. "Logan may be a powerful alpha in his own right, but he can never lead this pack. Not without the mark. So all these fears you're brewing are not valid."

Archer sat down and covered his face, but he stopped spouting off excuses, even though his frustration boiled under the surface. The front door opened, and he recovered quickly. He wiped his face and leaned back in the chair.

Kyle stepped into the room with Logan at his side. He had been tasked with coming home with his brother instead of at his normal time to help us out.

"Daddy," Logan cried and ran toward him, but skidded to a stop before he crashed into his father. That joyous burst fizzled.

I wanted to smack my son for the chill in the air.

"How was school?" Archer looked from Logan to Kyle, clearly dismissing the younger child.

"Good," Kyle said. "Why don't you tell Dad about your project?" he said to Logan, trying to keep his younger brother in the conversation.

Kyle was being the perfect pack leader by including Logan in the conversation. It saddened me that his father couldn't offer that same type of support.

Logan launched into his day like any enthusiastic four-year-old, entertaining all of us with his antics...except his father, who stared on with a stoic expression, only brightening up when Kyle spoke.

J.E. Taylor

HUNTER'S MOON
Chapter 24

ARCHER NEVER DID WARM up to Logan again. His parenting style varied from offering sharp feedback to ignoring Logan altogether while he praised Kyle whenever possible. It seemed Cheryl's death always loomed between them, no matter how many years passed. And Archer never fully recovered from her loss.

alpha position to him, and I recommended Archer as my replacement on the council, hoping that would thaw the bitterness that had crept in and made a home in his heart.

The council requested a transition period that would include both me and Alessandra in attendance for at least the first meeting and then in an advisory capacity at meetings until we were fully ready to step away and retire.

I scoffed at the idea, but Alessandra thought there was some merit in her advising Kyle until he was a little older and more experienced.

As the annual council meeting started, I scanned the alphas. Most remained the same as they'd always been. But there were a handful of transitions happening, especially considering we were all getting on in age. Frankly, we wanted to relax and let someone else lead for a change.

Just before Archer pounded the gavel to start the meeting, the door opened and Robby Young slipped inside without his alpha. His commanding presence blanketed all of us, and he offered a smile of embarrassment for cutting it close. Another minute and he would have been considered late.

His gaze found mine, and I gave him a nod from my position between Archer and Alessandra at the table. He acknowledged it with a tilt of his chin.

The council went through normal business updates, including Archer's appointment to the council and Kyle's promotion to alpha within the pack, and then Archer asked whether there were any other items to discuss.

Robby stepped forward and cleared his throat before speaking. "As you all know, Rick Johnson

Hunter's Moon

passed away a few weeks ago." Murmurs and nods filled the room. "I'd like to take the position of alpha for the Allegany pack again."

Archer's face scrunched with distaste. "Your mate wasn't a wolf."

My gaze snapped to my son. I don't know where the hell that prejudice came from, but it irked me. He had mentioned it once when Robby and Rick had informed the council of the demise of the Monster Defense Agency. Both Alessandra and I had been disappointed then, and from the look on her face right now, we were in that headspace again.

I never cared who someone mated with. I only cared that they were decent and respectful and put their pack first.

"What the hell does that have to do with me taking over as alpha?"

Robby's question was valid, and we all turned our attention to Archer.

"You have half-breed children."

Robby's face turned red, and the growl that came out of him made me quiver. "Again, what does that have to do with leading my pack?"

I had enough of this prejudice bullshit.

"Robby is an exceptional alpha." I shot a glare at my son and his unacceptable behavior before I addressed the rest of the alphas in the room. "He led the pack for years before his captivity. And they thrived under his exceptional leadership. When he was thought to be dead, his best friend and beta was named alpha. Upon Robby's return, he did not challenge his friend. Instead, he honored Rick's station as alpha and operated as the pack beta all these years." I paused and scanned the room. I didn't know one alpha in this room who wouldn't do the same for their beta if they were in the same circumstance. "I do not have a problem with Robby Young taking over the pack again."

Out of the corner of my eye, I saw the other council members nodding.

My son's glare made me wonder whether I had made the right decision about offering him the council position. If he couldn't be just and compassionate, then the council wouldn't be as effective as we were for all these years.

"All in favor," Archer said through clenched teeth. Everyone but Archer raised their hand.

He didn't bother asking for any opposed show of hands. He would have been the only one in the room who didn't approve of the ask.

"Motion approved," he grumbled. "Anything else?" When no one stepped forward, he said, "Meeting adjourned."

I rolled out from behind the table with my anger simmering. I approached Robby before he left the room. "I'm sorry about that." I hooked my thumb back toward the table where the council was still talking.

"I'm used to it. How are you doing?"

"Tired lately." I smiled and shrugged. My ailments drained me on a daily basis, but I wasn't going to give Robby a rundown of my failing health. "How are your kids?" I thought back to the one time I met them. Unfortunately, it was at their mother's funeral, but his daughter was the cutest thing I had ever seen. I even treated her to a wheelie in my chair before Alessandra scolded me into behaving for the rest of the funeral.

"They are good. It was a tough go for a while, but I think they've been able to move forward without their mother." He ran his hand through his hair. "I appreciate that you and your wife came to Sarah's funeral. I'm not sure I said that to you."

"No need to thank us. We are always here for our friends." I looked him over. Outside the dark circles under his eyes, he appeared to be solidly in control of his emotions. "You seem to be doing okay, too."

He shrugged. "I don't have the luxury of wallowing in sorrow. I have two kids who need me and a pack that needs a leader."

And that was why I backed him for the position.

He lost his wife a while ago and then his best friend a few weeks ago, and he wasn't thinking of his loss. No, his focus was on his children and his pack.

HUNTER'S MOON
Chapter 25

"**H**EY GRANDPA," LOGAN SAID as he waltzed into the room with his legal attaché case under his arm.

I pressed the button on the bed, lifting the head of my side of the mattress up to take him in. My health had taken a sharp turn recently, and the doctor wasn't optimistic. It seemed the paralysis finally caught up to me, with infections and kidney failure. "You delivering subpoenas again?"

"Yup." He smiled. "I need money for a car and my dad thought this would help with my college resume."

"He's right." At least Archer had pressed Logan to go to school and make something of himself instead of continuing to beat the boy down on a daily basis.

Logan sat next to me and leaned his elbows on his knees. "I need to ask you a question."

"Okay." I smiled, even though I felt like death warmed over. "What can I help you with?"

He shifted in the seat and cocked his head as if trying to figure out how to ask. "Do you think I'll ever be alpha?"

"You would make a superb alpha, but that isn't in the cards in this pack." He knew his brother held the mark of a leader and that he could never challenge him and be accepted as the alpha of our pack.

He deflated before me as if I just shot his dreams to hell. He stared at his folded hands.

I couldn't let him give up his dreams. "Logan, the world is a big place."

His head snapped up, and he met my gaze.

I smiled and continued. "You should find your place to shine. You are strong. Stronger than your brother. But the gods chose him to mark as alpha of this pack."

"Are you telling me to leave?" Hurt filled his voice.

"To reach your full potential, yes." I knew it was hard for him to hear. This was his home, and everything he loved was here within our pack.

He blinked a sudden mist out of his eyes and his chin trembled.

"Look, Logan. I love you with all my heart. I don't want to see you go, but I also don't want you to become a bitter shell like your father. You have a mate somewhere out there. Find her and find your place as an alpha. If an opportunity presents itself, don't pass it up to live in your brother's shadow, or worse, live as a rogue because you can't be a follower."

"Who says I can't be a follower?" He crossed his arms and leaned back in the chair with a stubborn jut of his chin.

I raised an eyebrow at him. Logan was a natural leader and could be even more cocky than his grandmother. He was not prone to submission, even when ordered to, and that had caused a lot of sibling scraps between him and Kyle over the years. Even when Alessandra was alpha, once he hit thirteen, he could ignore her orders, which reminded me too much of myself. I could ignore Alessandra for days on end if I didn't agree with her, but I still felt the sting of her orders whether I liked it or not. But I never saw a flinch in Logan when he ignored her or his brother's directives.

As his brother put it, Logan was almost too perfect not to be a leader somewhere. And I prayed he'd get that chance someday.

"Are you scared?" he asked, pulling me out of my reverie.

The worry and sadness in his eyes tightened my throat, and I thought about the question.

Was I scared to die?

My wheelchair caught my eye. Fifty years tied to that miserable thing was long enough. I slowly shook my head.

"I've been able to help a lot of people over the years. And I've had a full life with the woman I love more than life itself." I smiled. "And as a beautiful bonus, I've seen my grandchildren grow into fine young men."

"That's because of you."

I didn't argue. Their father had become a ball of bitterness that none of us really could stomach being around for long. I didn't know whether the man had smiled or laughed since his wife died, and I didn't know why he couldn't get out of his own way to see that there were people around him who cared.

I shrugged. "I've had a good run, Logan. Just remember what the important things in life are as you navigate this world."

"I will. I love you, Grandpa."

He leaned over and kissed my cheek. The sheen in his eyes nearly overflowed. He squeezed my hand and hurried out of the room, grabbing his bag before he left without another look back. But his sorrow lingered on the air.

ALESSANDRA CAME INTO THE room after Logan left. She carried a plate of food, and I shook my head. That shit wouldn't stay down, and I didn't want to throw up again.

I had said my peace to Archer and Kyle earlier in the day before they went off to work. But I hung on to speak with Logan. I am glad he asked me the question first, because telling him he should look for opportunities outside the pack with no lead-in would have been more like a sledgehammer than a suggestion.

My time was coming. My body ached with fever, and my organs were slowly shutting down on me. I would have rather gone in my sleep, but I didn't have that luxury.

Dying wasn't fun in any condition. But it was time.

I reached out, took Alessandra's hand in mine and brought it to my lips, kissing it tenderly before I pulled her toward me and captured her mouth in a lingering kiss. I wanted to taste her forever.

She pulled back, and concern crinkled her forehead. "I love you, Jacob Blaez."

Darkness edged my vision, but the tear slipping from the corner of her eye captivated me. "Don't cry, baby. Just think about the next time I see you. I will dance with you and run with you and make sweet, sweet love to you. I promise we will take advantage of all that heaven offers." I smiled. "I love you, Leigh."

My vision faded into overwhelming brightness, and with my last breath, I muttered, "I'll see you on the other side."

THE END

Acknowledgements

I wanted to take a moment to thank all of the folks involved in my Kickstarter. You who cheered for me and helped fund my Kickstarter. And this retail version was born out of that experience.

Thank you! I cannot begin to express my gratitude for all those who supported me during this wild ride.

I hope you enjoyed Hunter and Alessandra's story!

If you want to explore more of Robby's story, check out my Shades of Night series. And if you want to know a little more about where Logan ended up, check out the Shades of Night sequel – Pack Magic!

J.E. Taylor

About J.E. Taylor

J.E. Taylor is a USA Today bestselling author, a publisher, an editor, a manuscript formatter, a mother, a wife, a retired business analyst, and a Supernatural fangirl. Not necessarily in that order. She first sat down to seriously write in February of 2007 after her daughter asked:

"Mom, if you could do anything, what would you do?"

From that moment on, she hasn't looked back.

Besides being co-owner of Novel Concept Publishing, Ms. Taylor also moonlights as a Senior Editor of Allegory E-zine, an online venue for Science Fiction, Fantasy and Horror.

She lives in New Hampshire with her husband and during the summer months enjoys her weekends on the shore in southern Maine.

Visit her at www.jetaylor75.com!

You might also enjoy other werewolf romance stories from J.E. Taylor's backlist:

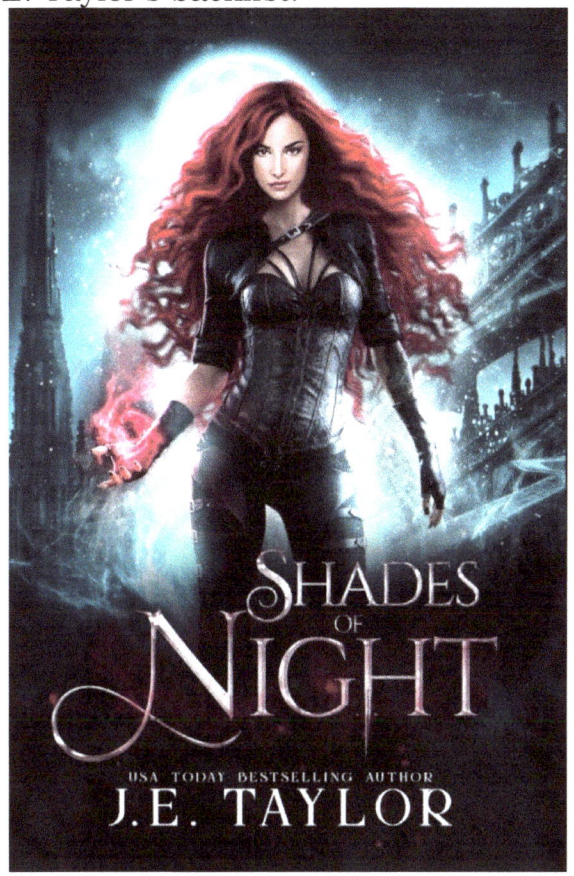

SHADES OF NIGHT

The Monster Defense Agency demands loyalty, and once you become an agent, the only way out is in a body bag.

When Sarah Stone and Robby Young train together at the agency's academy, sparks fly. And when they are paired as partners, they must muzzle their attraction, or they will face a firing squad.

All their pent-up frustration sharpens them into finely tuned monster hunters. Their ability to neutralize entire nests of vampires becomes the stuff of legends.

But hunting vampires has its own risks. Especially when Sarah and Robby uncover duplicity and corruption at the highest echelon within the Monster Defense Agency.

With a bull's-eye on their backs from both the agency and the vampires they hunt, Sarah and Robby's only hope is to take down the Monster Defense Agency.

But two against an ancient organization that trains monster-killers and knows all their tricks is even harder than it sounds. It's going to take all their skill and intelligence to kill this beast.

And being caught is not an option.

Shades of Night delivers forbidden mates, cool magic, and a kick-ass heroine in this fast-paced urban fantasy series.

Books included in this special edition hardcover:
Young Blood – A Shades of Night Prequel
Wicked Heart – Shades of Night Book 1
Crooked Soul – Shades of Night Book 2
Tainted Mind – Shades of Night Book 3

PACK MAGIC

She's a hybrid alpha scorned by her pack, until he arrives.

Daughter of a tribrid and a flame-touched alpha werewolf, Erica Young's course in life should be set. Except no one wants a phoenix-werewolf with a taste for blood to be their alpha.

When the head of the werewolf council shows up with a possible candidate to take her place in the pack, sparks fly.

Logan Blaez, the prodigal son of the council head, is willing to challenge Erica for the role of alpha, even if that means a fight to the death. Until he lays eyes on her.

Now he wants to claim Erica as his mate and rule as her alpha.

Too bad Erica isn't willing to submit, or give up her birthright.

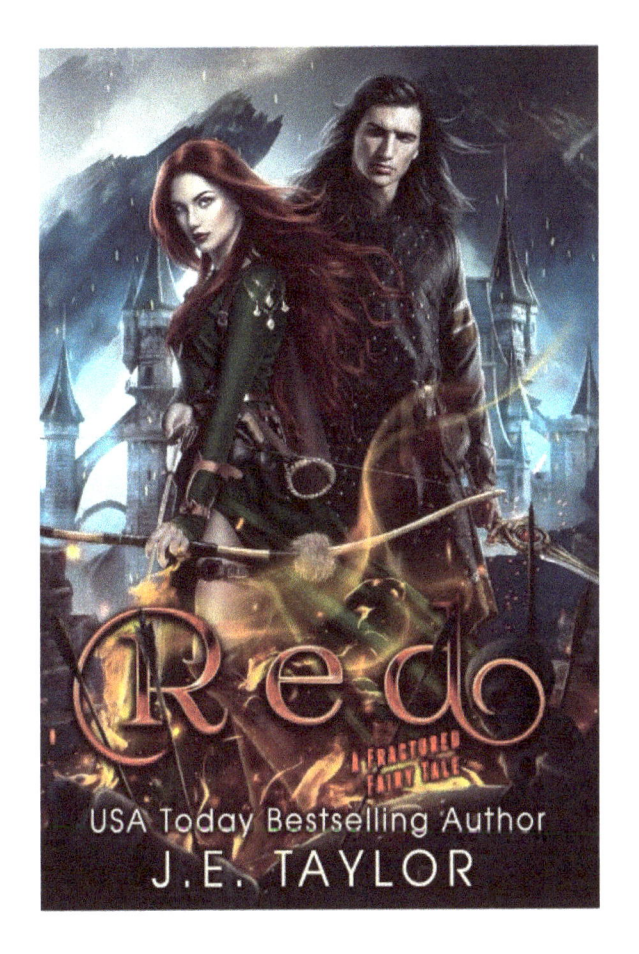

RED

What happens when a werewolf hunter falls for her prey?

Red Locklear regularly hunts all manner of woodland prey, but her favorite kill is the beast that tore her parents apart when she was a little girl.

The werewolf.

Now that Red is all grown up, these horrid creatures are terrorizing Dakota Territory once again. As a member of the elite Dakota Guard, Red has a duty to extinguish the life of every last wolf she sees. Failing to do so is a death sentence.

When her grandmother doesn't come back from a foraging run, Red dons her quiver of silver arrows and breaks town law, heading into the forest after sunset to search for her.

The dark woods test her hunting skills as well as her loyalty to the Dakota Guard, and she's left wondering if there is any way out of this alive.

Fans of *Once Upon a Time* and *Grimm* will devour RED.

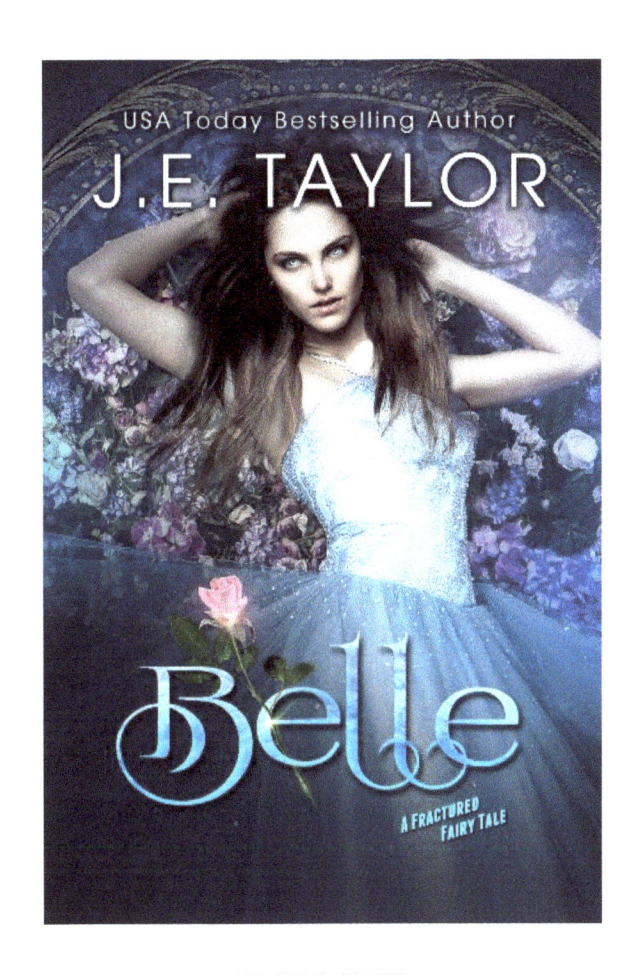

BELLE

Can a cursed shifter find the love needed to be cured?

My name is Belle Denton, and I was looking forward to finding my mate at the annual Shifter's Ball. Unfortunately, my petty side had to strike out at a homely patron who was not dressed for a ball. She looked more like the one hired to pick up after the horses. And I said so, loudly as my friends snickered at my dark wit.

That's when karma struck.

That homely patron wasn't as she seemed. She was a powerful sorceress who laid a vanity curse on me which made me partially shift into this monstrosity that pulls screams from grown men and cringes from my family and friends.

If I had just kept my cruel words to myself, I would not be exiled to my grandfather's dilapidated estate searching for a way to break this curse without getting killed in the process.

If you like fairytale retellings, you can get all ten including RED and BELLE in A FRACTURED FAIRY TALE – Books 1-10

AFRACTURED FAIRY TALE

Little Red Riding Hood, Cinderella, Brave, Rapunzel, Frozen, Snow White, Sleeping Beauty, Aladdin, Beauty and the Beast and Peter Pan – all fairy tales you know and love, but twisted, fractured into something new.

Shifters and magic claw through the pages of these fractured fairy tales, giving you a thrilling take on an old tale.

Will the heroine survive whatever the evil villain has in store? Or will Love conquer all?

Grab your hard cover copy of A Fractured Fairy Tale – books 1-10 and find out!

A Fractured Fairy Tale books 1-10 includes:
Red, Cinder, Brave, Tangled, Frozen, Snow, Spindle, Jasmine, Belle, and Hook

Find these titles and other fantasy and suspense titles on J.E. Taylor's website!

www.JETaylor75.com